MURDER IN
THE MONASTERY

S

MURDER IN THE MONASTERY

LESLEY COOKMAN

Published by Accent Press Ltd – 2013

ISBN 9781908917751

Printed and bound in the UK

Cover design by Sarah Ann Davies

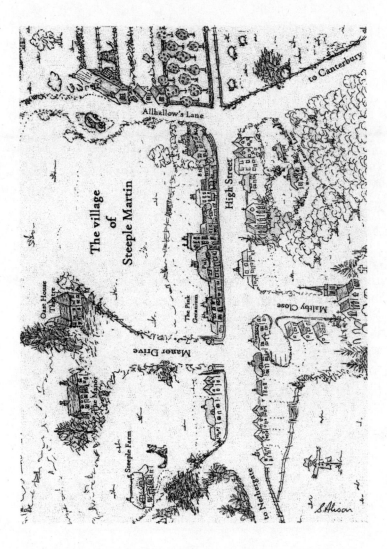

The village
of
Steeple Martin

Allhallow's Lane

High Street

to Canterbury

Oast House
The Cure

The Pink
Geranium

Manor Drive

The Manor

Maltby Close

Steeple Farm

to Nethergate

S. Alison

Acknowledgements

Once again, I have to thank Suzanne Sutton and the Reverend Frances Wookey for their invaluable help. If I've got any particulars of the workings of an Anglican Benedictine Abbey wrong, I sincerely apologise, as I do, as usual, to the fine British Police Force for taking such liberties.

Thank you also to Peter Oliver who put me right on the name of the Tredega Relic and Seraphina Moody who allowed me to use her Arte Umbria courses. Lastly, to my indefatigable editor, Bob Cushion.

WHO'S WHO IN THE LIBBY SARJEANT SERIES

Libby Sarjeant
Former actor, sometime artist, resident of 17, Allhallow's Lane, Steeple Martin. Owner of Sidney the cat.

Fran Wolfe
Formerly Fran Castle. Also former actor, occasional psychic, resident of Coastguard Cottage, Nethergate. Owner of Balzac the cat.

Ben Wilde
Libby's significant other. Owner of The Manor Farm and the Oast House Theatre.

Guy Wolfe
Fran's husband, artist and owner of a shop and gallery in Harbour Street, Nethergate.

Peter Parker
Ben's cousin. Free-lance journalist, part owner of The Pink Geranium restaurant and life partner of Harry Price.

Harry Price
Chef and co-owner of The Pink Geranium and Peter Parker's life partner.

Hetty Wilde
Ben's mother. Lives at The Manor.

Greg Wilde
Hetty's husband and Ben's father.

DCI Ian Connell
Local policeman and friend. Former suitor of Fran's.

Adam Sarjeant
Libby's youngest son. Lives above The Pink Geranium, works with garden designer Mog, mainly at Creekmarsh.

Lewis Osbourne-Walker
TV gardener and handy-man who owns Creekmarsh.

Sophie Wolfe
Guy's daughter. Lives above the gallery.

Flo Carpenter
Hetty's oldest friend.

Lenny Fisher
Hetty's brother. Lives with Flo Carpenter.

Ali and Ahmed
Owners of the Eight-til-late in the village.

Jane Baker
Chief Reporter for the *Nethergate Mercury*. Mother to Imogen.

Terry Baker
Jane's husband and father of Imogen.

Joe, Nella and Owen
Of Cattlegreen Nurseries.

DCI Don Murray
Of Canterbury Police.

Amanda George
Novelist, known as Rosie.

Chapter One

'How's the self-catering business going?' The Reverend Patti Pearson kicked her way through last autumn's leaves that still lay at the side of the path.

Libby Sarjeant frowned. 'Not brilliantly. Steeple Farm's got a six month let at the moment, but the Hoppers' Huts don't seem to have taken. I think they're too small for self-catering.'

'And still no thoughts of any more writing or painting weekends at the Manor?'

Libby shuddered. 'No. Put us right off, that last one did.'

'So you haven't got much on at the moment?'

Libby turned and looked at her friend suspiciously. 'Why?'

Patti laughed. 'I was just hoping to save you from being bored.'

'You're not going to rope me into another church thing, are you?' Libby had helped devise a nativity pageant for Patti's church, St Aldeberge's, last December.

'Not exactly.' Patti stopped by a stile and leant her elbows on the top. 'What a lovely view.'

Libby surveyed the wooded valley before her. 'Yes, it is. I forget how pretty our part of the world is, sometimes.'

'I wish Anne could get up here.' Anne Douglas, who lived in Steeple Martin, Libby's home village, was confined to a wheelchair.

'Aren't there any country walks suitable for her chair?'

1

said Libby.

'A few, but they're all rather sanitised and landscaped.'

'Yes, I suppose they would be.' Libby turned to face Patti. 'Come on then, what did you want me to do?'

'It isn't exactly important,' said Patti. 'It's out of interest, really. Have you heard of the Tredega Relic?'

'No. Is it Cornish?'

'The name's Welsh,' said Patti, 'because that's where Saint Eldreda came from. At least, they think so. Have you heard of her?'

'No.' Libby shook her head. 'You talk in riddles, woman. Let's get back to the car and head for a pub.'

It was a Wednesday afternoon, Patti's regular day off, when she joined Anne for dinner and stayed overnight. However, Anne, working for a library in Canterbury, didn't get home from work until later, so Patti had taken to coming and spending time with Libby first, after finishing her stint in the St Aldeberge community shop.

'St Eldreda,' Patti continued in the car, 'was an obscure saint who came from Mercia on what is now the Welsh borders. As far as anybody can tell. I don't suppose she was actually anywhere near Tredegar, but that's what it's become known as.'

'What has?'

'The relic. St Eldreda married a nobleman who brought her to Kent and after he was killed, Egbert, who was King of Kent, gave her some land and she set up a house of prayer. He did the same for Domneva of Minster.'

'Who?'

Patti sighed. 'Sorry, I'll keep it simple. Well, St Eldreda's monastery became quite famous after her death because miracle cures began occurring after pilgrims had visited her tomb. But then the first chapel was destroyed by fire, it being made of wood, we assume. So St Eldreda's

2

relics were removed for safe keeping.'

'Ewww! Do you mean her skeleton?'

'Yes. Now this bit is where things get complicated. It appears her family wished her bones returned to Mercia, but somehow a compromise was reached and they were only given a finger. Which is now known as the Tredega Relic.'

'Ah, got it. So what's the mystery?'

Patti shot her a quick look. 'Who said it was a mystery?'

'You wouldn't have mentioned it to me if it wasn't.' Libby beamed smugly and turned her gaze to the passenger window. 'Look there's a pub. Shall we stop?'

'Libby, I can't have a drink at four thirty in the afternoon! Let's go back and you can make me a nice cup of tea.'

'Oh, all right. But it looked a nice pub,' said Libby wistfully.

'You can get Ben to bring you here one evening. If you're not rehearsing anything, of course.'

'You know we're not at the moment,' said Libby. 'Go on then, about these bones?'

'The Tredega Relic was housed in an abbey church in Mercia, but when dear old Henry tore everything down, it appears the Relic was lost.'

'Dissolute Henry's dissolution. What about the remaining relics in Kent?'

'They're still here. Somehow, the Augustines, who were good at that sort of thing, got them moved to Canterbury Cathedral, and they were left intact. When, centuries later, the nuns returned to their site, which of course was practically ruined, they, or their mother house, managed to raise enough funds to build a small house. It's now St Eldreda's Abbey, and,' said Patti, pulling into the side of the road, 'it's over there.'

At first, all Libby could see were rather typical stone ruins. Then she made out other buildings, including what looked like a modern church.

'They incorporated a farmhouse that had been built on the land by a previous owner, and subsequently they've built a marvellous new chapel.'

'So that's why you wanted to come out here today. To show me this. But I still don't know what the mystery is. And anyway, you're an Anglican, not a Catholic.'

'They are now Anglican Benedictines,' said Patti, 'and one of them is an old friend, Sister Catherine. And the mystery is that the Tredega Relic has turned up.'

'Turned up? How?'

'In an auction catalogue. Bold as brass, apparently. And the girls want to find out what's going on. They've applied to the auction house who can't, or won't, tell them anything about the supposed seller.'

'The *girls*?'

'The nuns,' giggled Patti. 'They're a jolly bunch.'

'I always thought,' said Libby, 'that nuns would be totally against female priests.'

'Well, Catherine isn't. Would you like to meet her?'

'Now?' Libby looked nervous.

'Actually no, not now. They have visiting hours which stop at four. We could make an appointment.'

'We'll see. Come on, I want that tea now. And you can tell me what delights you have in store for me.'

'The nuns want to find out more about the seller of this supposed relic,' said Patti, settled in front of Libby's fireplace later.

'I expect they would,' said Libby, busying herself with wood and firelighters. 'Still cold for April, isn't it?'

'Look, Libby, are you interested or not? It doesn't matter if you aren't.'

4

Libby sat back on her heels and grinned up at her friend. 'Of course I'm interested. You – and they – want me to find out who the seller is and what the provenance is for this relic. I haven't got a clue how I'll go about it, but it sounds just what I need at the moment.'

'Oh?'

'Yes, Patti. You were right. I'm bored.' She got up and made for the kitchen. 'Just going to make the tea.'

She came back with two mugs to find Sidney the silver tabby happily purring on Patti's lap.

'He is a tart, that cat,' she said, handing over one of the mugs. 'Come on, then, how do I start with this business? I know next to nothing about convents, nuns, relics or saints. Or auctions, come to that. And how come just a bone is in an auction?'

'It's in what's called a reliquary that was made for it when it went back to Mercia. It's a gold and jewelled box, very rare. They were usually pieces of jewellery, pendants and so on, that could be worn. They are also far more common, if that's the word, in the eastern forms of Christianity, and more even than that in the eastern religions. Anyway, presumably because it was so precious, someone hid it away very carefully when it went back to Mercia and even the Cromwells didn't manage to get hold of it.'

'And now it's appeared?'

'Someone browsing the online site of a very respectable auction house spotted it and looked it up. The whole story was there, but not how it had come into the possession of the seller. This person then looked up the Abbey and sent them an email asking if they were the sellers.'

'And they weren't, of course,' said Libby.

'No, and the auction house won't tell them who the seller is.'

'Well, there's nothing to say it's illegal,' said Libby. 'Whoever hid it back whenever it was could have kept it in the family and it could have become an heirloom. The Abbey wouldn't necessarily have a claim on it, would they?'

Patti frowned. 'I suppose not. But they are interested in where it's been. After all, it could have been stolen all those years ago, not hidden by one of the nuns or monks.'

'So you just want me to look into its provenance? They don't want to get it back?'

'I'm not sure, but it is a bit idolatrous in my opinion. I think they just want to know.'

Libby stared into the fire. 'I don't see what I can do apart from ask the auction house, and maybe have a look back at the history of the old abbey in Mercia. It might be interesting.'

'You haven't got the constraints of living as a nun,' said Patti. 'They've got computers, of course, but they are bound by the routines of their days and haven't got the freedom to travel.'

'Hmm. I don't see me travelling to Wales to find things out, you know.'

Patti put her head on one side and grinned. 'You're thinking it might not be what you want to do after all, aren't you?'

'I am, a bit,' said Libby with a shamefaced grin. 'But I'll do a bit of background research and see if I get anywhere.'

'Right.' Patti stood up. 'I'm off to Anne's. Coming for a drink later?'

'Of course. Are you eating at Harry's?'

'Of course. My weekly treat, The Pink Geranium.'

'See you later, then,' said Libby.

The Pink Geranium, the mainly vegetarian restaurant in

Steeple Martin, was owned by Harry Price, who lived with Peter Parker, cousin to Ben Wilde, Libby's significant other. Libby's son Adam lived in the flat above the restaurant when he wasn't staying with Sophie Wolfe, stepdaughter to Libby's best friend Fran, in the seaside resort of Nethergate. Peter, Ben and Libby had fallen into the habit of meeting Patti and Anne in the pub on Wednesday evenings, and Harry would join them if the restaurant permitted.

This evening, before Patti and Anne arrived, someone else appeared at their table.

'May I join you?' asked Dominic Butcher.

Libby allowed herself an inward sigh. Dominic Butcher had recently been cast in an Oast House Theatre production, and as a former professional actor, thrown his weight around until stopped by the director. He also had the temerity to have the same name as Libby's eldest son.

'Of course.' Peter politely shuffled his chair closer to Ben's.

'Dominic.' Ben nodded and turned back to Libby. 'So what exactly do these nuns want you to do?'

'Find out the provenance of this relic – sorry, reliquary. I don't see how I'm going to do it.'

'St Eldreda's Abbey,' said Peter dreamily. 'Lovely place. Very atmospheric.'

'Oh, you know it?' Libby said in surprise. 'I'd never heard of it.'

'They allow occasional drama performances there,' said Peter. 'Even Murder in the Cathedral. I wonder …'

'What?' asked Ben and Libby together, somewhat nervously. Peter's projects had occasionally been known to lead to as much off-stage drama as on.

'Murder in the Cathedral,' said Dominic, obviously not liking to be left out of the conversation. 'I was in that myself, you know, a few years ago –'

'I could write a play about St Eldreda, couldn't I?' Peter turned bright blue eyes on his cousin. 'And if we could find anything out about this relic –'

'Reliquary. Who's this "we"?' asked Libby.

'If the nuns gave me permission, I'd naturally help you.' Peter gave her his most charming smile.

'I suppose we could ask Patti what she thinks,' said Libby.

'What do I think?' Patti pushed Anne's wheelchair up to the table. 'Evening all.'

'I was just telling them about St Eldreda and the reliquary,' said Libby.

'And I thought it would make a great play to put on in the Abbey ruins,' said Peter.

'Oh.' Patti looked surprised. 'I suppose it would. Tell me more.'

Ben pulled out a chair and introduced Dominic. 'And I'll go and get your drinks,' he said, 'while Peter persuades you to use your good offices in his cause.'

By the time Ben got back with a tray of drinks, Peter had finished.

'I think it's rather a nice idea,' said Anne. 'Can we talk to Catherine about it?'

'She's a friend of yours as well?' said Peter.

Anne and Patti looked at each other and smiled.

'Of course,' said Patti. 'I'll ring her tomorrow. She'll want to talk to Libby, anyway.'

Libby opened her mouth and shut it again.

'Well, I'm happy to offer my services if it comes off,' said Dominic. 'I've done a bit of directing you know, as well as the telly.'

Anne looked at him curiously. 'Were you on television?'

8

Dominic smiled deprecatingly. 'I was Alf in *Limehouse Blues*.'

Anne looked blank.

'It's a TV soap,' Patti explained. 'Anne doesn't watch much television.'

'Ah. Well, I'm actually thinking of going back to my former profession now, anyway,' said Dominic, glad to be in the forefront of the conversation at last.

'Oh.' Patti gave it the downward tone to convey lack of interest, but Dominic carried on.

'I was a Senior House Officer,' he said.

Libby shuddered to think of a patient under the alcoholically shaking knife of Dr Butcher.

'If it gets off the ground, Dominic, I shall direct it myself,' said Peter. 'And Libby's an ex-professional too, you know. She'll be on hand.'

'And we just hope,' said Ben, 'that the combination of you two doesn't lead to any more murders.'

Chapter Two

Apart from a little desultory internet research on reliquaries, St Eldreda and auction houses, none of which revealed anything of great use, Libby did nothing much on Thursday. She was working on a series of small paintings for Guy Wolfe's gallery-cum-gift shop, most of which she had done before, but visitors seemed to love them. Nethergate was a very old-fashioned British seaside resort that had changed little since the nineteen fifties, and many of the tourists it attracted preferred genuine paintings of the area to more normal holiday mementoes.

But on Friday Peter phoned.

'I've got the go-ahead,' he said.

'For what?'

'Murder in the Monastery.'

'What?'

'The play. In the Abbey ruins.'

'Oh!' Libby sat down on the stairs. 'You really meant it?'

'Oh, yes. I could do with having a chat about it, if you're free.'

'What, now?'

'Harry's open for lunch. I'll treat you, if you like. How can you refuse?'

'In that case, I shall go and put a face on,' said Libby, standing up.

Fifteen minutes later she joined Peter at the big pine table in one of the windows of The Pink Geranium. In front of him he had a notebook, a laptop and an open bottle of red wine.

'I shouldn't drink at lunchtime,' said Libby, eyeing the bottle.

'Yes, you should, dear heart.' Peter poured her a glass. 'Cheers. Here's to the new project.'

Libby drank obediently. 'Go on then, tell me all about it.'

'St Eldreda was granted land to build a monastery, and it is the remains of that you can still see. At least, some of it. Some of it was rebuilt after the Norman Conquest.'

'Thus Murder in the Monastery. So how did you get permission? Did Patti ask her mate?'

'No, I did. I called yesterday and spoke to the lady. She asked me to put a proposal into an email for her, which I did, and she called me this morning and said it had been approved, as long as they get to see the script before it's performed.'

'That was quick.'

'It just happened that the timing was right. It's the thirteen hundredth anniversary of Eldreda's death in 712 so they felt it was appropriate.'

'But what's it going to be about? She wasn't murdered, was she?'

'There actually was a suggestion that she was. And then the chapel burnt down –'

'Patti mentioned that.'

'And it was thought to be a deliberate act to destroy the relics.'

'Good job they were moved, then. So who dunnit?'

'That was never proved. I've undertaken to provide some alternative theories for the sisters and they can decide which is most –' Peter frowned and drummed his fingers on the table.

'Seemly?' suggested Libby. 'Well. It all sounds terribly complicated. What about the reliquary?'

'That will come into it. I may even be able to work it that Eldreda's Welsh family had something to do with the burning of the chapel in order to steal the relics.'

'You can't malign people like that!' Libby was shocked. 'You'll have to invent someone.'

'That's why I've got to put it before the sisters, in case I've stepped on someone's toes.' Peter grinned and lifted his wine glass.

Harry appeared with two plates of soup.

'No Donna?' asked Libby.

Harry pulled a face. 'She's gone part-time.'

'Well, she is seven months pregnant,' said Libby. 'I don't suppose the standing does her much good.'

'She's doing the books and admin at home though,' said Peter. 'Just as you suggested.'

'So all you need is a new waitress? Shouldn't be too difficult. Have you still got that lad you bullied?'

'He bullies them all. Likes to pretend he's a chef off the telly,' said Peter.

'Jacob?' said Harry. 'Yes, but he's part-time, too, and can't work during the week. He's good at prepping in the kitchen at weekends, though. I think he prefers that.'

'He used to look terrified out here,' said Libby. 'Poor child.'

'So,' she continued, when Harry had gone back to the kitchen, 'what did you want my help on?'

Peter looked surprised. 'Well, everything. The script, the characters, the story …'

'Oh.' Libby looked alarmed. 'But I don't want to get into research. I'm supposed to be looking into this reliquary thingy.'

'But that will help, won't it?' said Peter. 'Can't you get

in touch with the sale rooms and ask if you can see it, and if they have any information on its background for the play in the actual place it came from? I bet they'd let you see it, and they might part with a bit more info than they would to the nuns.'

'Maybe ...' Libby thought for a moment, sipping her soup. 'Perhaps I could. I'll have to ask Patti which sale rooms it is. What else?'

'I don't know whether to use St Eldreda as a character or if the sisters would see that as – oh, I don't know – blasphemous in some way.'

'You could set it immediately after her death and concentrate on the investigation,' suggested Libby.

'That's what I thought. So it becomes a proper murder mystery.'

Libby looked at him sharply. 'Don't forget what happened last time you recreated a real-life murder.'

'I know, I know, but the murder wasn't even connected in the end, was it?'

'Everybody connects the two,' said Libby. 'Anyway, go on.'

When they'd finished their soup, Harry brought them cheese and joined them while they thrashed out a few more points on the story.

'When do you want to perform it?' he asked.

'It will have to be in the summer because of the weather,' said Peter.

'That doesn't give you long, it's April now,' said Libby. 'You've got to write it, get it passed by the sisters, cast and rehearse it.'

'Three months if we aim for July,' said Peter. 'Should be able to do it.'

'After all,' said Harry, standing up, 'it only took God a week to create the world.'

Peter frowned at his departing back. 'Sarcasm doesn't suit him.'

'It's true, though, Pete. And think of all the early medieval research you're going to have to do.' Libby shook her head. 'If you want to do it, why don't you find an easier subject?'

'I can't write about Murder in the Monastery unless there is one, can I?' said Peter reasonably.

'What about the current problem? Or something in the more recent history?'

Peter sighed. 'I'll ask Sister Catherine. I'm going to see her to get some background tomorrow. They have a sort of open house between eleven and twelve.'

'In that case,' said Libby, 'I shall wait until you report back before doing anything further.'

It wasn't until quite late on Saturday afternoon that Peter sent Libby a text.

'On my way home. Can I call in?'

He knocked on the door ten minutes later bearing a large folder.

'Lots of info,' he said, 'and very interesting.'

'Do you want tea?' asked Libby. 'The kettle's on and Ben will be back in a minute.'

'I'd love a cup. I had a very small cup of coffee when I first arrived at the Abbey and that was it.'

'Have you been there all this time?' Libby's eyebrows shot up.

'Not quite.' Peter threw himself languidly on to the cane sofa, which creaked alarmingly. 'But I was there for a good time. They let me look through some of their books. Fascinating. Especially the story of the re-establishment of the order.'

'Oh?'

'Go and make that tea, dear trout, and I'll tell you.'

Libby made the tea, brought it back into the sitting room and turfed Sidney out of the armchair.

'Tell all,' she said.

'Well,' said Peter, sitting upright and sipping his tea, 'in the first place the auction site that the reliquary was found on isn't quite that. It's a specialist antiquities dealer's website. I'm sorry to say I didn't even know such things existed. I thought items such as Anglo-Saxon brooches and Viking swords would be Crown property.'

'No,' said Libby, with a wealth of knowledge derived from watching archaeology programmes on television, 'sometimes an item found on someone's land is returned to him and he can sell it. Although I'd be surprised in this instance. All items like that must be reported to the coroner within fourteen days and he decides if it's officially treasure which can then be claimed by the Crown. There's something about percentages of gold and silver and age, but I don't know the exact details.'

'Well, this website states quite categorically that it has authenticated the reliquary and has the provenance. Apparently it was in the hands of a private collector from the eighteenth or nineteenth century.'

'But it won't say who?'

'They wouldn't be able answer any questions, would they?'

'No, but who was the collection left to?'

'The person selling the reliquary, I suppose.' Peter sighed. 'Now listen, before you get any more hot under the collar about that, I must tell you about the re-establishment of the order, which you suggested I should find out about.'

'And?'

'Patti told you that the buildings had gone into private ownership, didn't she?'

Libby nodded.

'Apparently, the last private owner wanted to sell, but was having trouble. A local vicar suggested that, as it had been a monastic organisation, it should be offered to English monastic houses. As it happened, this community of Anglican Benedictine sisters had been living in rather cramped quarters somewhere else, and with all sorts of outside financial help, managed to buy it. I believe there was a substantial legacy from one particular woman, but I can't remember who, exactly.'

'So they aren't really anything to do with the original St Eldreda?' said Libby.

'Nothing at all. And they don't necessarily want the reliquary back, they just want to know where it's been.'

'Oh, so a bit of a damp squib, then?' said Libby, putting down her mug.

'Not really. They still use her name, and, as I told you, they're celebrating her anniversary this year. But,' Peter grinned wickedly, 'that isn't the best bit.'

Libby sighed. 'Go on. What is it?'

'There really was a Murder In The Monastery.'

Chapter Three

'There was? Who? St Eldreda?'

'No, no, much more recent. At the time of re-establishing the monastery, the reliquary turned up.'

'What!'

'This is one of the main reasons they want to find out who's selling it now.'

'But why didn't Patti tell me all this in the first place?' said Libby.

'She didn't know all of it. Apparently, Sister Catherine simply told her about the reliquary turning up on the website. Patti looked up the story of the original relic herself.'

'So did Sister Catherine know Patti had asked me to look into it?'

'Oh, yes. It was then she told me the story.' Peter finished his tea and peered into the mug hopefully. 'Any more?'

Libby sighed. 'Lucky I keep the kettle on the simmer!' She took the mug and returned in a few moments with a fresh one. 'Now, go on, tell me the story.'

'Well.' Peter settled back into the corner of the sofa and Sidney jumped on his lap. 'It was at the time the order bought the Abbey and the farmhouse, back in the seventies.'

'It was that recent?'

'Yes. I was surprised, too. There are a couple of nuns still there from that time, but most have joined more recently. After the order had been offered the Abbey, they had to raise enough money to buy it. They sold their previous home quite easily, but had to find the shortfall quickly. It was then that they were offered the Tredega Relic.'

'Really?' Libby frowned. 'Who by?'

'An anonymous donor, who suggested they sell it to raise funds.'

'How extraordinary! What happened?'

'Their solicitor began to look into it, and eventually the potential donor suggested he bring it to show them to prove its existence. He had already sent photographs.'

'He?'

Peter nodded. 'The day before the meeting had been set up with the solicitor and the Mother Abbess, the body of a man was discovered in the ruins of the Monastery. He had on him the correspondence between himself and the community, but no relic or reliquary.'

'Blimey.' Libby was wide-eyed. 'So was he identified as the man who'd written the letters?'

'Yes, by his wife, who knew nothing about it.'

'But why,' said Libby, still frowning, 'had he offered them the relic? And how had he come by it?'

Peter shrugged. 'No one knows. The police investigated at the time, but didn't find anything. The sisters weren't informed of any progress, and of course, things were very different back then.'

Libby was silent for a moment. 'How did they raise the money in the end?'

'A couple of gifts and, finally, a legacy from a nun who died. Of course, they tried to find out from the police why the man had been in the ruins of the Monastery when he died.'

'And did they? Or how he died?'

'Sister Catherine doesn't know.' Peter grinned. 'And she's just as curious as you are!'

'So that's why she let Patti mention it to me?'

'Yes. I don't think they want the relic – after all, it belongs to a different order and a different era, but it's connected to their building and their name.'

'Right.' Libby leant back in her chair and looked at the ceiling. 'So we need to know all the details of the offer of the relic in the seventies. How would we do that?'

'Sister Catherine says she's already tried to find out on the internet and found a list of unsolved murders from the seventies to see if she could find the name of the man, but it wasn't very conclusive. She also said she didn't have unlimited access to the internet, either.'

'I don't suppose she has. So did she find a name?'

'As far as she could make out, it was Bernard Evans. She hasn't gone any further.'

'So now it's up to me, eh?' Libby sat up straight and grinned. 'Well, this makes it a slightly more interesting project. And will you write your play about this murder?'

'No, about the early medieval period. And they will let us do it in the Monastery ruins. They aren't at all precious about it, and I was right, they have staged Murder in the Cathedral there. The whole place was deconsecrated when it went into private hands, so they're quite cheerful about it all. They have music concerts there, too.'

'You know, the police should have been informed about this antiquities website,' said Libby. 'It's probably enough to make them re-open the case.'

'That's a thought.' Peter quirked an eyebrow at her. 'Going to phone Ian and tell him?'

'I might. I could also invite him to dinner.'

'He'd smell a rat,' said Peter.

Chief Detective Inspector Ian Connell had tolerated

19

Libby's so-called help in several of his cases, not least because Fran Wolfe, Libby's best friend, was a reluctant psychic, whose "moments" had been instrumental in significant breakthroughs. He had, at one time, been rather romantically interested in Fran, but despite her choice of artist Guy Wolfe as a husband, he had remained a friend to both of them.

'I'll just give him a ring, then. Ask him who would be the right person to contact.'

'Cold Case squad, I expect,' said Peter. 'Which will mean it won't be Ian getting involved.'

'True. Still, they should be informed, shouldn't they?'

'Certainly.' Peter grinned. 'Go on, then. Ring him.'

Libby squinted at the screen of her mobile and found Ian's private number. To her surprise, he answered.

'Is this a social call?' he asked.

'Well, not exactly,' said Libby, and heard him sigh.

'Go on. What is it?'

'Who would I tell if I had information that related to a crime committed in the 1970s?'

There was a momentary pause, and Ian spoke in a completely different tone.

'What information on what crime?'

'The murder of – we think – a Bernard Evans in St Eldreda's Monastery. Or Abbey, as it is now.'

'And what,' asked Ian cautiously, 'is this information?'

Libby explained about the reliquary.

'And you just happened to come across this?' Ian was now definitely suspicious.

'No, Sister Catherine at the Abbey asked me to see if I could find out who was selling the reliquary. She'd asked the antiquities dealer, who wouldn't tell her.'

'Why on earth would a nun ask you –' Ian paused. 'Miss Pierce.'

'Pearson,' corrected Libby. 'Yes, she was at college with Sister Catherine.'

'But aren't nuns Roman Catholic?'

'I thought that, too, but apparently not. These are Anglican Benedictines. So what do we do?'

Ian sighed. 'I'd better speak to Sister Catherine and then get on to the dealer. They'll tell me who the seller is, believe me.'

'You? Wouldn't it be the cold case unit?'

'It's been reported to me, hasn't it? Let's just see what happens.'

'There.' Libby sat back and switched off the phone. 'Now we just sit back and let Ian do his stuff.'

'And you've lost yourself a nice little mystery,' said Peter, standing up. 'I'd better get back and make a start on this while everything's fresh in my mind. Can I send you a rough outline when I've done it?'

'OK,' said Libby. 'It'll give me something to do.'

When Peter had gone, she called Patti to tell her.

'So it look as though I won't be doing a thing. Ian will find out who the seller is as it relates to an old murder, and that will be that.'

'Oh, pity. It would have been interesting for you.'

'Kept me out of mischief, you mean,' giggled Libby. 'Actually, Peter's got permission from your Sister Catherine to perform his play in the Monastery ruins, so helping him with it over the next few months will do that.'

'Excellent. How did he find her?'

'Do you know,' said Libby in surprise, 'I didn't ask him. And he didn't say, but they obviously got on all right.'

'You'll have to meet her soon,' said Patti. 'She was very interested in our little mystery from last year.'

'How morbid of her.'

'Oh, come on, Libby. That's rather pot and kettle isn't it? She doesn't get much excitement.'

'I suppose so. Anyway, I'm bound to meet her once Pete starts rehearsing over there. I expect we'll do the first part in the theatre. We've only got a few one-nighters until the June production.'

Libby relayed the news to Ben when he arrived home.

'That's a pity,' he said, waving a bottle of gin at her. 'I thought that was going to be a nice quiet little mystery where you wouldn't get into any trouble.'

'That's what Patti said. Sorry to disappoint you all.'

Ben grinned and handed her a gin and tonic. 'I expect something will come along.'

Sunday was something of a ritual. Ben's mother Hetty, who lived at his family home, the Manor, cooked an enormous roast dinner and expected anyone who was around to come and help eat it. Libby, Ben and Peter were always there, Harry if the restaurant wasn't opening on a Sunday lunchtime, which, in April, it wasn't, Peter's younger brother James, sometimes with a girlfriend, more often without, Hetty's brother Lenny and his partner, Hetty's best friend Flo Carpenter, and occasionally, Fran and Guy Wolfe. This Sunday they were all there, and Hetty looked round the long kitchen table with satisfaction.

'Beef and Yorkshire today,' she said. 'Pop down and get the good claret, Ben.'

Hetty and Flo shared a palate for and knowledge of good wines, learnt from their respective late husbands, which put their younger friends and relatives to shame. Under the influence of the good claret, the conversation turned to the reliquary and Peter's play.

'I've already done a working synopsis which I've emailed to Sister Catherine,' he said.

'You can email nuns?' Hetty's bushy eyebrows rose in

surprise.

'Yes, Auntie,' said Peter, using a title she hated. 'They've all been dragged into the 21st century by their habits.'

'So how long will it take you to write, once the nuns approve it?' asked Libby.

'I thought I might do a slightly more detailed synopsis of each scene, cast it and use an improvisation technique.'

Everyone looked at him in astonishment.

'Aren't we a bit traditional for that?' asked Ben. 'And won't it be a bit difficult to improvise in early medieval English?'

'Old English is actually more or less Scandinavian,' said Peter.

'Anglo-Saxon,' put in Harry.

'Clever.' Peter gave him an amused smile. 'Anyway, no one would be able to understand it, and we might as well use modern language, avoiding any slang and sticking, as far as we can, with the proprieties of the era.'

Lenny was looking puzzled. 'Come again?'

Peter fell into a long explanation which appeared to baffle his uncle further.

'Will you audition?' Fran asked Libby, helping herself to more roast potatoes.

'I expect so. There must be a Mother Abbess or something. Would you like to have a go?'

Fran looked across at her husband. 'What do you think, Guy? I haven't done it for years.'

Fran, like Libby, had been a professional actor at one time, and had, in fact, performed at The Oast House Theatre in pantomime a few years ago.

'Long way to go for rehearsals,' said Guy, 'but it would be an experience, wouldn't it?'

'You wouldn't mind?' Fran looked doubtful.

Guy exchanged looks with Ben and they laughed.

'I'd mind far less than I mind you getting mixed up in murders,' said Guy.

'Oh, well, I might then.' Fran grinned at Libby. 'It might be fun.'

'Both of you?' Peter returned to the main conversation. 'What about you, Ben?'

'Are there any men?'

'Of course. The monks who took the reliquary to Wales and those that took the other relics to Canterbury.'

'Well, maybe.'

'Your lead actor Mr Butcher will want to be in it,' said Harry.

'Dominic? Yes, I suppose he will,' said Peter gloomily. 'The trouble is, if it's going to be based on improv he'll go on and on for ever.'

'Make him a Trappist,' suggested Harry.

'You watch out there isn't a real murder in the Monastery, then,' said Flo. 'He's an annoying bugger.' She lifted her glass. ''Ere's to success then. Make sure we got somewhere dry to sit.'

Chapter Four

Rehearsals for *Murder in the Monastery* began as soon as Sister Catherine and the Mother Abbess had approved Peter's outline. Libby, Fran, Ben and Dominic Butcher were all in the cast, along with several other members of the Oast House Theatre's regular company. Patti brought Sister Catherine to one of the first rehearsals, where she entertained them all with a highly embellished story of Saint Eldreda and her relics, and put them right on a few matters of both religion and language. She also promised to send them information on costume.

'Early medieval is difficult,' she said, 'because, as you know, it's a period also known as the Dark Ages, and people aren't quite sure what was being worn when. But we've got material in the archives, even though it wasn't our Order.'

'Isn't she nice?' whispered Libby to Fran. 'I somehow imagine her with a lot of long, blonde, curly hair.'

'I know what you mean.' Fran looked at the bright, interested face of Sister Catherine, leaning forward from her seat on the edge of the stage, waving her hands as she described something. 'And so young.'

'Well, Patti's quite young, and they were at college together.'

'I still can't understand what makes a pretty, intelligent young woman decide to become a nun,' said Fran, with a sigh. 'It's unnatural.'

'Not to them,' said Libby, fearing an anti-religious

lecture from her friend.

Fran turned to her and smiled. 'No, I know. And since we've known Patti I think I've become more tolerant.'

'Good.' Libby turned back to where Peter was helping Sister Catherine to her feet. 'We'd better go and say goodbye and thank you.'

'I wanted to say thank you to you, actually,' said Sister Catherine, clasping Libby's hand between both of hers. 'It was kind of you to look into our puzzle, and ask the police to become involved. We don't necessarily want it back, we're an Anglican Order, but it would be nice to see the relic back with the rest of poor Eldreda.'

'And find out who committed the most recent murder,' said Libby, 'not to mention find out who has profited from selling it. The reliquary looked quite beautiful – if macabre.'

Sister Catherine smiled wryly. 'I doubt if any of the money would come our way, and we wouldn't want to profit by it, especially if it had been the reason for – well, for murder.'

'Come on, Cathy,' said Patti, coming up behind them, 'we've got to get you back to the Abbey.'

'OK.' Sister Catherine gathered up her habit in one hand and held her other out to Fran. 'Good bye. I shall look forward to seeing the play when it's a bit further advanced.'

Within a few days, Patti had called to say that Catherine had discovered that the day usually said to be St Eldreda's Day was July 13th. Peter felt this was auspicious for the first performance of Murder in the Monastery and stepped up rehearsals. The at-first improvised script had been refined and written down, and submitted to the Mother Abbess for her approval (and from her to the Bishop – just in case!). The relic itself seemed to have faded into the distance.

It was June when Ian joined Libby, Patti and the theatre group in the pub after rehearsal one Wednesday.

'Surprise, surprise!' said Libby, as he bent to kiss her cheek. 'Where have you been hiding?'

Ian made a face. 'Behind a desk, mostly.'

Ben handed him a pint. 'Any news on our reliquary?'

'That's why I came by.' Ian took a grateful sip of his beer. 'After a good deal of negotiating, an officer from the Arts and Antiquities Unit at the Met was able to get in to see the antiquarian site offering the item. There is actually a proper little gallery, not just a website, although it's hidden away down one of those London alleyways and has no shop front.'

'Well,' said Fran, 'I suppose you wouldn't want to advertise all that priceless stuff, would you?'

'They definitely don't, and they were extremely put out by any suggestion that they were handling stolen goods.'

'I bet they were.' Ben looked amused. 'What happened?'

'Eventually, the owner of the gallery, or whatever it's called, gave in, probably because he could see himself up on a charge. He produced all the documentation on the object and Arts and Antiquities arc looking into it.'

'What about us and the Abbey?' said Libby indignantly.

'He's copying me in on everything, don't worry, but it's easier for them to look into it. They're on the spot, they're experts and they've got the contacts.'

'I suppose so,' said Libby grudgingly.

'He's right, Libby,' said Patti. 'After all when the Abbey tried to look into it they got nowhere, and you would have thought that their credentials were enough to get them in.'

'So what's the latest?' asked Dominic Butcher, on the

outskirts of the group, from where he'd been listening.

'Mark, my Arts and Antiquities contact, is looking up the solicitor who's handling the sale. Apparently, it's a probate sale.'

'Someone's died?' Libby wrinkled her brow.

'But we don't know who. Normally the solicitor would handle it on behalf of the estate of the deceased, which would be stated, but this time it isn't.'

'Isn't that suspicious?' said Dominic.

Ian shrugged. 'Not necessarily. Anyway, in this case, because of its history the solicitor will be forced to tell Mark who owned it and show what provenance they have.'

'Good,' said Libby with satisfaction. 'Have you told Sister Catherine?'

'I've left a message. I expect they were all at prayers, or something. I've suggested she get in touch with one of you.'

'Excellent,' said Patti. 'So once we know who the person was, we can try and find out how he got it.'

'That's what I meant when I said they'd have to show provenance.' He smiled slightly. 'But I don't suppose there's any harm in you doing a little digging once we've got a name.'

Libby, Fran and Patti looked at each other and grinned.

'Blimey,' said Libby. 'Permission.'

Patti called Libby the following afternoon to say Sister Catherine had been on the phone very excited.

'It's the thrill of the chase,' said Patti. 'She doesn't get much excitement.'

'Well, we'll keep her in the loop. She might find out things better than we could because of her status.'

Finally, Ian called Fran on Friday and asked her to pass on the news that the solicitor had divulged the name of his dead client.

'A collector called Marshall,' Fran reported to Libby, 'who bought it way back in the seventies from someone who claimed to be a descendant of the original owner.'

'St Eldreda? Wouldn't have thought she'd had any descendants.'

'No, there was some tale about it being held in trust by the monks.'

'Ah!' said Libby. 'The monks who spirited it away during the dissolution.'

'Anyway there was enough to convince Marshall that it was genuine, and the solicitor apparently had the whole story of St Eldreda down pat.'

'Hmm,' said Libby thoughtfully. 'Seventies. That's when that bloke was murdered in the monastery and the reliquary was stolen.'

'And then,' said Fran slowly, 'it was sold on.'

'And the murdered man – Bernard Evans, I suppose – had offered it to the order. He obviously thought it should go back to where it came from.'

'Yes, but he was suggesting they sold it to raise funds to buy the monastery.'

'Well, good for him, poor sod,' said Libby. 'So presumably, whoever knocked him off sold it to this collector, pretending to be descended from the monks.'

'Not very good title, is it?' said Fran. 'If the monk's family pinched it.'

'They were looking after it,' said Libby. 'I expect that would be their story. I wonder who they were?'

'I wonder if there's a history of the Tredega monastery, if that's what it was called.'

'Worth a prowl round the internet,' said Libby.

'OK. Let me know if you find anything and I'll do the same.'

But there was no Tredega Monastery, Abbey or

anything else. Libby found a site where she could look for historical sites by century, and although there were plenty in Wales, none were near Tredegar. Libby tried the Tredega Relic, which she'd tried before, but there were only vague references to it. Searching for St Eldreda was similarly ineffective, although she did have a brief history of her life online. There wasn't even much on the rather limited website of the current Abbey. Libby sighed in frustration and went to make a cup of tea.

She was sitting in the bar/foyer of the theatre that evening waiting for Peter to start rehearsals, when Fran came in with a smile of triumph.

'Found it!'

'You haven't?' Libby was frankly disbelieving. 'I couldn't find anything, whatever search terms I used.'

'Did you try Mercia?'

'No! I never thought of it.'

'Well, I did.' Fran sat down opposite Libby and pulled some papers from her bag. 'You told me Patti said Eldreda had come from Mercia and the relic, although called the Tredega Relic, was probably from nowhere near the actual place.'

'Yes.'

'Well, Mercia is the modern day Midlands and doesn't go into Wales. The other thing is, the Mercians and their king Wulfhere were only Christian from 658, so any monastic institutions would be after that.'

'So? The relic wasn't stolen until the dissolution.' Libby frowned.

'But there must have been someone back then who wanted her relic.'

'But it could have just been her family. It could have been a chapel, or something that became a monastery later. I wonder,' said Libby slowly, 'if it was her family.'

'What? Who wanted the relic back?'

'Well, yes, but whose name was Tredega – not the place?'

'Well!' Fran sat back in her chair. 'Of course, that could be it. But they didn't have Christian and surnames as we do back then, did they?'

'No, but perhaps they *came* from Tredegar originally. Anyway – you said you found it. Where was it?'

'I *think* I've found it, and it's in Herefordshire, and it was one of the first Anglo-Saxon Christian religious houses. There's an eighteenth century church on the site now, but they've excavated the Anglo-Saxon building and a Tudor one.'

'Why do you think it's our one?' asked Libby.

'Because the website mentions Eldreda.'

'So how come Sister Catherine didn't know that?' said Libby.

'She didn't know much, did she? Her order are Anglican Benedictines, not the original Augustines. But she got the area right. It is on the borders of Wales, near one of the castles that were built to keep the Welsh out of England, although it pre-dates that. I suppose everyone assumed it was near Tredegar as there actually is a place called that.'

'Can we find out if Eldreda's family were called Tredega?' said Libby.

'We can have a go. Might have to take a trip to the area to look at any written records there are – although there won't be many.'

'But what we really want to know,' mused Libby, 'is who took the relic during the dissolution and kept it for all those years.'

'Or how it turned up with poor Bernard Evans.'

'And was in the hands of the late collector.'

Fran and Libby looked at each other and grinned.
'On the trail again!' said Libby.

Chapter Five

Fran called Libby the following morning. 'How about a day out at the seaside?'

'Do you want me to do something?' asked Libby warily.

'Yes, go through the research on our relic. I thought we could do it together. It's a lovely day, and we could have lunch outside The Sloop.'

'Oh.' Libby brightened. 'OK, be with you in about an hour.'

It was indeed a lovely day, the road to Nethergate from Steeple Martin was thickly bordered by a mass of green hawthorn, blackthorn and alder. The sea came into view sparkling like cheap sequins as the car crested a rise, with the long, dark shape of Dragon Rock hunkered down in the middle of the bay. Libby smiled with pleasure.

She managed to find a parking spot in Harbour Street not too far from Coastguard Cottage and met Fran leaning over the sea wall contemplating the beach.

'Nice 'ere, innit?' she said.

Fran turned and smiled. 'I'm lucky aren't I?'

'The cottage, the sea, Guy and me. Yes, you are.'

Fran punched her lightly on the arm. 'Come on, see what I've found. Or would you like an ice cream from Lizzie's first?'

Lizzie had a small booth selling indescribably beautiful ice cream just along from Guy's gallery.

'Oh, go on, then.'

Returning to the sea wall with their cones, Libby said,

'So what have you found out, then?'

'Believe it or not, there's the whole story on the estate website. I suppose it was concealed at the time and only got publicised with the advent of public openings and so on.'

'So the church belongs to the castle estate?'

'No, the estate of a stately home called Maidenhaye. It seems to be a sort of Chatsworth or Castle Howard set up – you know, villages still part owned by the estate, farm shop, all sorts of events going on.'

Libby sucked the last dollop of ice cream out of the soggy end of the cornet. 'Come on then, let's go and have a look.'

Maidenhaye was beautiful. The house, smaller than either of those to which Fran had compared it, still contained the sort of paintings and treasures associated with the British stately home, and within the estate boundaries there were villages, shops selling only produce from the estate, estate farms, woodyards and craft shops, not to mention several properties available for holiday lets.

That, of course, was quite apart from the archaeological digs that seemed to be an ongoing process.

'Here we are,' said Fran. 'Dissolution.'

An early monastic house had been excavated, after the excavation of the supposedly 12th century monastery, the ruins of which had stood in the grounds for as long as anyone could remember. And with the excavation had come the examination of accompanying documents held in the family's archives.

And there was Eldreda.

'No mention of Tredega, though,' said Libby.

'No, but it tells the story. How her relic was brought back to the monastery and the reliquary was designed to hold it. Miracles were supposed to happen if the faithful came and prayed to it. And then how this monk – what's his name?'

'Brother Thomas.' Libby peered at the screen.

'Yes, him. Fled from the monastery when he knew Henry's thugs were on their way and gave it into the family's safekeeping.'

'It even explains what happens next,' exclaimed Libby. 'It's not even a secret.'

'Yes, the family lost everything – or nearly – and sold the relic after the South Sea Bubble burst. And there they lose sight of it.'

'Right.' Libby sat back. 'So who are the family who lived at Maidenhaye? Does it say?'

'The family are still there. It was entailed, and somehow they repaired their fortunes and hung on, even after the last war.'

Libby scrolled back through the pages. 'The Beaumonts. That sounds Norman-ish. Were they the family who brought back the reliquary?'

'I should think the original Anglo-Saxon family married into a Norman family,' said Fran. 'So it probably is the original family.'

'Who are still there. Should we ask them about it?'

'We ought to ask Sister Catherine if she's done that already,' said Fran.

'But she's so difficult to get hold of.' Libby gazed out of the window. 'Let's ask Patti.'

'Go on, then, give her a ring. Then we can go and have lunch.'

But Patti didn't know.

'I'm sure if she'd have known all that she'd have told me when we first spoke about it. But if they sold it after the South Sea Bubble – when was that? 1720s? – they wouldn't know its whereabouts now, would they?'

35

'They might know who they sold it to,' said Libby. 'Anyway, it's all become a bit academic now. After all, the antiquities dealer has quite happily admitted he's got the relic, and he's told Ian who they're handling it for. We're just interested.'

'As usual,' said Patti, amusement palpable in her voice.

'All right, nosy,' agreed Libby, 'but after all, you did set us on the trail.'

'And gave your Ian a link to a cold case,' said Patti. 'Just watch out that the curse of the relic doesn't come after you!'

'I still think we have to get in touch with the Beaumonts,' said Libby, as she and Fran walked down Harbour Street towards The Sloop Inn. 'Peter needs to if he's writing a play about St Eldreda. He might need to get their permission.'

'That's a point. You'd better tell him ASAP. Are we rehearsing tonight?'

'Yes. And I'll leave a message for Ian. I find it odd to say the least that the Arts and Antiquities people haven't got this far in their researches.'

Peter went into a very uncharacteristic panic when Libby told him the news and rang off saying he was going to call the Maidenhaye estate immediately. To the message she left for Ian, she received no reply.

When she arrived at the theatre that evening, Peter was in the bar with his laptop and several sheets of paper, frowning furiously.

'Good job you told me about the Beaumonts,' he said, looking up. 'They're very happy for me to go ahead, but they knew nothing about the reappearance of the relic. They've given me access to the few documents they hold when ever I want to go down, which means I'd better go this weekend. Want to come?'

'Well, yes, but – Ben …'

'Oh, for goodness' sake, Lib. You're not tied at the hip. Fran could come too, if she liked.'

'If I liked what?' Fran came up behind Libby, who explained.

'No, I'll leave it to you two, I have to help in the shop in Saturdays, and Guy's being very forbearing about all this rehearsing I'm doing.'

Ben appeared carrying a ladder.

'You don't mind if Libby goes down to Herefordshire with me on Saturday, do you, cousin dear?' Peter called across the lobby.

Ben raised his eyebrows in surprise. 'No, why?'

'We've found out more about the relic,' said Libby. 'Well, Fran did, actually.'

'So who did you speak to at Maidenhaye?' asked Fran.

'Eventually the household manager, who put me on hold while she spoke to someone else. The Beaumonts are in residence, apparently, and she managed to convey the fact that they are very interested. Wonder why?'

'Who wouldn't be? Something from your family's past turning up as part of a puzzle. If you count poor Bernard Evans as a puzzle, that is.' Libby looked over Peter's shoulder at the pieces of paper. 'Script changes?'

'There will have to be, now. These are preliminary notes. Meanwhile, we can go over the stuff that won't be affected.' He stood up. 'Is everybody here?'

'Nearly everybody,' said Ben. 'Except Dominic.'

'I don't know how he kept a job in television,' muttered Peter. 'I've never known anyone so unprofessional.'

The errant Dominic turned up halfway through Peter's explanation of the prospective script changes and annoyed everybody by asking for the whole story to be repeated. Peter refused and chivvied everyone into position for the start of the scenes he proposed to rehearse.

'I do think he might have explained properly,' Dominic said in an aside to Fran. 'It might have an effect on my character.'

Fran gave him a disgusted look. 'You're playing a thoroughly disreputable priest. Nothing much is going to change that.'

Dominic looked thoughtful. 'No. Much more fun playing baddies.'

Fran rolled her eyes and edged away.

When Libby and Ben got home, Libby found the Maidenhaye website and showed it to Ben.

'It looks beautiful,' he said. 'Perhaps we should book into one of their hotels and make a weekend of it.'

'That's an idea,' said Libby. 'That looks nice.'

The Maidenhaye Arms, predictably, stood on the edge of a village called Haye, just a stone's throw from the main house and the archaeological site. Ben called Peter's mobile, apologising for the lateness of the call, and made his suggestion.

'Looks good,' said Peter, after calling up the site on his own computer. 'Do you think it's too late to ring now?'

'We'll email. A double and a single? Hal won't be able to come will he?'

'No, pity. If we get in, don't forget to tell Hetty we won't be around for Sunday lunch.'

Friday morning, and an email accepting the booking was in Libby's inbox.

'Now you need to tell the Beaumonts we're coming,' said Libby, when she called Peter to tell him. 'And hope they don't mind hangers-on.'

She had barely switched off the phone when a sharp knock on the door indicated someone in a bad mood.

'Hello, Ian,' she said.

'What's all this about the Beaumonts and Maidenhaye?' he demanded, sweeping past her in to the sitting room.

'I told you in the message. Peter, Ben and I are going down there, tomorrow.'

'And you didn't think to ask me first?'

Libby was outraged. 'I bloody did! We didn't decide to go down there until last night after Peter had spoken to them. By which time you'd had my message since lunchtime. Besides, I don't have to ask your permission to do everything in my life.'

'All right, calm down, I'm sorry.' Ian pushed his hand through his hair.

'And you did say there was no harm in us digging,' said Libby, slightly mollified.

'Yes, I did. I've said I'm sorry.'

'Shall I put the kettle on?' asked Libby. 'Come into the kitchen and you can tell me all about whatever it is that's brought this on.'

'Mark – you remember? – got on to Marshall the collector's solicitor, who is handling the sale. He was able to state chapter and verse and make the solicitor realise that the reliquary had been stolen from Bernard Evans. He genuinely didn't know, and showed Mark all the relevant documentation for its provenance. The trouble is, the documents *were* genuine. They just dated from a century before.'

'No!' Libby paused in the act of pouring water on to tealeaves. 'So they were stolen, too?'

'Unfortunately we can't find that out. At the moment we're trying trace the person who provided them and sold the reliquary. All we have is photocopies of the documents, which Mark has verified.'

'It gets more and more complicated, doesn't it?' Libby fetched milk from the fridge. 'So why were you cross that we'd been in touch with Maidenhaye?'

'Because the documents appear to come from the Beaumonts.'

Chapter Six

'So what exactly was he cross about?' asked Peter, as Ben manoeuvred the four by four out of the Manor drive the following morning.

'He felt he should have approached the Beaumonts first – or Arts and Antiquities should.' Libby put her feet up in the back seat and prepared for a relaxed journey.

'I can see why he felt that. How did you talk him round?'

'By pointing out that anyone could have found out as much as we had about old Eldreda without knowing anything about Bernard Evans's murder. We were simply nosy researchers. He eventually conceded we might be able to find out more than he could. The Beaumonts don't, after all, know what we're looking for.'

'What *you're* looking for, you mean,' said Peter, sending her a disapproving look over his shoulder.

'So are you, really, whatever you say.' She peered through the gap between Peter and Ben. 'How long did you say this would take?'

'About four and a half hours, according to the route planner.' Ben eyed his satnav with disfavour. 'And if this doesn't take us up a farm track by mistake.'

'I shall follow the map on this,' said Peter, waving his smart new tablet. 'And give you updates on the news if you should want it.'

'No thanks,' said Libby. 'I have thought about a smartphone, though. It would be quite good for the old social networking.'

'I can't believe,' said Ben, looking over his shoulder as he pulled on to the main Canterbury road, 'that only a few years ago I had to help you buy your first computer. And now listen to you talking about social networking.'

'A lot's happened in the last few years,' said Libby. 'And Fran and I couldn't possibly have carried out our investigations without the internet.'

Peter and Ben exchanged amused grins.

'Anyway, to get back to the subject, are we allowed to tell the Beaumonts about the documents that were found?' Peter asked.

'Yes, I think so. After all, unless they somehow got the relic back, they'll be as much in the dark as we are, and they ought to know that someone has misappropriated some of their documents.'

'They probably don't know of their existence if they haven't noticed they're missing,' said Ben. 'Oh, great. Here's the first traffic jam.'

Including a brief stop at a motorway service station, the journey actually took five hours; they pulled up in the Maidenhaye estate car park at half past three.

Libby uncurled stiff limbs from the back of the four by four and stretched. Ben was already looking in the windows of the estate shop, sited handily in what appeared to be an old barn right next to the car park.

'Look at that beef,' he said. 'And that bread.' He turned to Peter and Libby. 'Do you think we should have an estate shop?'

'We wouldn't want to take away the livings of Joe and Nella at Cattlegreen,' said Libby, 'or Bob at the butchers. And they have organic stuff. The only thing the village hasn't got is a baker, and I can't see us doing that.'

'Hmm.' Ben turned back to the shop. 'Lovely range of

home-made jams and pickles they've got, and look at their cheese counter.'

'All right, all right,' said Peter, 'we'll go in and buy everything when we leave. I shall take cheese back for Harry. Now where do we have to go?'

They discovered the entrance to the main house and explained that they were there to see the Beaumonts and didn't want to buy the (expensive) tickets to see the house. The woman behind the desk looked dubious but lifted her telephone and pressed a button.

'Mr Beaumont will be down in a moment,' she said addressing a spot just behind Peter's left shoulder.

Libby looked round for a seat, but in the large hall the only seats were behind the desk. She wandered over to a huge portrait of a typically bland-faced gentleman in eighteenth-century clothes. 'I wonder if it was this one who lost the family fortunes?'

'It certainly was,' said an amused voice. Libby spun round to see that a tall man in slightly disreputable clothes had joined Peter and Ben.

'I'm sorry,' said Libby, going forward and holding out a hand. 'I'm Libby Sarjeant and I always say the wrong thing.'

'And I'm Alastair Beaumont.' The man took her hand with a friendly smile. 'Do come upstairs and meet my wife. We're dying to hear your story.'

Libby, Ben and Peter followed his rather stooped figure down a corridor and through a door marked private, where they climbed a well polished staircase to another door marked private.

'Sorry about this, but if we didn't keep a tiny bit of the house to ourselves, we'd go mad.' Alastair Beaumont opened the door and ushered them into a room with huge windows overlooking the park, with a view in the distance of what looked like ruins.

'Jennifer,' he said, 'here are our guests.'

A short woman with greying brown hair and a bright pink cardigan came forward with an equally bright smile.

'So good to meet you all,' she said. 'And we're dying to hear all about the relic. I boiled the kettle while Alastair was downstairs fetching you, so we can all have tea.'

When they were all settled in armchairs surrounding the empty fireplace with cups of tea, Libby began the story as it had gradually unfolded to them.

'It's intriguing,' said Alastair when she had finished, assisted by Peter, who told of his visit to the Abbey and the forthcoming play. 'We knew nothing about the documents. How did your policeman know they were genuine?'

'Actually, I don't know,' said Libby. 'I mean, they were authenticated by someone in the Arts and Antiquities department as being original old paper and ink – apparently they can practically tell what year the ink is from – and they have the Beaumont crest on them. Further than that, I don't know. But I expect Chief Inspector Connell will be in touch to ask you to verify them.'

'And these documents are where, now? Or rather, where were they found?' asked Jennifer Beaumont.

'They were provided by the solicitor handling the estate of a Mr Marshall, the collector who died,' said Peter. 'We think he bought it in all honesty. The documents would certainly make it appear legitimate.'

'So we don't know who sold it to him?' Alastair Beaumont frowned at his tea cup. 'And you say someone was murdered, too?'

'Yes, a Bernard Evans back in the seventies, but we don't know where it came from then. He had inherited it, we think.'

'I wonder if he's a distant connection of ours?' said

Jennifer Beaumont. 'We have Evanses in the family, don't we dear?'

Alastair laughed. 'I should think everyone in England has Evanses somewhere in their families, Jenny.'

'All right, I know I'm a bit dim.' Jennifer smiled comfortably, not at all put out.

'Well, when we've finished our tea we'll go down to the muniment room and you can see what I've dug out so far since your phone call,' said Alastair.

A white-painted arched door led into the muniment room, which was not, as Libby had thought, a dim and dusty dungeon, but a light room with tall windows, shelves on the walls, also white-painted, and a polished round table in the middle. Library steps stood against one set of shelves which held what appeared to be modern brown storage boxes, while against one wall stood a beautiful apothecary's chest and an ancient telescope. More boxes could be seen through a cupboard door which stood open.

'As you can see,' said Alastair, 'we're trying to catalogue everything and make everything more accessible, especially since we've had the archaeologists around. And we already had these out after the discovery of the earlier monastic house.'

On the table were fragile documents in what could have been Sanskrit as far as Libby was concerned.

'These are the letters brought back with St Eldreda's finger after she died. Very rare. Then these,' Alastair lifted a leather bound book which looked as though it might fall apart at a sudden breath, 'are the reports of Brother Thomas bringing the reliquary here. We'd always wondered why he came here, but of course St Eldreda had a connection with this place, although we don't actually know what that was.'

'And it was quite safe here from thereon?' asked Libby.

'Well, actually, no, it wasn't.' Alastair smiled wryly. 'It has a chequered history, and we can't sort it all out. Before it was sold by the family after the South Sea Bubble adventure, it had gone missing twice, both times having been recovered.'

'And how had that happened?' asked Peter. 'Someone stole it?'

'Yes, both times it was a member of the family who needed money, and both times it was sent back by whoever had bought it. The members of the family by the time it was finally sold decided it brought bad luck. The people who'd sold it both came to bad ends, and it was assumed that whoever had bought it had also had bad luck and returned it, only for the family to lose almost everything in the eighteenth century.'

'But we don't know where it went after that?' asked Ben. 'No more bad luck?'

'Not until this poor chap Bernard Evans you told me about. Someone seems to have stolen it then, yet it's now being sold with Beaumont documentation.' He shook his head. 'You don't know exactly what these papers are?'

'No.' Libby looked round the room. 'What could they have been, do you think?'

'Probably,' said Peter, 'the original documents of sale from the eighteenth century.'

'But,' said Libby, frowning, 'that's not possible. If the family sold it all bona fide, in 1720 whatever, whoever bought it had the documents. He either left it to someone or gave it to someone with the documents. Eventually it was left to our Bernard, and then it was stolen. But we don't know that the documents were stolen with it.'

'They must have been,' said Ben. 'He was taking it to the Abbey, wasn't he? He would have brought the provenance with him.'

'Hmm.' Libby was still frowning.

'It's the only thing that makes sense,' said Alastair. 'And the person who stole it then sold it to the collector who has just died.'

'It's such an obscure item, though,' said Peter. 'It's almost as though someone has been tracking it through the years. How would anyone know about it? This is the first time it's gone on sale – or even view – to the public.'

The four of them looked at each other.

'That's true,' said Alastair slowly. 'And of course, the only people who could possibly have known anything about it would be the members of my own family.'

Chapter Seven

Ben, Libby and Peter shifted uncomfortably.

'I wouldn't worry about it,' said Alastair, sounding amused. 'Our family has more than its fair share of villains and ne'er-do-wells. If a member of the family found out that Bernard Evans had it in the seventies, he, or she, could well have stolen it from him. A bit much to murder him, I'd have thought, but perhaps it was an accident.'

'But we come back to "how did they know",' said Libby. 'Bernard was left it, apparently. We still don't know by whom.'

'Well,' said Alastair, pulling a chair out from the table and indicating that the others should do the same, 'we could start by looking at who it could have been from my family.'

'That's a bit extreme,' muttered Peter. 'Families can be –'

'Tricky.' Ben nodded. 'We know all about that, Alastair.'

Alastair quirked an eyebrow, but said nothing.

'Your family must have been quite widely – er – disseminated by then, Alastair,' said Libby hurriedly.

'Oh, yes.' He pulled a scroll towards him and began to unroll it. 'Peter, could you weigh down the other end?'

'This is a family tree we had drawn up a few years ago. I got this out as well to see if I could see any connections, and now we've got Bernard Evans's name we could look for him.'

Libby shook her head. 'I can't see him being a member of your family.'

'He could be the issue of someone who married into it. If only we knew where it went after it was sold in the seventeen hundreds,' said Ben.

'We know who it was sold to,' said Alastair.

The other three stared at him.

'But you said ...' said Libby.

'I didn't say anything.' Alastair smiled. 'We do know who it was sold to, but the family lost sight of it after that.'

'So who was it?' asked Peter.

'A man rejoicing in the name of Bartholomew Tollybar, who I've always thought must have been a bit of a crook.'

'And who was he?' asked Libby.

'We don't know. We simply have the deed of sale –' he reached across to pull another document forward '– here.'

'Bartholomew Tollybar – is that esquire?' Libby pointed to a squiggle.

'Yes, and that's all we know about him.' Alastair sat back in his chair and smiled at the other three. 'I can't see that it helps at all.'

'I can,' said Libby. 'We can look into Bartholomew's family tree. Find out about him. You know, censuses and things.'

'They didn't start until the next century,' said Ben. 'You found that out before, didn't you?'

'Oh, yes. Well, let's see.' Libby thought for a moment. 'Street directories?'

'Possibly,' said Alastair, 'but I'm not sure why you want to trace him.'

'It's a link,' said Libby. 'We need to trace the progress of the reliquary until it reaches where it is now. It might help find out who killed Bernard Evans,' said Libby.

'We haven't looked at the family tree yet,' Peter pointed

out, 'and I'm still holding the other end.'

'Sorry.' Libby bent towards it. 'This is you, is it, Alastair?'

Alastair pointed the way through the generations of Beaumonts, past the impecunious member who had sold the reliquary, and back into far more sparse accounts. Brother Thomas appeared, but as a secondary branch of the family, and then, in the early fifteenth century, the line seemed to peter out.

'And do we know who the black sheep were who pinched it before it was sold?' asked Ben.

'Not definitively. That tends to be passed down orally, but as far as we can tell it's never been anyone of the direct line.'

'Son of a younger son?' suggested Libby.

'Something like that. You can see we've got many offshoots now, not all of them followed up.'

'So all we've really got to follow up is old Bartholomew Tollybar,' said Libby, as Peter and Alastair carefully rolled up the family tree.

'If it helps.' Alastair put the documents back inside a cupboard. 'I was wondering, if the reliquary was up for sale, if the family might buy it.'

There was a surprised silence.

'You said the nuns don't want it?'

'Well, not really.' Libby looked at Peter. 'They don't, do they?'

'They regard it as idolatrous,' said Peter. 'They're an Anglican order. They were just interested.' He looked at Alastair. 'Do you regard it as rightfully belonging to your family, then?'

'No, because we sold it, but it did once belong to this family,' said Alastair reasonably.

'Not really,' said Libby. 'It belonged to the monastery

50

where St Eldreda came from.'

'But that's here in our grounds,' said Alastair, 'and she came from here.'

'Yes.' Libby nodded. 'So, do you want it back?'

'Legitimately, if we could. Don't you think it would be fitting?'

The other three looked at each other.

'It would,' said Peter,' but I've got a feeling our Chief Inspector Connell won't let it go anywhere just yet.'

The Maidenhaye Arms was comfortable, old-fashioned and quiet. After a wash and brush-up, Libby met the two men in the bar.

'So what do we think of all that, then?' asked Peter, while Ben went to fetch drinks. 'Nice bloke?'

'Yes, very nice,' said Libby. 'I was a bit bothered by him wanting to buy the relic, though.'

'I think it's quite natural,' said Peter.

'But whatever that old document said, we can't be sure that St Eldreda came from his family, can we?'

'No, because it looks to me as if the Beaumonts are descended from a Norman line who wouldn't even have been here then.'

'And what about the original abbey or whatever it was?'

'There are more than one sets of archaeological remains there, aren't there,' said Ben, putting three gin and tonics on the table. 'I think it's safe to say that was where she was taken. Or rather, the reliquary was. And transferred to the newer one before the dissolution.'

'So did we actually find anything out?' said Peter. 'Only who the reliquary was sold to three hundred years ago.'

'We really needed to know how those documents were stolen, and where from,' said Libby. 'Then we could find out who took them.'

'And when,' said Ben. 'If they were forged back then,

51

perhaps when one of the Beaumonts pinched the reliquary, it wouldn't help.'

'But Alastair said it had been stolen *before* it was sold. And we don't know exactly when those documents were dated.' Libby took a sip of her drink. 'Oh, dear, this is most confusing.'

'Actually, I don't think there's much more we can learn here,' said Peter. 'I suppose we could talk to the archaeologists, but they won't be able to tell us about anything.'

'Wasted journey, then?' said Ben.

'No, because we know about jolly Bartholomew Tollybar,' said Libby. 'That's a good starting point for finding out where it went after that.'

'It's a long shot,' said Ben.

'I wish we'd been able to take a copy of that family tree,' said Libby thoughtfully. 'If we could trace perhaps a rogue line ...'

'How would that help?' said Peter. 'All we'd get is a lot of names we don't know.'

'Yes.' Libby sighed heavily. 'Oh, well, at least we can report back to Ian that we haven't done anything he wouldn't like.' She looked round the bar. 'Are we eating here?'

The food was good, basic British cooking, made from ingredients from the estate shop.

'Is this place owned by the Beaumont estate?' asked Libby, when their plump, smiling host brought coffee to their table.

'We lease it from them,' he said. 'No restrictions except that we use estate produce. Which we're happy to do anyway.'

'And what's it like living here? It's almost feudal, isn't it, with the estate owning whole villages?'

He laughed. 'It sounds like it, doesn't it? But actually, there are privately owned properties, apart from the leased ones. And ex-estate workers who have their properties for life.'

'So he's a benevolent despot, Alastair Beaumont?' said Ben.

'Indeed he is.'

'You're a benevolent despot, too, aren't you, darling?' said Libby, patting Ben's arm as the manager left them.

'I only have a couple of tenant farmers,' said Ben. 'And I leave them alone as much as I can.'

'You seem to have a lot of work to do in the estate office,' said Peter.

'We've still got the woodyard and the staff who look after our own bit of ground that isn't leased out,' said Ben.'

'Do any of them have tied cottages?'

'Why the sudden interest?' asked Ben, amused. 'You've never asked before.'

'I've never thought about it before,' said Peter. 'Have they?'

'No, we don't own any property except the two farms, and they only revert to us if none of the family want to continue in the business.'

'So the farms are more or less theirs for ever?'

'That's it. If either of the families decided to leave, which they may well do, seeing that farming's going through such a bad time, especially dairy, we'd have to sell up.'

'Where would they go?' asked Libby. 'If they left?'

'Both families have bought property away from the farm,' said Ben. 'They're sensible.'

After dinner they took a stroll round the village, which impressed them with its neatness and prettiness.

'It's like a village in a story book,' said Libby. 'Very

chocolate-boxy.'

'Not untidy and slapdash like our village?' said Ben with a smile.

'I like us as we are,' said Libby. 'This all looks a bit repressed.'

'I know what you mean,' said Peter. 'I don't think they allow rowdy parties here.'

'You don't do rowdy parties,' said Libby, tucking one arm through his and the other through Ben's. 'Come on, let's go back to the pub and have a drink.'

The following morning they returned to Maidenhaye itself to say goodbye to Alastair and Jennifer.

'You will let us know about any developments?' said Alastair. 'And remember, if it really is for sale, we'd certainly be interested to buy it.'

Ben and Peter browsed the estate shop and bought various treats, while Libby tasted a couple of the estate wines.

'We could do something at the Manor,' she said as they finally pulled out of the car park to start the journey home. 'I know we supply some of the meat for the butcher's shop and there's Nella and Joe at Cattlegreen, but maybe cheeses and marmalades and things.'

'Are you offering?' asked Ben, grinning at her in the rear-view mirror.

'Not exactly,' said Libby, 'but what about a farmer's market sort of set up? Then Bob the Butcher and Nella and Joe could sell stuff.'

'Where, though? They both have shops in the village already, as you said yesterday. And personally, I wouldn't like to have to go into retail at this time of life. If we were to start making anything at the Manor or on the farms, I'd rather they sold it themselves or through the eight-til-late.'

'You've changed your mind,' said Libby, settling back

in her corner. 'It just looked nice there.'

'It did look nice, but don't forget there aren't any other shops in that village. We've got several. We're lucky.'

It was when they were on the home stretch of the journey, having circumnavigated Canterbury, that Libby's phone began to ring.

'Libby, it's Patti.'

'Patti? It's Sunday. Why aren't you ministering?'

'I'm going to one of the other churches for evensong in a minute, but listen. You'll never guess what!'

'What?'

'They've offered to let St Eldreda's display the reliquary while the play's on!'

Chapter Eight

'How did that happen?' asked Peter, when Libby relayed Patti's conversation.

'I'm not sure. Sister Catherine wasn't either, apparently. She said the solicitor for the estate rang to say he'd received a request from someone. It wasn't you, was it?'

'Libby! Of course it wasn't. I wouldn't know who the solicitor was.'

'Well, the nuns don't know, but whoever sent the request did them and us a favour. The nuns are delighted, even though they wouldn't like to keep it. We are to keep it to ourselves, though, until nearer the first night.'

'Security risk,' said Ben. 'It must be worth a small fortune.'

'I wonder,' said Libby slowly, staring out of the window at the familiar road ahead.

'What?'

'I wonder if Ian's done it.'

'Ian?' Peter's head whipped round. 'Why on earth would he do it?'

'To see if someone else takes a shot at it.'

'So someone else can get murdered?'

'Well, it might bring someone out of the woodwork, mightn't it?'

'Whoever killed Bernard Evans in the seventies isn't likely to still be around,' said Ben.

'Why not? We were all around then and we still are.'

'Yes, but he'd be likely to be older than we are, so a

fairly geriatric murderer.'

'Oh, that's true,' said Libby. 'Still, it's a thought.'

It being Sunday, Hetty had cooked her usual roast, but re-scheduled it for seven o'clock. As Harry was shut on a Sunday evening, he joined them, and they all relaxed round the large kitchen table with glasses of one of Hetty's fine wines.

'So that's where we are now,' Libby concluded, having brought Harry and Hetty up to date with the events of the past few days.

'Estate shop sounds good,' commented Hetty.

'That's what I said! But Ben says no,' said Libby.

Hetty fixed her son with a gimlet eye. 'Not going to put the village shops out of business. Home-made produce. Get the farmers to provide it. One of 'em keeps bees, don't he?'

'I did say that might be the answer,' said Ben grudgingly.

'But you said they'd have to sell it themselves or through the eight-til-late,' said Libby. 'I bet Het could work out something better than that.'

Looking pleased, Hetty simply grunted and got up to fetch the rib of beef that had been resting on top of the Aga.

'I think I'd put my money on Lib and Hetty together,' said Harry. 'We could even sell some stuff in the caff.'

'We've got a local vineyard, haven't we?' said Peter. 'Could we sell their wines, too?'

'Hey, wait a bit,' said Ben, holding up a hand. 'I haven't said yes, yet. And I'd have to look into all the legal side first.'

'Oh, the boring bit,' said Harry. 'OK, change the subject. Who do you reckon asked those solicitors to lend old St Edie's finger?'

'No idea.' Peter shook his head. 'There aren't many

people who know about it, after all.'

'All of us and the cast of the play,' said Libby, 'Fran and Guy, Patti and Anne, the nuns and – I say – do the nuns have servants?'

'They have oblates, or alongsiders, women who live and work with them, some for a short period, some for longer,' said Peter. 'I met a couple of them when I went to meet Sister Catherine.'

'So there's them, too,' said Libby. 'Do they live in or out?'

'In. And there are occasionally guests who are on retreat. They have guest accommodation.' Peter fetched a dish of roast potatoes and carrots to the table.

'Most of those are mine,' said Harry. 'To make up for the meat.' He cackled and drew the dish towards him.

'There's more,' said Hetty.

The subject of the reliquary was abandoned until after the beef had been finished and the treacle sponge demolished.

'Pouff,' said Libby, leaning back in her chair. 'The Maidenhaye Arms couldn't hold a candle to that.'

Hetty looked pleased, but said nothing.

'Speaking of Maidenhaye,' said Ben, 'you ought to let Ian know what happened, Lib. After all, he wasn't altogether pleased about us going down there.'

'It can wait until tomorrow,' said Libby. 'If Ian's got a Sunday off he won't appreciate a call from me.'

But on Monday morning it was Ian who called Libby.

'I've just been speaking to Alastair Beaumont. He tells me he'd like to buy the reliquary.'

'Yes,' said Libby, surprised. 'He told us, too. I was going to ring you to report.'

'Of course you were.' Libby could almost hear him grinning. 'Anyway, it appears that there's no knowing when or from where those documents were stolen. I described them to Mr Beaumont and he confirms that they sound genuine, but he doesn't have a clue where they might have come from, except that to him they sound later than the document of sale he showed you.'

'Dear old Bartholomew Tollybar? Really?' Libby frowned.

'Which argues that, if our provenance documents are genuine, the reliquary must have been back in the possession of the Beaumonts *after* Tollybar bought it.'

'Suggesting that yet another renegade member of the family pinched it back?'

'Another?'

Libby explained about the previous thefts of the reliquary.

'It forms a pattern,' said Ian. 'For some reason, some members of the family think the reliquary should always be in their possession, and others use it for personal gain.'

Libby tried to think this through. 'I think I understand,' she said. 'So what you're saying is Bernard Evans was left the thing by a family member and it was pinched by another one. Bit convoluted, isn't it?'

'I'm not sure about who left it to Evans. I think that was probably someone who'd bought it from a family member, and someone else wanted it back.'

'I've got a picture of all these little Beaumont figures throwing the reliquary around like a football,' said Libby. 'You need to see Alastair's family tree. It's vast.'

'That's what I thought. You see, there will always be offshoots of a family who resent the main branch. Wouldn't you say it could have been one of those who played fast and loose with this thing?'

'Maybe,' said Libby doubtfully. 'It all sounds a bit far-fetched to me. In fact, why are you so interested?'

'Because,' said Ian, 'the item was stolen from a murder victim within living memory, and it has now shown up. That means we have to investigate. You know that. You told us about it.'

'But the history …'

'Libby, you're always the one who wants to look into the history. Now, did you hear that the estate is to loan the reliquary to the Abbey for the duration of the play?'

'Yes, Patti told me yesterday. How did that come about. Was it you?'

'How did you know?' asked Ian, after a pause.

'I couldn't think that anyone else requesting it would have been indulged,' said Libby. 'Is it bait?'

'I wouldn't put it quite like that,' said Ian, sounding uncomfortable.

'But you want to see if it draws anyone out.'

'In a way. We thought if it was publicised –'

'Isn't that dangerous?'

'It will be well guarded, and only on view during performances. The rest of the time it will be in secure custody.'

'Police, or a security company?'

'Whatever resources can stretch to. There has been interest from a Kent museum since the news leaked out –'

'Leaked out?'

'You couldn't expect this to stay under wraps, and, as I say, this museum might undertake to keep it temporarily.'

'Hmm. I suppose it will be all right, as long as the nuns aren't put in danger.'

'We'd never do that. So you carry on with your rehearsals, and we'll make all the arrangements. We'll let you know if any developments occur.'

'So that's that,' said Libby to Sidney, as she switched off the phone. 'Thank you and good night.'

She called Fran, then Patti, Ben and Peter and relayed the news.

'I expect Ian will tell Sister Catherine himself,' she said to Patti, 'so there's no need for me to bother her.'

'I expect so,' said Patti, 'but he'll have a fight on his hands.'

'He will?'

'The nuns want to keep the reliquary in the Abbey for the duration. They don't want it going anywhere else. They feel it's their right, even though they won't keep it afterwards.'

'Right. This should be interesting, then, but as I said to Ian we don't want to put the nuns in danger.'

'Not many people break into an abbey,' said Patti. 'Especially one with a good security system!'

The subject of the reliquary gradually disappeared from daily conversation over the next couple of weeks, until the first rehearsal took place at the Abbey in the ruins of the monastery.

'Apparently,' said Peter, as he drove Ben and Libby to the Abbey, 'the reliquary is already there, in a special glass case and they've appointed a private security company to look after it at night.'

'Only at night?' said Libby.

'There'll be people around it all the rest of the time,' said Peter, 'and it's a high-security case.'

'Are they opening it to the public?' asked Ben.

'Only the public who come to the play. And since there's been a bit about it in the local press ticket sales have shot up.'

'Really?' Libby was interested. 'Has our Campbell been on to you yet?'

'Not yet. I doubt if it's quite TV news-worthy.'

Campbell McLean was a reporter for the Kent and

Coast television network.

'Jane ran it in the *Mercury*,' said Peter. 'I sent her the press release myself.'

Jane Baker was assistant editor at the *Nethergate Mercury* and was a long-standing friend.

'In that case Campbell won't be far behind,' said Libby. 'He picks all Jane's stories apart.'

When they arrived at the Abbey, Peter parked on the gravel sweep in front of the modern building as Sister Catherine and a woman in a blue pinafore dress came out on to the steps.

Sister Catherine seemed delighted to see them, and very excited about both the play and the reliquary.

'Oh you must come and see where we've put it,' she enthused, 'but I forget myself! This is Martha, our resident alongsider.'

The woman in the pinafore dress stepped forward and held out her hand.

'I'm so pleased to meet you,' she said with a smile. 'Of course, I've already met Mr Parker.'

'Peter, please,' said Peter. 'And this is Libby and Ben.'

'Hello,' said Libby taking the outstretched hand. 'Lovely to meet you. I must say, I'm curious.'

Martha's dark eyes twinkled. 'Most people are.'

'Come on then,' urged Sister Catherine. 'I want you to see the reliquary at last.'

She led the way through the Abbey, from a wide entrance hall along a corridor to a modern glass-enclosed cloister. Double doors at the end of this opened into an atrium which, in turn, looked out on the ruins of the monastery, and in the centre of which stood a glass case on a high wooden plinth.

'Not too close,' said Martha, 'as we've got the lasers switched on.'

'Lasers?' Libby stopped short.

'If no one's around we switch them on. The security patrol checks it at night. They have access through the monastery grounds, not through the Abbey of course,' said Sister Catherine.

'And it's not lit at night, of course,' added Martha, her head on one side appreciatively. 'It looks wonderful there, doesn't it? As though it belongs.'

And it did. The reliquary itself was worked gold, set with coloured stones which Libby assumed were real emeralds, rubies and sapphires. It was small, only about six inches long by about two inches deep, and mounted on what looked like a battered piece of wood.

'I'll turn off the lasers, shall I, Sister?' asked Martha. 'After all, I shall be here with the actors.'

'Thank you, Martha.' Sister Catherine smiled gratefully. 'I don't know what we'd do without Martha, really I don't. She's volunteered to give up Compline every night you're here to act as – well, as hostess, I suppose.'

'The other oblates will help,' said Martha. 'We have two living here at the moment and three who are part of the family but live in their own homes. We aren't constrained to the life of daily prayers as the sisters are.'

'I must go to prepare for Compline now, so I'll leave you in Martha's hands,' said Sister Catherine. 'Good night and God bless.'

They all watched her go back through to the cloister, a tall, gliding black figure suddenly lit by a shaft of late sun through the cloister glass.

'I don't know how they do it,' murmured Libby.

'To tell you the truth,' said Martha, coming back from where she'd deactivated a concealed switch, 'neither do I.'

'But you live with them, you share in their daily life,' said Ben.

'But only as much as I want to,' said Martha. 'Yes, I'm devout, but I need a certain amount of freedom.' She smiled round at them. 'I'm so looking forward to this play. It'll be exciting to meet so many different people.'

'I just hope you don't regret it,' said Peter.

Libby looked at him sharply, but didn't say anything.

'So where do we go?' asked Ben. 'We'd better start setting up shop.'

'I know the way,' said Peter. 'I've got it all mapped out.'

'Our garden store has been cleared for you,' said Martha. 'There won't be much privacy, but it's the best we could do. We do have another building a bit further away which we use – or rather – is used – for weddings.'

'Oh, yes, I heard you had weddings here,' said Libby.

'We don't, exactly, they are civil ceremonies because the monastery is actually owned by a Heritage Trust, not the Abbey. But the land is still ours. It's a very complicated situation.' Martha opened the glass doors of the atrium. 'We'll keep these locked while the public are here, but the reliquary will be spotlit so they'll be able to come and look at it. It's quite a centre piece, isn't it?'

'It certainly is.' Libby went out through the doors and turned back. 'Thank you so much, Martha. Will you be around if we need to ask anything?'

'Yes, of course. We've put our public toilets at your disposal, which are also used by visitors to the monastery, and they're over there.' She pointed.

'She's nice,' said Libby to Peter as they strolled slowly towards the monastery ruins and their performance area. 'What did you mean when you said you hoped they don't regret it?'

Peter stopped and stared up at the grey stone arches.

'I just hope nothing goes wrong. I've got a rather nasty feeling that something might.'

Chapter Nine

The other actors, including Fran, began to arrive. They all drifted over to look at the reliquary, exclaiming or shuddering, according to temperament. When they had all assembled, Peter called them to order and showed them the layout of the performance area.

'The only place you will be able to go to when off-stage is behind the Abbey building over there.' He pointed beyond the atrium. 'The gardener's shed has been cleared for our use, but there isn't much in there except a couple of benches. That's where we'll have to change, so don't bring masses of belongings and make up – there just isn't room. Right, now, everybody ready?'

'It's going quite well, isn't it?'

Dominic's voice in her ear made Libby turn sharply.

'Yes. Although we'll have to stop soon because the light's going.' Libby peered through the grey ruins to where Peter stood on the far side. 'I hope he's organised the floodlights.'

Dominic turned towards the atrium. 'Makes the thing stand out though, doesn't it? The dusk.'

Libby looked across. The reliquary in its glass case glowed under the spotlight. 'Certainly does.'

'Doesn't look very safe there, though.'

'Oh, it's very well guarded,' said Libby. 'Lasers and all sorts. And a security patrol.'

'Just as well,' said Dominic. 'It looks valuable. Oh, hey, that's me. I'm on.'

Libby watched him stride on to the "stage" and declaim his lines. He was a pest in a lot of ways, but she supposed his heart was in the right place.

Peter called a halt ten minutes later.

'No use rehearsing in the dark,' he said. 'Luckily, the ruins have floodlighting, which we may have permission to turn on early, and we've also got more lights being loaned to us by the theatre's lighting people. We won't have those until the week of the performance, though, so I'm keeping my fingers crossed for the early floodlighting. Off you go.'

'I'll go and find Martha and tell her to lock up the reliquary,' said Libby. 'And someone's got to lock the gates to the grounds.'

She went into the atrium and called. Martha appeared immediately from a door to the left.

'I've been watching out of the window,' she said 'It's fascinating, isn't it? I shall ask if we can put the floodlighting on as soon as you come for your next rehearsal.'

'That's just what Peter was hoping for! Who do we have to ask?'

'Don't worry, I'll sort it out,' said Martha. 'Are you ready for me to lock the gates?'

'You do that, too, do you?' Libby watched Martha switch off the spotlight and switch on the security.

'When the heritage people aren't here, yes. The whole site has to be kept secure. It's not like Whitby Abbey where you can just wander in.'

The main car park for the ruins was empty by the time Martha and Libby arrived, and Libby marvelled as the huge electronic gates swung slowly shut.

'Your car's in front of the Abbey, isn't it?' said Martha. 'Come on, we can cut through here.'

'The grounds are beautiful, aren't they?' said Libby,

67

peering around her through the dusk.

'Glorious. As long as the rain keeps off you'll have a lovely week. Here we are.'

They emerged on to the forecourt, where Peter and Ben were waiting by the car.

'Thanks for everything, Martha,' said Peter. 'We hope we won't be too much trouble.'

She beamed. 'Of course you won't. We're delighted to have you and the reliquary here.'

'It's going to work, isn't it?' said Libby, as Peter drove them out on to the main road. 'It's a lovely setting. And Martha's going to ask for the floodlighting to be switched on early for us.'

'Great. All I need to do now is finalise the paperwork with the heritage people,' said Peter.

'I was wondering about insurance,' said Ben. 'The Abbey surely can't afford it for the reliquary?'

'Apparently the estate are funding that. The main beneficiary has agreed that, and is actually coming to see the play.'

'Bloody hell!' said Libby. 'So why haven't we heard anything about this beneficiary before?'

'I don't know, but apparently he or she thinks it's good exposure for the pesky thing, and will increase the chances of a good price. It's going up for auction, now, rather than a private sale.'

'Alastair Beaumont might not be able to afford it, then,' said Ben. 'Pity.'

Rehearsals rolled on and were often blighted by rain. Final preparations were made, hundreds of yards of cabling were hidden among the ruins, and several large padlocks bought for the gardener's shed, where all the lights were kept overnight. The security company patrolled the outside walls twice a night, and inside, using a side entrance at random times.

'Wouldn't want any Tom, Dick or Harry learning our routines, would we?' said one of the security guards to Libby one evening as they packed up to go.

'Must be costing a fortune,' said Fran, as they arrived back at the pub in Steeple Martin, where Guy was meeting them.

'It's the beneficiary who's paying again,' said Libby. 'He doesn't want his precious bauble nicked before it makes a fortune at auction.'

'Have you heard any more from Ian?'

Libby shook her head. 'Nothing. It's as though he's dropped the case.'

'I don't suppose he has, but it's very different looking into a forty-year-old murder to one committed yesterday,' said Fran. 'He's probably trying to track down whoever left the thing to – what was his name?'

'Bernard Evans. Yes, I expect so. I hope he remembers to tell us what he finds out.'

As Libby had predicted, Campbell McLean had been in touch and had already done a piece on the local news about the reliquary and the play, and on the first night was to bring a camera crew and interview Peter before the play began. However, he wasn't allowed to film the reliquary, only to show the auction catalogue photograph.

'Another security thing, I suppose,' said Peter, telling them in the pub after the dress rehearsal. 'It's been a bit of a pain, hasn't it?'

'Oh, I don't know,' said Libby. 'It hasn't been too bad at all. And Martha and the other oblates have been having a high old time.'

Bob the Butcher leant forward. 'Exactly what *is* an oblate?'

'Someone who works alongside the nuns. They're lay

people, but very religious, and not bound by all the regulations that apply to the nuns. Also called alongsiders,' explained Libby. 'Martha's the permanent resident, but they have others who come for short periods and live in, and others who live out.'

'Doesn't seem much of a life to me,' said Bob. 'No wonder they're enjoying us lot.'

'They go out and about helping people,' said Libby vaguely. 'At least, I think they do.'

'Anyway, the publicity's been good for ticket sales,' said Ben. 'We've almost sold out for all four performances.'

'It does seem a lot of work for just four performances,' said Libby.

'It was all we were allowed if you remember,' said Peter reprovingly. 'And don't forget most of the cast have day jobs.'

'Oh, I know,' said Libby. 'Which is why we're so thin on the ground in here tonight.' She looked round. 'Not many of the usual group.'

'And we haven't got our lovely bar to drink in after the show each night, so I don't suppose we'll get many any night,' said Ben.

'Until the last night,' said Peter.

'Well, of course. We're having the after-show party in the theatre and it will be a Saturday,' said Libby.

Peter grinned at her. 'It'll be worth it. I can't believe how beautiful the production looks.'

'Glad you're pleased.' Libby patted his arm. 'Come on, then. Early night before the big day tomorrow.'

Ben, Libby and Peter arrived early at the Abbey the following day and stood looking at the graceful grey stone arches and carvings which would be their set.

'I hope we do it justice,' said Peter. 'And I hope all the

lighting won't detract from it.'

'It enhances it, what do you mean?' said Libby in surprise.

'I mean the physical lights. I hope they don't intrude.' Peter shrugged. 'Oh well. I'm going to get them out of the shed and begin setting up.'

Libby trailed behind the two men and found Martha in the unlocked atrium polishing the glass case. She turned and smiled.

'Big day today.'

'It is.' Libby peered into the case. 'I've got quite fond of this old thing. Pity we never did find out its history.'

Martha sighed. 'Well, you did find out quite a lot. Just not who stole it and murdered that man.'

'Do you think it brings bad luck?' Libby looked at the calm sensible face beside her.

Martha stared into the case. 'N-no, not exactly,' she said. 'I just think it should have stayed in the monastery in the first place.'

'What? Do you mean not gone back to Wales?'

'Well, this was where she died.'

'But the rest of her went to Canterbury, so this wouldn't have stayed here anyway,' said Libby.

'No,' said Martha with a sigh.

'And she would have been lost in the Dissolution in any case.'

'True.' Martha turned with a sad smile. 'My trouble is, I'm a bit of a romantic. Not the right thing, I suppose, for someone who lives as I do.'

'Oh, I don't know. Even if you don't want it for yourself, you can appreciate romance in others – although you're not exactly talking about that sort of romance, are you?'

Martha laughed. 'No, I wasn't, but I know what you

71

mean. I've been married, you know.' She turned and gave the glass a last polish.

'Oh – I'm sorry –' began Libby.

'No, no, it's quite all right.' Martha tucked the cloth into the large pocket in her pinafore. 'I believed in the sanctity of marriage – he didn't. In fact –' she looked away '– I'm still married.'

'Ah.' Libby gazed fixedly out of the doors to where Ben and Peter between them were carrying two lamps and a quantity of cable.

'Sorry.' Martha gave a little laugh. 'That conversation went a bit astray, didn't it?'

'Not at all,' said Libby with relief. 'They do, sometimes. Anyway, I'd better get over there and help with the set-up. Will you be staying here?'

'I'm going to sneak over to watch the performance. I can lock this up while it's on, can't I?'

'Good idea,' said Libby. 'Hope you enjoy it.'

In dribs and drabs the rest of the company trickled in. Sister Catherine appeared to wish them luck and announced that all the sisters had been given dispensation to watch the performance. This rather increased the nerves of the cast and Peter in particular, who started fidgeting round the lights and muttering.

'God,' said Libby inappropriately, as she adjusted her habit and wimple, 'if he doesn't shut up he's going to have the whole cast collapsing from sheer fright.'

Outside the shed the light was beginning to fade. The floodlights were switched on, and the security guard radioed through that the first of the audience had arrived and the gates were being opened.

'No one outside now,' Peter said, coming through the door of the shed, fair hair flopping over a deep frown. 'Sorry it's so bloody crowded in here.'

72

A chorus of assurance lifted the frown a little, and he nodded and went out to see if the reliquary was safe.

'Martha will be standing by it while members of the audience go and peer at it,' said Libby, 'then she'll lock it up and come and watch us.'

'Isn't that a bit dangerous?' asked Dominic. 'Leaving it alone with all these strangers here?'

'Not a bit,' said Ben. 'Anyone trying to get up to the atrium would have to get past us – or through us, come to that. There's no other way, unless they go through the Abbey itself, and that's locked up tighter than a drum.'

'Why a drum?' mused Fran, gazing out of the door. 'I've always wondered.'

Libby smiled fondly at her.

The buzz of the audience grew louder and at last Peter came back to give them the three-minute call. The audience went quiet and the lights came up. Libby felt sure her heartbeat was visible though the thick black of her habit, and swallowed nervously. 'Break a leg, everyone,' she whispered, and moved forward.

An hour and three-quarters later they stood together bowing incessantly to a rapturous crowd. Eventually, Peter resolutely shepherded them back through the dark arches to their shed and surprised them by producing champagne.

'Did you hear anything from the audience?' Libby asked him as he topped up her glass. 'Any comments, I mean?'

'The only one I had to answer properly was why our nuns wore modern habits.' He grinned. 'I pointed out that medieval paintings showed monks and nuns in almost the same clothes as they wear now. At least we didn't put you all in those dowdy grey jobs.'

'The shorter ones, you mean? No, they lack a certain gravitas, don't they?' Libby sipped appreciatively. 'Good idea, this.'

By the time they were all changed and the technical apparatus locked away there was no sign of either Martha or the sisters. The atrium was dark and the floodlights off. Libby and Ben stayed with Peter as he did his final locking up, and bade the security guard on duty goodnight.

'How did your interview with Campbell go?' asked Libby, as they climbed into Ben's four by four. 'I forgot to ask.'

'Oh, fine. Just a little bit about its history and how we came to be doing the play. It's only a filler, I think.'

'Do we know when the beneficiary of the will is coming? Or was he there tonight?' asked Ben.

'I've no idea. We don't even know if it's male or female. I wonder if it will introduce itself?'

'It might simply want to check the security arrangements,' said Libby. 'We might never know.'

The Thursday and Friday performances were equally well received, and glowing reports appeared in both Jane's *Nethergate Mercury* and the large county newspaper. Ben reported a large number of requests for tickets sadly turned down, and all cast and crew members had friends and family trying to get in on their coat-tails.

'A bit like the pantomimes,' said Libby, as they drove, for the last time, towards the Abbey, 'and the fight for tickets to them. Perhaps we ought to reprise this at the theatre.'

'No.' Peter shook his head firmly. 'It was written to be performed at the Abbey, not in a theatre. And that reminds me, we shall have to organise a work party to go tomorrow and do the get-out. We can't take it all tonight.'

Martha met them when they arrived, a frown on her face.

'What's up?' asked Libby.

'It's the owner. Well, the person who will be the owner,' said Martha. 'He wants to take it away tonight.'

'The reliquary?' said Peter, as they all stopped dead. 'He's here, then?'

'I don't know. I suppose he must be on his way. Sister Catherine had a phone call.'

'But that might not be genuine,' said Libby. 'Oh, for goodness' sake! It will take hours to dismantle the lasers and the case – and you can't just let someone walk off with it on the say-so of a phone call.'

'No, that's what we all thought. Sister Catherine said the security company are contracted to deliver it back to the antiquarian auction place, and they won't allow it out of their sight.' She sighed. 'So it will be here until tomorrow morning. What I can't understand, if that phone call was genuine, is why? This person volunteered to loan the relic, and even paid for the security company – why go against that?'

'That's what makes it seem phoney,' said Ben. 'I think you're wise to keep it here.'

'Yes,' Martha turned a wistful face towards the atrium. 'I shall miss it.'

The usual end-of-term feeling pervaded the cast as they changed and got ready for the last performance of Murder in the Monastery.

'The last ever, probably,' said Bob, adjusting his tonsure-wig. 'Shame.'

'Couldn't Peter ask the beneficiary of the estate to lend it for another performance next year?' asked Dominic.

'It will have a new owner by then,' said Fran.

'Well, why not ask them. It might be those people you went to see, Libby.'

'And it might not. No, I think this is the last we'll see of it, Dominic,' said Libby. 'And it'll be gone by the morning.'

At the end of a triumphant last performance, Peter produced more champagne and an invitation back to the theatre bar. 'And we need a work party for tomorrow, don't forget,' he warned.

Libby went to find Martha, who was locking the atrium for the last time.

'I'll see you tomorrow,' she said, 'but I expect this will be gone by then.'

'I expect so,' said Martha. 'I'm handing over my keys very early.'

'You look sad,' said Libby.

Martha smiled. 'I know. I am. I've so enjoyed this week – and the weeks leading up to it. When this goes it will seem like the end of something lovely.'

Impulsively, Libby leant forward and kissed her cheek. 'You've been great,' she said. 'If they ever let you out you must come to Steeple Martin and see us all.'

This time Martha laughed. 'Oh, they let me out, all right. And perhaps I will.' She made shooing motions. 'Go on, they'll be waiting for you.'

'I'm going,' said Libby. 'Bye Martha.' She waved at the dark atrium. 'Bye St Eldreda.'

But in the morning, when the security guard arrived, St Eldreda was still there, which was what he expected. What he didn't expect was to find Martha spread-eagled on the floor in front of it, and outside, lying in the shadow of the great stone arches, a body in a monk's habit, its skull smashed like a crushed snail shell.

Chapter Ten

Peter called Libby early on Sunday morning.

'Pete? It's only half past six!' Libby unglued her eyes to peer at the clock.

'Lib, listen, this is serious.' Libby could hear the shake in Peter's voice. 'Dominic's dead.'

'Dom?' Libby's voice rose to a shriek.

'Not your Dom.'

Libby's heart rate slowed. 'You mean Dominic Butcher?'

'Yes. At the Abbey.'

'Oh, God.' Libby closed her eyes. 'Where? What happened?'

'All I can tell you is what Sister Catherine told me. The security guard found Martha next to the reliquary case and Dominic dead in the ruins.'

'Martha? She's not –?'

'No, but she's in hospital. Critical, Sister Catherine thinks. It looks as though she foiled a burglary attempt.'

'By Dominic?' Libby was frowning. Ben was sitting up and trying to listen.

'I don't know,' said Peter helplessly. 'He was wearing his costume.'

'The habit?'

'Yes.'

'And the reliquary? You said Martha foiled …'

'It's still there. But Martha was next to the case and Dominic was some distance away, so it looks as though

77

there may have been a third person.'

'What do we do?'

'Wait for the police to get in touch. We can't go and do the get-out.'

'Oh.' Libby digested this. 'The police will want to talk to us, then?'

'Yes. Sister Catherine has given them my number and yours.'

'Oh, good.' Libby looked at Ben. 'Here we go again.'

'I'm going to the theatre to make a start on clearing up the bar,' said Peter. 'It'll keep me busy.'

'Good idea,' said Libby, swinging her legs out of bed. 'Give me a chance to have a cup of tea and I'll follow you up.'

Three quarters of an hour later, Ben and Libby joined Peter at the theatre. All the glasses from the previous evening's last-night party were already stacked on the bar, chairs were piled on tables and Peter was manipulating the vacuum cleaner out of its cupboard.

'Sister Catherine called again,' he said, straightening up. 'Apparently Martha's still unconscious, and there's a police officer by her bed.'

'How ill is she? Did Catherine say?'

'I don't think she knows. And I don't suppose the police will tell us. I wonder who's in charge?'

'It won't be Ian,' said Ben. 'The Abbey isn't in his jurisdiction.'

'Oh,' said Libby gloomily. 'We won't get any inside information, then.' She went behind the bar and turned on the tap. 'Might as well wash up, then.'

Peter switched on the vacuum cleaner and Ben began to root about for forgotten glasses parked on windowsills and behind pillars.

The vacuum cleaner was suddenly silent and Libby

looked up, startled, as she heard Peter's voice.

'Can I help you?'

In the doorway stood two people. A large and uncomfortable-looking man with close-cropped greying hair, and a petite woman with a mane of suspiciously bright blonde hair.

'Oh, lord,' muttered Libby. 'Big Bertha.'

'You Peter Parker?'

'Yes? And you are?'

'Superintendent Bertram. This is DI Davies.'

Peter's chin lifted. 'Identification?'

Big Bertha looked astonished, but scrabbled in her shoulder bag before bringing out her ID. DI Davies beat her to it.

'You knew Dominic Butcher and were instrumental in bringing that antique to St Eldreda's Abbey. Why?'

Libby strolled out from behind the bar, wiping her hands on a tea towel.

'Don't worry, Pete. She always puts people's backs up.'

Superintendent Bertram turned a furious gaze on Libby. 'Oh, for f ...' she began.

'Yes, nice to meet you again, Superintendent. Remember me? Libby Sarjeant with a J?'

'I remember you,' snarled the smaller woman.

Peter raised his eyes as Ben, coming through from the auditorium, joined the group.

'The murder at Lewis's place,' explained Libby. 'We met then.'

'Are you involved in this?' snapped Bertram.

'In the play that was put on at the Abbey? Yes.'

'We all were,' said Ben. 'This is our theatre. We put the play on.'

'What do you mean "our theatre"?'

Libby, Ben and Peter looked at each other in surprise.

'What I said. Our theatre.' His amusement showed. 'We own it.'

Looking a trifle discomfited, Bertram cleared her throat.

'What connection do you have to the Abbey?' asked DI Davies.

'Only that we put on a play there based on the story of the original St Eldreda,' said Peter. 'I'm sure Sister Catherine has already told you that.'

'Why did you ask for that – that thing?' Big Bertha's voice was even more like a cheese grater than ever, thought Libby.

'The relic? Because that was how we knew about the story,' said Libby. 'Sister Catherine asked me to look into the reliquary –'

'She did what?'

Libby smiled tranquilly. 'Yes. It's all right, DCI Connell from Canterbury knows all about it. In fact, it was him who asked for the reliquary to be loaned for the play.'

'He what?'

'Did Sister Catherine not tell you? He's spoken to her several times.' Libby crossed her fingers, hoping it was true.

DI Davies put away his notebook, and Big Bertha sighed.

'I'll call him. Meanwhile, if you can all give me statements about your movements last night and what you know of Butcher and the other woman –'

'Martha,' said Libby helpfully. 'Let's sit down.'

Davies, Ben and Peter lifted chairs off tables and they all sat down. Libby's eyes went to the coffee machine, but she decided it would only prolong things if she offered.

The interviews were straightforward, each of them giving as thorough an account of their movements the previous night as they could, unnecessarily so, in Libby's case, and their candid opinions of Dominic Butcher.

'And the woman?' said Bertram.

'Martha is an oblate. She lives at the Abbey with the nuns, but isn't quite as bound by the monastic life, so she was in charge of us while we were there. She was also in charge of security for the reliquary,' explained Libby. 'The last thing I said to her last night was that I hoped she'd come and visit us in Steeple Martin.'

'The – what did you call it?'

'Reliquary,' supplied Ben. 'It contains part of St Eldreda's finger.'

Davies looked gobsmacked, Bertram nauseous.

'Why were you looking into it?' Bertram looked back at Libby, who explained.

'As I said, DCI Connell knows all about it.'

'We'll have more questions.' Bertram stood up abruptly. 'Meanwhile, don't get in my way.'

Davies smiled at them weakly and followed his tiny blonde warlord out of the theatre.

'You did enjoy winding her up,' said Peter admiringly.

'Dangerous thing to do, I reckon,' said Ben. 'But at least we might get Ian on the job. Coffee?'

'She's like a Jack Russell – makes up for her size with full-blown aggression,' said Libby.

'That's giving Jack Russells a bad name,' said Peter. 'Coffee's a good idea. Anyone got any coins?'

They finished the clearing up and discussed how to tell the rest of the company.

'Some of them said they'd be in to help this morning,' said Peter, looking at his watch, 'because we thought we'd be going to the Abbey. Shall we wait for them?'

They filled in the time by going into the workshop to tidy up – Ben, bottling up behind the bar – Peter, and ambling aimlessly around the little garden outside the bar –

Libby. While she ambled, she called Fran.

'Did it happen this morning?' asked Fran after a moment.

'I don't know. Sometime during the night, I supposed.'

'Then why was Martha there? Did she stay up all night with the thing? Was she dressed?'

'I don't know.' Libby was bewildered. 'Why?'

'If she was dressed it would either be before she went to bed or after she got up this morning.'

'It couldn't be before she went to bed because the security guard would have found her on his rounds.'

'So it must have been this morning,' said Fran slowly. 'But Dominic could have been killed earlier. He wouldn't necessarily have been seen if he was in a habit among the ruins.'

'No,' agreed Libby, 'and the security guard wouldn't have been looking there, anyway. He was only there to check on the reliquary.'

'Were the atrium doors open?'

'Fran, I don't know! All I know is what Sister Catherine told Peter. Big Bertha didn't tell us anything.'

'Oh, no!' groaned Fran. 'Is she on the case?'

'Yes,' giggled Libby, 'and she didn't know about Ian's involvement. She wasn't half cross! Oh, look, Fran, I've got to go. The others have turned up and we've got to tell them.'

The members of the company who had arrived, somewhat blearily, to help with the get-out, were told of the tragedy and expressed varying degrees of shock and horror.

'Like that business with The Hop Pickers,' muttered someone who'd turned a pale shade of Eau de Nil. Peter shot her a withering look. And Libby remembered him saying he thought something could go wrong.

'But at least it wasn't until after the run,' she told herself, and then felt ashamed of the thought.

'Harry says to go to the caff for a restorative,' said Peter, pocketing his phone after the other members of the company had gone. 'Are you going to Hetty's for lunch?'

'No, she's going to Flo and Lenny,' said Ben. 'Harry's open today, isn't he?'

'Yes, he is. Closed this evening and all day tomorrow. He's finally making his hours regular, rather than opening at random times. Come on.' Peter looked round the little foyer, switched off the lights and held open the double glass doors.

Chapter Eleven

Steeple Martin high street was bathed in sunshine. Harry had opened the front door of The Pink Geranium, although the closed sign still hung there.

'Thought I'd give the place a good airing,' he said. 'Is it too early for a nice bottle of red?'

'Save it for lunch time,' said Ben, 'if you've got room for us, that is.'

'Not going to Hetty's? I'm honoured.'

'She's going to Flo and Lenny's,' said Libby. 'Don't get above yourself.'

Harry went off to fetch coffee, and Ben, Peter and Libby seated themselves at the big round pine table in the window, where Harry had already spread the Sunday broadsheets.

'Good job it missed the papers,' said Peter, moving a *Telegraph* to one side.

'It'll make the news today,' said Libby. 'And we'll have Campbell and Jane on our tails.'

'Well, let's hope Jane can act as a stringer before the nationals descend,' said Ben, 'although I doubt it.'

'What do we know about Dominic's family?' asked Libby. 'He's never mentioned a wife.'

'I don't suppose anyone would put up with him,' said Peter. 'I think he was married, but I don't know much about him. He only moved here – what was it? Last year?'

'I don't even know where he lives,' said Libby.

'Somewhere off New Barton Lane,' said Peter. 'I got

the impression he was renting.'

'The only time I really had anything to do with him was when he helped with the set building for panto,' said Ben. 'He was full of his professional career and very little else.'

'So what was his actual job?' Libby frowned down at the *Sunday Times*. 'I assume he had one.'

Ben and Peter looked at one another.

'I've no idea,' said Peter. 'All I know is his mobile number which I had to have. I hope the police have more success.'

'Is his number in your phone?' said Ben. 'Why don't you call it? See what happens?'

'It'll go straight to voicemail,' said Peter, fishing his phone out of a pocket. 'Told you. It did.' He put the phone away.

'Interesting that the police didn't answer it,' said Libby.

'They might not have it. He may not have carried it in his habit.' Peter shook his head. 'I just can't understand what he was doing there and in costume.' He pushed a lock of lank fair hair off his forehead and leant back in his chair, scowling.

'Here we are, poppets,' said Harry, placing a large cafetière on the table along with four mugs. 'I shall join you. Why the long face, treasure?'

'We were talking about Dominic Butcher and realising we knew hardly anything about him,' said Libby.

'You knew enough about his illustrious career,' said Harry, pushing down the plunger on the cafetière. 'Bloody *Limehouse Blues*. He even talked to me about it.'

'Really?' said Libby. 'When?'

'Once or twice when I went into the pub before you lot came in. Introduced himself as a "friend" of yours. And he came to the caff a few times.'

'Was he with anyone?' asked Ben.

Harry shook his head. 'Always came in with a book, but keen to talk to anyone who would listen.'

'And did you find anything out about him?' said Libby.

'Like what?'

'What he did for a living, for instance?' said Peter, leaning forward to pick up the cafetière.

'Nah. He gave the impression he was resting.'

'He said something about returning to his former profession once, do you remember?' said Libby.

'God, yes, as a doctor. But they'd never have him back.' Peter poured coffee into the four mugs.

'We perhaps ought to tell the police that,' said Ben. 'It might be significant in tracing his family.'

'You can tell Ian, then,' said Libby. 'I'm not telling Big Bertha anything.'

'Big Bertha?' Harry rocked forward on his chair. 'That blonde bird you met before?'

'The same, apparently. All last night's eye make-up and split ends,' said Peter.

'Miaow,' said Libby. 'By the way, Fran asked some interesting questions on the phone.'

'And they were?' asked Peter.

Libby repeated what Fran had said.

'I expect the police will have gone into all that by now,' said Ben. 'Their first action would be to find out what times the security guard went round. Where was he actually stationed?'

'In the lodge at the Abbey gates. It has a view of the gates into the monastery ruins, but he had to walk right up the drive to get to the atrium, by-passing the ruins on his left,' said Libby.

'So no one could have got into the whole site from the road without being seen by him?' said Harry, drawing an invisible map on the table.

'Unless they waited for him to go on his rounds,' said Peter.

'So they'd have to know when that was?'

'But it may have been random,' said Libby. 'Don't they say that if those sort of things are done at regular times it gives criminals an advantage?'

'I don't know,' said Ben, 'but it makes sense. But do we think it was Dominic who got in?'

'Wait!' Libby held up a hand. 'Did anyone see him at the party last night?'

Everyone looked at everyone else.

'No,' they all said together.

'So that's something else to tell the police,' said Ben.

A little later, Ben and Libby strolled back to Allhallow's Lane to change before returning to The Pink Geranium for lunch.

'It looks as if Dominic was trying to steal the reliquary,' said Ben, 'or is that what we are meant to think?'

'I don't know, but it looks as if Martha was defending it, and Dominic was too far away for it to be him she was defending it from, if you see what I mean.'

'Yes. But we are agreed he must have hidden after we all left last night?'

'Oh, yes,' said Libby, 'and I believe he'd done it before. Remember after the dress rehearsal I commented that not many people had come back for a drink? And Dominic always came for a drink.' She shook her head. 'Poor sod. I wish I'd been nicer to him.'

While Libby struggled to find something to wear, Ben left a message for Ian on his official police mobile.

'If he's managed a day off today, I didn't want to disturb him on his personal one,' he explained, as they left the house again, Libby avoiding the affronted, glaring eye of Sidney, who clearly thought they should be staying in with him.

'I wonder if we'll hear anything else from Big Bertha today?' she said. 'He must have had some sort of ID on him, cards or something, so I suppose that's how they identified him.'

'It was poor Sister Catherine who was dragged out to look at them both, and all she and the security guard knew was that Dominic was a member of the company.'

'How do you know all that?' asked Libby in surprise.

'Oh – I forgot – Patti called while you were in the shower. She wanted to know anything we knew and exchanged gossip. The nuns are in a flat spin, apparently.'

'I bet they are,' said Libby. 'Oh, dear. I'm sure Patti feels guilty now.'

'What for?'

'Asking me to look into the reliquary's provenance. If she hadn't, none of this would have happened.'

'In that case you ought to feel guilty, too. You told Peter, Peter wanted to write the play, Dominic was in it ...'

'So we all ought to feel guilty,' said Libby, scowling at him. 'Gee, thanks.'

'What I was trying to point out was that it's simply a chain of events. If Hitler's father hadn't met Hitler's mother, World War Two would never have happened. See?' Ben tucked his arm through hers. 'Come on. I bet Harry's done Pollo Verde just for you.'

Peter joined them for lunch, and to their surprise, so did Patti and Anne.

'How have you escaped the clutches of your parish?' asked Libby, as Patti sat down.

'I'm on holiday! Anne and I are off to Umbria the day after tomorrow.'

'Oh, lovely. Hang on – where's Umbria?'

'Next door to Tuscany,' said Peter. 'Just as beautiful, if

not more, and less touristy.'

'You've been?' Anne, her small face lighting up, leant forward in her wheelchair.

Peter smiled at her. 'Yes, several times, although it was a long time ago when I actually worked for a newspaper before I went freelance.'

'Newspaper?' Patti frowned. 'What did you do?'

'He's now a freelance journalist. He used to work for one of the more prestigious newspapers,' said Ben. 'I'm quite proud of him, really.'

Libby laughed as Patti and Anne exchanged slightly puzzled looks. 'Ben's Peter's cousin,' she explained. 'That's how the Oast House Theatre is a family business. Ben did the conversion and Peter is the artistic director. I'm just a hanger-on.'

'So where are you staying in Umbria?' Peter asked.

'We're doing a painting holiday at a beautiful villa,' said Anne.

'It's called Arte Umbria,' said Patti. 'We both loved art at school and have never had a chance to do it properly since.'

'Excellent,' said Libby. 'Send us pictures, won't you? And now, if it's not too touchy a subject, what did you think of the play?'

Patti sighed. 'I thought it was excellent, and I felt very proud that I'd been instrumental in bringing it about. And now look what's happened.'

'I know.' Libby shot an "I told you so" look at Ben.

'It was very good,' said Anne. 'I thought it was brilliant the way you managed to convey the suggestion of ancient language while keeping it comprehensible.'

'Thank you.' Peter looked surprised.

'Anne can actually read Chaucer in the original,' said Patti, smiling at her fondly. 'I can barely master basic

Latin.'

'You don't need Latin in the Anglican church, surely?' said Ben.

'No, but it's very useful for the history of the church. We did it at college.'

'Can you stop now?' complained Libby. 'I'm feeling really inadequate.'

'Nobody can act like you, though,' said Ben, patting her hand while everyone else laughed.

'That's a double-edged sword,' said Libby.

By tacit agreement, the subject of murder was not mentioned for the rest of the lunch. Harry was able to join them for a drink at the end, grumbling that since Donna, his former right-hand woman, had at last produced her first baby, he'd had far too much to do.

'She's still doing the books at home, isn't she?' asked Libby. 'And surely you should have been able to find a capable waitress or waiter by now? People are crying out for jobs.'

'But not jobs with unsocial hours,' said Harry. 'I need most help at weekends, when they'd rather be out clubbing.'

This remark produced an uneasy silence.

'What did I say?' Harry looked round the table in surprise.

'Dominic,' said Ben.

'And Martha,' added Libby.

'Oh,' said Harry. 'Is that how …? Oh.'

'We think so,' said Patti. 'Martha, anyway.'

'Come to think about it,' said Libby, 'no one's told us how Dominic died.'

'They don't,' said Harry, 'then when you say "I've never used a Toledo Stiletto in my life" they leap up with the handcuffs.'

'Very funny,' said Libby.

'Sorry, just trying to lighten the atmosphere.'

'A bit hard to do that under the circumstances,' said Peter, 'even for you, dear heart. Do you know, I feel an alarming sense of resentment against poor Dominic for spoiling my play.'

Libby and Ben murmured agreement.

'I think that's perfectly normal,' said Patti. 'Even if you knew who'd killed him and felt resentment towards them, Dominic still seems to have put himself in danger.'

'I've just thought of something,' said Libby. 'If Dominic had planned to stay behind for whatever reason, who would know? And if no one knew, it was an opportunistic murder by someone who also shouldn't have been there.'

'On the other hand,' said Ben, 'he could have arranged to meet someone just like poor Bernard Evans did. Someone who said he was someone else.'

'But what was he, or she, offering?' asked Libby. And what did Dominic have to give?'

Chapter Twelve

This question occupied Libby for the rest of the day, until Ben got thoroughly fed up with her and went to see his mother. Denied an ear, she called Fran.

'I think Ben's probably right. Lured by someone, just like Bernard Evans.'

'But with the promise of what?' Libby shook her head. 'I don't get it. In fact, I don't get it at all.'

'Have the police been back to see you?'

'No. I expect they'll want formal statements from all of us, including you, but Big Bertha was going to liaise with Ian, so which of them will be in charge I don't know.'

'Big Bertha, the murder's her case. Ian's concerned with the reliquary and the cold case of Bernard Evans.'

'I wonder if the media will link the two?' Libby stared at the newsreader mouthing silently on the television screen.

'Not so far,' said Fran. 'I watched the main and the regional news at lunchtime, and there was only a brief mention of Dominic's murder on Kent and Coast by the anchor person.'

'What's the betting Campbell will be on to it in the morning? On to us, I mean.'

'Of course he will, so will Jane. And if Campbell links it to the Bernard Evans murder, which he will, it will go national.'

'Oh yes,' said Libby. 'You're right.'

The three phone calls arrived hard on each other's tails

the following morning. Jane was first, Campbell second and the police third. Libby refused to say anything to either Jane or Campbell and nervously agreed to the police that she would be in later that morning.

'Yes,' said Fran, on being appealed to, 'I got the calls, too. Jane understands and just wants an exclusive if ever we're able, Campbell got pushy, and the policeman just sounded uninterested.'

'Same here,' said Libby. 'Do you know who's coming to interview you?'

'I expect it will be someone from the local police station here. I'm not close enough to the enquiry to warrant anything else. What about you?'

'No idea. How close are Ben and I to the investigation, do you think?'

'Close. You're both on the board of directors of the theatre, for a start, and you took on Dominic. And Peter, because he wrote the play and had quite a lot to do with the nuns. Although it was only Sister Catherine, not the others. In fact, we hardly saw any of the others, did we?'

'No,' said Libby gloomily. 'But we don't know the murder was anything to do with the reliquary.'

'With Martha sprawled in front of it? Suggestive to say the least.'

To Libby's perturbation, she and Ben were interviewed separately, she at number 17 and Ben at the Manor. Two solid and dependable-looking detective constables, both young enough to be her own sons, interviewed Libby, and accepted tea.

'How well did you know the deceased, Mrs Sarjeant?' asked detective A.

'Not very well.'

'But he was in your play.' Detective B squeezed his eyes together suspiciously.

'So were a lot of people. I don't know all of them very well. People audition, we don't check them for a criminal record.'

'Pity you don't.' Detective B bristled.

'Sorry – what I meant was, he auditioned for a part last year when we put out an open call, so we had his name and address – at least we have somewhere – but that's about it. He never volunteered anything about his life to me, although he used to see us in the pub sometimes. He'd been a professional actor.'

'Open call?'

'For a play. We advertise for actors in the local press and on the internet.'

'Don't you vet them?' Detective A was surprised. 'They could be anybody.'

'We don't pay them. We have no right to go delving into their personal lives,' said Libby.

'Well, we have to,' said Detective B. 'We know he and his wife were separated, he was in debt and out of work.'

'He was talking about going back into medicine,' said Libby.

'Medicine?' Both detectives looked up.

'He had been a house surgeon, I believe, before he got his break on television.'

'*Limehouse Blues*.' The detectives looked at one another. 'Not exactly a favourite of the police force.'

'I can imagine.' Libby grinned. 'I don't watch it myself.'

'Glad to hear it, madam,' said Detective A, with the suspicion of a smile. 'So you didn't know Mr Butcher well. Did he ever show any interest in this – er –' he consulted his notebook, 'this relic?'

'Only as much as we all did,' said Libby. 'I remember him commenting once on the security arrangements. Most of the cast and crew knew what was going on with it as it was the whole reason the play was being done.' She sighed. 'It's such a shame. It was a good play.'

'It wasn't the play that died, Mrs Sarjeant,' said Detective B.

'No,' said Libby, feeling hot colour sweep up her neck and into her face.

'What about Cornelia Fletcher?' asked Detective A.

'Who?'

'The woman who was attacked.'

'But her name's Martha!'

'Not according to her bank statement.' Detective B looked up from his notebook. 'You didn't know?'

'Of course not! Sister Catherine introduced her to me as Martha, their resident alongsider –' Libby caught Detective B's frown '– or oblate, as they're known. And that's all I've known her by. I suppose she took Martha as a sort of Christian *nom-de-la-vie.*'

Both detectives looked at her disapprovingly.

'You never saw her away from the Abbey?' Detective A was back in charge.

'No. She looked after us, and always locked up the atrium and the reliquary. She and the security guard were the only ones allowed anywhere near it. There were lasers – and – and – and things.'

'Yes. They were turned off.' Detective B looked at Libby accusingly.

'Well, I didn't do it,' said Libby indignantly. 'And how come the security guard didn't see anything?'

'He did,' said Detective A. 'He saw Ms Fletcher and Mr Butcher.'

'Oh.' Libby shifted on the sofa.

'Now, Mrs Sarjeant,' continued Detective A, 'tell us what you know about this – relic. We understand you have been enquiring into its – um –'

'Provenance,' supplied Libby. 'Yes.' She sighed, offered more tea, was refused, and settled down to relate the entire circumstances of her knowledge of the reliquary, including the trip to Maidenhaye and as much of the history of St Eldreda as she could get away with.

'However,' she concluded, 'I expect you know all that, as DCI Connell does, and is investigating himself.'

This time she'd thrown them a curve ball, Libby could see it in their suddenly rigid faces. They didn't know, she thought with glee. Big Bertha didn't tell them.

Detective B made up their collective minds. 'Very well, madam,' he said getting massively to his feet. 'That will be all for the moment. No doubt we'll be in touch.'

'No doubt,' said Libby sweetly, holding the front door open for them, before rushing to the phone to warn anyone who had not been questioned yet of this delightful fact.

'I've got Superintendent Bertram herself,' hissed Peter. 'Here now. Go away!'

'I can see two large gentlemen approaching the front door,' said Ben. 'I shall wave Ian in front of their noses.'

'I've already had a couple of uniforms who were completely uninterested,' said Fran. 'Told you.'

'What did they ask you?'

'How well I knew Dominic and when did I last see him. Did he seem to have any particular interest in the reliquary – although they couldn't pronounce it.'

'Neither could mine, and the same questions. They hadn't been briefed properly, unless Big Bertha is genuinely trying to keep Ian out of the investigation.'

'She can't hope to do that,' said Fran. 'She'd know one of us would tell him, or the other officers.'

When the phone rang ten minutes later, Libby nearly fell over in her eagerness to snatch it up.

'Ben?'

'No, Libby, another of your gentlemen,' said an amused Ian.

'Oh! Sorry, Ian, I was expecting Ben to report on his questioning by Big – Superintendent Bertram's men.'

'Oh, they've been, have they?'

'Yes, to me first, then Ben, and Peter's got the lady herself. And, Ian, my two didn't know about you!'

'That was silly of her, wasn't it? I take it you put them right?'

Libby repeated her conversation with the two detectives. 'It completely put them off,' she finished gleefully.

'I bet it did. Well, I thought I'd better put you in the picture, as I'm pretty sure the superintendent won't. She obviously had to get in touch with me, but sadly for her I was on a day off and for once, out of range. She had to leave a message with the team. I did actually receive the message from one of my sergeants, but I decided, as I wasn't SIO, I would only respond this morning.'

'After she'd had a chance to make a fool of herself?' suggested Libby.

'Of course not,' said Ian, sounding shocked. 'However, I was able to give her some background detail.'

'Oh? Are you going to tell me what it is?'

'You know what it is. The murder of Bernard Evans.'

'Oh.' Libby was disappointed. 'Nothing more on that?'

'A little, but I think I'll keep it to myself just now. What did you tell the police?'

'Well, actually, that's rather odd. Big – Bertram came to the theatre yesterday morning and interviewed Pete, Ben and me, yet we've all had separate interviews going over the same ground this morning. Why would that be?'

'I expect she decided to have another go at you all individually in case you changed your stories. And I expect she's digging really deeply into Peter because he wrote the play.'

'Surely she'll have questioned Sister Catherine about that? And what would that have to do with Dominic's murder?'

'Oh, come on, Libby! Dominic, on the face of it, was hidden in the Monastery in order to steal the reliquary and Martha looks as though she was protecting it from him.'

'That's mad,' said Libby. 'In that case, why was Martha attacked by the reliquary when Dominic was found at least ten metres away?'

'I've no idea, it isn't my case, but I expect that's what it looks like to Bertram. And if that's what she thinks, she'll put someone else in the frame to have killed Dominic.'

Libby frowned. 'But why, in that case, was the reliquary *not* stolen?'

Ian sighed. 'I've told you, it isn't my case. I'm only interested in case it links up with the murder of Bernard Evans.'

'I wish it was your case,' grumbled Libby.

'So you could get away with poking around?' Ian sounded amused.

'No, because Big Bertha is so horrible. She hates me.'

'Oh, I'm glad you've stopped watching what you call her! I don't suppose she's got over your – er – *help* on the Creekmarsh case.'

'I'm sure she hasn't.' Libby paused. 'Oh, Ian, I hated that case.'

'Do you actually like any of the investigations you've muddled your way into?'

'Well … you can't enjoy murder, can you? But Fran and I have quite enjoyed the process of investigation. It's just when it comes so close to home, or is so sad.'

'I know. It's satisfying in a way when a murderer is

brought to justice, but sometimes ...'

'Yes,' said Libby on a sigh. 'But this one – it's different, isn't it? I didn't like Dominic, but he's close to home, and the reason he was there is because Patti asked me about the reliquary, Peter got interested and wrote the play.'

'Stop right there, Libby, or you'll be taking the blame for the whole thing.'

'I know, I know. I said to Ben I bet Patti feels responsible, and she does, and I know neither of us should. Anyway, you didn't call to talk about Patti, did you?'

'No. I went to see your Alastair Beaumont and his wife.'

'Oh!' Libby was taken aback. 'Didn't you trust my reporting?'

'It wasn't that, Libby, and you know it. I wanted to find out how genuine the documents the solicitor has actually are. The date puts it well beyond the time when the Beaumonts sold to Bartholomew Tollybar, but I've got a sample, rather reluctantly given, I have to say, of a document of around the date it purports to be. If we can match it up, then it looks as though someone, either in the family or very close to it, has been up to no good.'

'Do you mean up to no good now? Or in the past?'

'In the past, I would say. That document went with the reliquary when it was sold to the collector whose estate it's in now, and that was a long time ago.'

'What, as long as Bernard Evans's murder?'

'No, some years later than that.'

'So,' said Libby slowly, 'it was stolen from Bernard Evans, then sold on later by a Beaumont?'

'Possibly. Or perhaps Bernard Evans also had the document. Perhaps the person who left it to him had it.'

'So have you found out who left it to him?'

'Not yet. We're trying to trace any relatives who might have known.'

'The beneficiaries of Bernard's will, perhaps?' suggested Libby.

'Well done. We're going through the website which has details of most of the wills in the last forty years.

'Do you really think the Beaumont family have something to do with all this?'

'I'm not sure. I would hate to think that Alastair or Jennifer have, but there are all sorts of other lines of descent, don't forget.'

'And what about Old Barty Tollybar? What about his will?'

'If you can find it, I'd be glad to see it,' said Ian, 'but at the moment, I've enough on my plate. I've an appointment with Bertram in an hour, and I need to marshal my thoughts before I see her.'

'And your forces,' said Libby. 'I felt sorry for the Inspector who was with her yesterday.'

'Davies? Yes, poor bloke. He's a good detective, but she won't let him do anything. Right, Libby. Don't forget to keep me informed.'

'What even on your work line?'

'Even that.' Libby could hear the smile in his voice. 'Now go and see if Peter survived his encounter.'

Peter wasn't answering his landline, so rather than interrupt if he was still being interviewed, she called Harry's mobile.

'He's here, dear,' said Harry. 'I'll hand you over.'

'Where are you?'

'In the caff in shock,' came Peter's voice. 'Harry came over here to get out of the way while I was grilled, so I've joined him for tea and sympathy.'

'Tea?'

'OK, alcohol. Do you want to join us?'

Ten minutes later Libby was sitting at the big table in the window watching Harry pour wine.

'I shall fall asleep this afternoon,' said Libby. 'Come on, then. What happened?'

'I was questioned about practically everything but the colour of my underwear,' said Peter wearily. 'It's obvious she thinks I got the reliquary down here to steal it but can't quite make it fit the facts because it wasn't me who requested the reliquary but Ian.'

'That's exactly what Ian said.' Libby recounted the substance of her conversation with Ian.

'So he thinks a third party killed Dominic and beat up Martha, but didn't steal the reliquary?' said Harry. 'That doesn't make any sense.'

'No, that's what he said Big Bertha will think. So she's trying to find someone to fit that third party.'

'And she's picked on me,' said Peter morosely. 'Great.'

'It's all right, chuck,' said Harry, 'you've got about a hundred and one witnesses to where you were until at least two in the morning.'

'What about after that?' said Peter. 'There's only you, and they would discount your evidence as being partisan.'

'They could look at cars and amounts of petrol,' said Libby. 'If your car has no petrol …'

'We don't exactly jot down how full the tank is before and after each journey, dear heart,' said Harry. 'Be your age.'

'Did she ask you about Ian and his investigation?'

'Not a word. She barely mentioned Sister Catherine and St Eldreda's. She was just focussed on me, the reliquary, if I knew of the security arrangements, and how well I'd known Dominic. She practically accused me of having an affair with him, at one point.' He shuddered delicately.

'I wonder where his family is?' mused Libby. 'Won't they be contacted? His ex-wife?'

'Oh, I expect they've done that already. Although she kept asking me questions about his background as though I'd lived in his pocket for years.' Peter shuddered again. 'What a woman.'

'Ian's got an appointment with her,' Libby looked at her watch, 'in about ten or fifteen minutes. I wonder what will happen?'

'He'll tell her all about the Bernard Evans investigation and she'll hijack it,' said Harry.

'Do you think so?' Peter looked thoughtful. 'After all, superintendents don't tend to go out in the field, do they? They stay at home and pull the strings.'

'So you think she might give it to Davies?'

'No, I think she might turn it over to Ian.'

Harry grinned. 'Oooh, lovely! Do you think they'll fight over it? I love a good fight.'

Ben appeared in the doorway.

'I guessed you'd be here.' He pulled out a chair and sat down. Harry fetched another glass.

'I texted you,' said Libby. Ben pulled out his phone.

'So you did.'

'How did your interview go, then?' asked Peter. 'I'm almost under lock and key.'

Ben's interview had gone along the same lines as Libby's, but he was indignant to hear about Peter's.

'The woman's deranged,' he said. 'She gives the police a bad name.'

'Let me tell you about the other stuff Ian told me,' said Libby, 'and what he said we could do.'

'We?' said three male voices warily.

'Well, me. He said if I could find Bartholomew's will, I was welcome to try.'

Chapter Thirteen

The smell of the sea wafted in through Fran's open sitting-room window, a window that had been immortalised in Libby's paintings more than once. The walls were a foot thick, so the windowsill was deep, and Fran always had a small vase of flowers there. The curtains, small too, to fit in the embrasure, were a light yellow cotton with a small and indeterminate pattern, vague as an impressionist painting. This afternoon they drifted in and out with the slight breeze. Libby sniffed ecstatically.

'Gorgeous. I could sit here all day.'

'So could I,' said Fran, 'which is why I only come in here if I've nothing else to do. Let's take the laptop into the kitchen.'

'I found that website Ian told you about,' said Fran, clicking on a link.

Libby lifted Fran's fat black-and-white long-haired cat, Balzac, off the table and onto her lap. He turned round once, purred, licked her hand and went to sleep.

'The one for wills?'

'Yes, it doesn't cover anything that far back, but I've finally found where to look. It would have been heard at an ecclesiastical court, and their probate records should be held at the National Archive. It's likely to be probated at the Prerogative Court of Canterbury, as we think he was a wealthy businessman.'

'Do we have to go there?'

'No – look.' Fran pushed the laptop towards her and there it was. The National Archives, wills between 1384 and 1858. 'Mind you, we'll have to pay for it, but I think we can see if it's there for free.'

And it was.

'Lucky he had an unusual name,' said Libby. 'Are we going to order it?'

'We can just download it,' said Fran, busily tapping away. 'Can you fetch the printer from the spare bedroom? I think I can afford a few pounds.'

'You realise,' said Libby, stumbling back into the kitchen with Fran's printer, 'if we find out who Bartholomew left the reliquary to, we'll have to find his will, and so on and so on.'

'Mmm.' Fran was frowning at the screen. 'But it isn't mentioned in dear old Barty's will.' She connected the printer and hit the button.

'It isn't? But that just means it's included in "all the goods of which I die possessed", doesn't it?'

'Look.' Fran passed Libby the first pages of the will as they emerged. 'It's got other items mentioned. Valuable items. But not the reliquary, unless he's described it as something else.'

Libby scoured the seven pages of the will for some mention of the reliquary, but in the end had to agree with Fran. It wasn't there.

'So what does that mean?'

'It means he either sold it on, and we have no idea who to, or it was stolen from him.'

'Alastair said the people who sold it before came to bad ends, and it always came back to the family. I wonder if a family member got it back from Barty?'

'You mean one of the secondary branches?' said Fran, standing up. 'I need tea.'

'So do I,' said Libby, lifting Balzac on to the floor. 'And yes, one of those distaff sides or something. And I wonder how Barty died? Did he come to a bad end?'

'We can't tell from the will,' said Fran, 'and he died too early to have a proper death certificate.'

'What about parish records?'

'We don't know where he died, the will doesn't say that either.' Fran, not such a stickler for real tea as Libby, poured boiling water on to teabags in mugs.

'Ah,' said Libby, snatching up the first sheet of the will, 'but it does say where he lived, silly! Look – St Dionis Backchurch. And it mentions his sister, Beatrice Retford. That's two more records we've got.'

'What do we do, then? Go and find St Wotsit Backchurch?' Fran fished out the teabags and added milk.

'No,' said Libby, back at the laptop. 'We can't do that. It was demolished in 1858.' She clicked through another few searches. 'Parish records went to another church, which has also been demolished. I doubt if they'll have survived anywhere else.' She pushed the laptop away. 'Damn. I thought we were on to something there.'

Fran sat down at the table. 'Has Ian talked to Mr Marshall's beneficiary yet? He or she must know where he got it from. And he or she allowed the thing to come to the Abbey.'

'Yes, he –' Libby stopped. 'Oh, My God!'

'What?'

'I can't think how I forgot! Martha told me the beneficiary was coming on the last night and wanted to take the reliquary back with him, or her.'

'You didn't tell me that!' said Fran.

'I didn't tell anybody. The nuns consulted the security people and said they had instructions it was only to leave the Abbey under lock and key with them.'

'So did the beneficiary come?'

'I don't know. If it had, it would have introduced itself, wouldn't it? No, Martha and I both thought it was a try-on, but by whom, I've no idea.'

'The murderer, obviously,' said Fran. 'Was it a man or a woman?'

'I don't know. Do you suppose Sister Catherine's told the police about it? I mean, I forgot – so might she have done.'

'Call Ian. He must be out of Big Bertha's clutches by now.'

To Libby's surprise, Ian answered immediately.

'Um – I forgot something.'

Ian sighed. 'Yes?'

'Martha told me on the last night that Mr Marshall's beneficiary had called to say he or she was coming down and would take the reliquary back with him, or her.'

'What? Why hasn't anyone mentioned this?'

'Martha's unconscious. Sister Catherine would know. We don't even know if it was male or female. Which is it?'

'Which is what?'

'The beneficiary. Man or woman?'

'His niece, a Mrs Chappell.'

'So it would have to have been a female voice,' said Libby. 'Although no one at the Abbey knew who the beneficiary was, so I suppose it wouldn't matter.'

'They didn't agree, did they?'

'No, of course not. They invoked the security company and, for all I know, the police as well.'

'I'll get on to Sister Catherine straight away, if I can between prayers.'

'You? What about Big Bertha.'

Libby heard the smile in Ian's voice. 'It's all right, Lib, you can relax. She's handed over to me.'

'What a relief.'

'This doesn't give you carte blanche to go haring off into an investigation, but you can keep your eyes and ears open as usual, and don't go forgetting anything else.'

'No, Ian,' said Libby. 'I suppose we couldn't talk to Mrs Chappell?'

'No!' Ian's voice made her wince. 'That would compromise the investigation, you know that. You'll just have to think of something else.'

'Go on then,' Libby said to Fran, as she ended the call. 'He says we'll have to think of something else. What?'

'To be honest, I don't think we need to. Ian's on the case, literally, and we've now told him everything we know. Or everything you know, anyway. So we might as well retire gracefully from the lists.'

Libby stood up and paced restlessly across the kitchen. 'How many times have we said that over the past few years? It's nothing to do with us so we'll let the police do their job. And how many times have we turned something up which has broken the case?'

'I know, I know, but we also know that the police always get there, too. In their own time.'

'Hmm.' Libby sat down again. 'Usually just in time to save us from a fate worse than death.'

'Mostly you,' said Fran. 'And our intervention often just complicates things.'

'No, it doesn't.'

'Look, Lib, think about it. How many times have the police had to turn out to rescue us? That wastes resources and probably costs money.'

Libby sighed. 'OK. But I can't just let it go. What aspect of this case do you think the police won't be concentrating on?'

'There isn't one.' Fran leant her elbows on the table.

'Listen. The reliquary. Ian was already looking into the theft and Bernard Evans's death. He already knows about the current – late – owner and his beneficiary. He's working to find out where Mr Marshall got it from. He will be looking into Dominic's circumstances, his ex-wife, his financial affairs – all that sort of thing. And how the murderer got into the Abbey.'

'The monastery. Didn't get into the Abbey.'

'In which case how did he attack Martha? She was found inside the atrium. And the doors were open.'

'Martha must have seen something outside and opened them. Anyway, Ian will be looking at that. And what time it happened. So what's left?'

'Martha? Could there be something there? In her background?'

'Good lord, how? She's an oblate, she was simply protecting the reliquary on behalf of the Abbey and the beneficiary. I did wonder,' Libby squinted at the open garden door, 'perhaps Dominic knew her –'

'If he knew her, why didn't either of them say so?'

'You'd hardly admit to it if you were going to kill someone, would you?'

Fran wrinkled her brow. 'What maggot's got into your brain now? They were both attacked. And they were at least fifteen metres apart.'

'I don't know. I'm grasping at straws.'

'You are.' Fran stood up. 'Come on, let's get an ice cream.'

They strolled along Harbour Street with their cones, Libby thoughtful and Fran contented.

'What about Dominic's wife?' said Libby suddenly.

'What about her? Did she somehow follow Dominic to the Abbey and kill him and attack Martha – for what?'

'Money?' said Libby doubtfully. 'If he's not paying

maintenance or something?'

'So she knows he's going to steal the reliquary – why stop him if that was going to get her money?'

'She had a conscience?'

'So she murders him to prevent burglary? Oh, come on, Lib.'

Libby sighed. 'I know. It's just so frustrating.'

'It is, but there's nothing we can do about it.'

'We can still try and trace the history of the reliquary. Just for interest's sake.'

It was Fran's turn to sigh. 'We could, I suppose. But we've just lost our last link to Bartholomew Tollybar, so where do we go from there?'

'I know!' Libby stopped dead and nearly lost her ice cream. 'Andrew!'

'Andrew?'

'Wylie. He's a historian, isn't he? He's helped us in the past. I bet he could ferret out some more documents. He'd know where to look. And he could probably interpret that will. There's sure to be a clue there.'

Professor Andrew Wylie, retired, was the occasional significant other of novelist Amanda George, better known as Rosie, erstwhile creative writing tutor of Fran's, who had been involved in previous adventures.

'Let's go and see him now.' Libby threw the remains of the ice cream cone into a bin. Andrew Wylie lived in a new block of flats on the outskirts of Nethergate.

'We can't just burst in on him,' said Fran. 'Besides, he might not be there.'

'Rosie's away at that writing festival, so he won't be with her. Where else would he be?'

'He has a life outside Rosie,' said Fran.

'Let's ring him.' Libby fished out her phone and found Andrew's numbers. 'Landline first,' she said.

Andrew answered almost on the first ring.

'Andrew, it's Libby Sarjeant. How are you?'

'Libby? This is a surprise. I'm fine, how are you? I take it this isn't just a social call?'

'Sorry, is it that obvious?'

Andrew laughed. 'It's usually to do with Rosie, but as she's away in the wilds of Westmorland or somewhere, it must be something else.'

'Oh, dear. That makes me sound awful.'

'Not at all. Do you need help with one of your investigations?'

Libby made a face at Fran. 'Yes, Andrew, that's exactly it. I don't suppose we could pop round now?'

'I'd be very pleased to see you. Are you in Nethergate?'

'Yes, at Fran's. Are you sure you don't mind?'

'Of course not. I'll put the kettle on.'

Ten minutes later Andrew, a smart, dapper little man who looked far younger than his years, opened his front door and twinkled at them.

'And you've brought a laptop,' he said. 'That means it's serious. Tea or coffee?'

When they had been settled on the diminutive balcony looking out over Nethergate below, Libby told the whole story from Patti's first approach to the researches of this afternoon and Bartholomew Tollybar's will.

'Let's see then,' said Andrew, and Fran showed him the downloaded document.

'Fascinating,' he murmured. 'How do I enlarge text on this machine?'

Fran showed him. He pored over the screen for a long few minutes while Libby fidgeted and Fran stared serenely out to sea.

'Well,' he said eventually. 'Old Bartholomew has quite a lot to tell us. I think you might be pleased.'

110

'Really?' said Libby and Fran together.

'Oh, yes. The names of family, and even where they lived.'

Chapter Fourteen

'But all we found was his sister, Beatrice Retford. No mention of where he died or anything,' said Libby.

'Can you honestly say you could read this document?' asked Andrew.

'Well.' Libby and Fran looked at each other. 'Not properly,' said Fran.

'Look.' Andrew turned the screen towards them. 'Beatrice Retford, wife of Jasper. Then later, here, Jasper Retford of Cheapside, who gets Bartholomew's house and "sundrie effects". There are a lot of bequests and details of how the estate is to be administered –'

'Are there?' said Libby, peering.

'Yes, but the language is fairly archaic. Finally, that the residue of the estate is to go to a Mary de Beauville – see, here? – who apparently has comforted him in his old age.'

'Housekeeper?' said Fran.

'I think more than that,' said Andrew.

'De Beauville?' said Libby. 'That's a bit like Beaumont.'

'I think that's a coincidence,' said Fran. 'Easy to read something into it. So what does it say about this Mary, Andrew. Does it tell us where she lived?'

'In Tollybar's house, but the residue of the estate is that she might live in comfort for the rest of her life. It also mentions her issue, Thomas.'

'His?' suggested Libby.

'Very likely. Not exactly acknowledged, but it appears

that he was looking after his own. Unusual in those days.'

'Perhaps he wasn't such a crook as Alastair Beaumont thought,' said Libby.

'The will is very detailed, and there seem to be several business ventures, but, as you say, no mention of the reliquary. But he left Jasper Retford his sundries, so it may be there.'

'Or in the residue of the estate to Mary?' said Fran. 'If it was valuable, and she seems to be the closest to him.'

'A private gift before he died is most likely,' said Andrew. 'Anyway, we've got all these names we can follow up –'

'We?' repeated Libby and Fran.

'Don't you want me to?' asked Andrew with a grin.

'But it would be a lot of work,' said Libby. 'And you're –'

'Bored,' Andrew finished for her. 'It would be an absolute pleasure, believe me. I can go up to Kew, and the British Museum, probably, and ferret about to my heart's content.'

'If there are any expenses,' began Fran.

'I shall bear them myself,' said Andrew. 'I shall be only too delighted.'

'Well.' Libby looked at Fran. 'Even if it doesn't get us any further with the murder, it would be terrific if you could trace the reliquary. The Beaumonts and the nuns would all be pleased.'

'Leave it to me,' said Andrew. 'Now, can you email me this will, so I have the link to go from?' He gave Fran the address and she duly sent the document as an attachment.

'There now.' Andrew sat back, looking pleased. 'And, I can tell you, it will be very good for our Rosie to come home and find me not ready to jump when she says jump.'

'That confirms what we know about dear Rosie,' said

Fran, as they walked back to the car. 'She uses Andrew as a diversion whenever she feels like it.'

'And to feed poor Talbot when she flits off,' said Libby, remembering the fat black-and-white cat who was so frequently left on his own. 'I wish he could find someone else.'

'I don't suppose he wants anyone else,' said Fran. 'After all, when we met him he was happily single and not looking for anyone. Perhaps she's as much of a diversion for him as he is for her.'

'Except that he does a hell of a lot more for her than she does for him.'

'It gives him something to do,' said Fran. 'And if he can find anything out about the reliquary it will be great.'

'It'll be fantastic,' said Libby. 'And I'm sure, somehow, that it went back to the Beaumonts at some point after old Barty got it. Alastair said it kept coming back.'

It was while Libby was concocting a hasty supper after her afternoon out that the phone rang.

'Libby,' Peter's voice sounded strained. 'Could you come round here now?'

'Now? What's up? I'm just starting supper.'

'I've got someone here. I need help.'

'Police?'

'No.' Peter's voice dropped. 'Dominic's wife.'

Libby sent Ben a text to tell him dinner would be delayed, shoved the makings into the fridge and left the house. On the way to Peter's, her mobile rang.

'I'm sorry, darling,' said Libby. 'Peter's got Dominic's wife with him and said he needs help. Sent out an SOS, in fact.'

'Shall I come too?'

'I don't know. Can we play it by ear?'

Peter opened the door before she got to the cottage,

looking harassed.

'What's the problem?' Libby whispered.

'She's been hysterical,' Peter whispered back. 'She seems to think it's all our fault.'

'But I thought they were estranged?'

'So did we all.' Peter made a face. 'I'm wondering if this isn't all about some sort of compensation culture.'

'She'll be lucky,' said Libby darkly, and went inside.

Estelle Butcher was sitting bolt upright on Peter's sofa, while Harry lurked behind her in the kitchen doorway.

'Mrs Butcher.' Libby went forward with her hand outstretched. 'I'm so sorry about Dominic. What can I do to help?'

'Who are you?' Estelle Butcher's red-rimmed eyes narrowed at Libby.

'Didn't Peter tell you? My name's Libby Sarjeant.'

'And what have you got to do with anything?'

'I knew Dominic. I cast him in his first production at our theatre.'

'Your theatre? Piddling little amateur set-up. Dom was a pro.'

'An ex-pro, yes,' said Libby, 'like myself and several others of our company.'

'Hmph,' sniffed Mrs Butcher.

'I can't quite understand why you're here, actually, Mrs Butcher,' Libby continued, trying to keep her temper. 'We don't know how Dominic died.'

'It was your play. You put him in this position. I'm not sure that isn't actionable.'

Libby and Peter exchanged a look.

'I'm quite sure it isn't, Mrs Butcher. Dominic was found where he shouldn't have been in suspicious circumstances. Nobody connected with either St Eldreda's Abbey or the Oast House Theatre has any connection with

115

or liability for that.'

'Exactly what are you suggesting?' Estelle Butcher looked as though she might fly at Libby at any moment.

'Nothing. We don't know why Dominic was there in his monk's habit –'

'Because he'd been in your bloody play,' snarled Estelle.

'The play had been over for hours,' said Peter. 'The monastery grounds and the Abbey had been locked after we all left.'

'Then you left him behind and locked him in to be murdered.' Estelle's voice was rising into a shriek, but Libby detected a false and theatrical note behind it.

'If Dominic was left behind it was his intention. He concealed himself, or else broke in somehow later. That's what the police are looking into,' said Libby.

'The police!' spat Estelle. 'You're making my Dom into a criminal. What was he supposed to have done?'

'We don't know, Mrs Butcher,' sighed Libby. 'And we thought you and he –'

'Were having a break, if you must know. He's been depressed since he left *Limehouse Blues*. We thought he should get away.'

'Ah,' said Peter. 'Dominic gave the impression the separation was permanent.'

Estelle's face was thunderous. 'No, he didn't.'

'I assure you, he did,' said Peter. Libby looked at him and raised an eyebrow.

'So we can't tell you anything more,' said Harry, moving forward. 'The police are the ones to ask, not us. Have you been to his house?'

'What's it got to do with you?' Estelle swung round to face him.

Harry shrugged. 'You seem to think it's got everything

116

to do with us, duckie. Now, why don't you push off and pester the police?'

Libby stood up and Peter moved a step nearer. Estelle glared up at the three people surrounding her and seemed to shrink a little.

'Come on,' said Harry, taking her arm, 'up you get and off you go.'

She resisted for a moment, then struggled to her feet, snatching her arm from Harry.

'You haven't heard the last of this,' she said, and made for the door. As she wrenched it open she came face to face with a surprised Ben and pushed past him.

'Well, well, well,' he said. 'What did you do to her?'

'Sit down, pet, and I'll break out the booze,' said Harry. 'G&Ts all round?'

While Harry fetched bottles, glasses and ice, Peter and Libby told Ben about the nasty little episode.

'Actionable? What on earth is the woman talking about?' he said when they'd finished.

'I think they really were permanently separated, but when she heard about his death she decided there must be something she could make out of it. I bet she booted him out after he lost the telly job,' said Libby. 'And I thought none of us really knew about his marriage, Pete? You said he'd told you.'

'He can't say he didn't now, can he?' said Peter, blowing a languid kiss at Harry while accepting his glass. 'I formed the same impression as you did. She needed taking down a peg or two.'

'And she obviously hasn't been to his house,' mused Libby. 'I suppose the police wouldn't let her.'

'I wonder if they've found evidence that their break-up wasn't amicable,' said Ben. 'If they've been questioning her, rather than just informing her of his death, that could

117

account for her attitude.'

'If you ask me,' said Harry, 'she's shit scared.'

They all looked at him. Then Peter reached out and patted his thigh. 'Quite right, love. She was.'

'She is, Harry. I wonder why I didn't think of that,' said Libby.

'Which means she's got something to be scared about,' said Ben.

'Come to think of it, how did she know where you lived?' asked Libby. 'The police wouldn't have told her.'

'If they've been questioning her they would have asked if she'd had any connection with the theatre and possibly named a couple of names. Easy enough to come here and ask around. Anyone could have told her, in any of the shops,' said Ben.

'So do we think she wanted to find out if we knew anything against her?' said Peter. 'Was it a pre-emptive strike?'

'Against what, though?' said Libby. 'We actually don't know anything about her except that she existed – vaguely.'

'She's afraid you do,' said Harry. 'She was threatening you with all that shit about being actionable. Or at least, she was trying to.'

Peter looked up at his beloved perched on the arm of his chair. 'You're being very intuitive this afternoon, my pet.'

'Because I'm not as involved as you all are,' said Harry. 'And I've seen that sort of woman before.' He sniffed. 'Common.'

The others laughed.

'I wonder if we could find out about her?' said Libby. 'I mean, was she in the business too?'

'If she was, dear, it was probably at the lowest possible end,' said Harry. 'If she wasn't a woman I'd say drag artiste on the pub scene.'

'The police must have found her, so why can't we?' said Libby.

'The police had access to Dominic's house. Even if they were separated, I expect they found at least an address. Or even letters from a solicitor,' said Ben.

'And they could have looked up his marriage certificate,' said Libby, thinking of Andrew and the National Archives.

'Or, of course,' said Peter, 'they could have discovered that they weren't really married.'

'And that would be a problem why?' asked Libby, frowning.

'Suppose she heard of his death before the police told her and came forward claiming to be the widow. All sorts of scams might be perpetrated.'

'And in that case,' said Libby slowly, 'how did she know about his death in the first place?'

Chapter Fifteen

'We're making bricks out of straw,' said Peter. 'All the scenarios we've just dreamt up could be true, but we aren't likely to find out unless the police tell us.'

Harry glanced at the grandfather clock in the corner. 'Coming up to dinner time,' he said. 'Why don't we all go and have a meal at the pub? Makes a change for me to be cooked for and waited on.'

'I'd started dinner,' said Libby half-heartedly.

'How far had you got?' asked Ben.

'I put the vegetables back in the fridge. I hadn't got any further.'

'That's it, then. We'll go to the pub.' Ben stood up. 'Good idea, Hal.'

Peter unwound himself from his chair and stretched. 'It is indeed,' he said. 'My lovely boy is spot on the money today.'

'I told you, it's just because I'm not as involved as you are. You've all had horrors since yesterday morning. Come on, finish your drinks and we'll push off before the hordes descend.'

The pub, picturesquely set in the middle of the high street, leant confidingly up against the two cottages between itself and The Pink Geranium. Apart from being the "local" it had earned itself the reputation of being a gastro pub, and therefore attracted customers from all over East Kent, which sometimes made it difficult to get a table. However, being early on a Monday they had their pick.

'When do you suppose we'll be able to go back to the Abbey to do the get-out?' said Peter. 'There aren't as many willing bodies during the week.'

'No idea,' said Ben. 'I expect we'll be told. I can probably drum up a couple of the estate workers to come and help, and, if it was Wednesday afternoon, Bob would come. He still shuts on Wednesday, doesn't he?'

'I think I might ask. Should I ring Ian?' said Peter.

'I'd just ring Canterbury nick and ask,' said Harry. 'You don't want to be seen currying favour.'

'True,' said Peter. 'I'll do it tomorrow.'

However, an hour later when they had finished their meal, Libby's mobile rang.

'Are you at Harry's?' asked Ian.

'No we're all in the pub. Where are you?'

'Outside your house. May I join you?'

'Ian's coming to join us. Must be off the record,' Libby said, switching off the phone. 'You can ask him about the get-out.'

Ian joined them and accepted coffee.

'I just wanted to tell you that you can go and take all your stuff away now. Forensics have done their worst.'

'Can we ask you about progress?' asked Libby.

'As usual, I'll tell you as much as we know so far, but it goes no further. OK?'

They all nodded.

'It appears that Butcher was hit several times with a large stone, which has been retrieved. But the puzzling thing is that Mrs Fletcher –'

'Who?' asked the other three men together.

'The woman you knew as Martha. She wasn't hit with the same weapon. In fact, she hit her head on the corner of the stone plinth. We assume she was pushed over, probably as she ran from the attacker. Or she could even have

121

tripped.'

'Have you worked out what time this was?' asked Ben.

'The security guard's previous round was at 4 o'clock, so somewhere between four and six. Butcher's death seems to have been earlier according to the doctor, but Mrs Fletcher's injury is put very close to six, so, again, there's a discrepancy.'

'So the killer had knocked off Dominic,' said Libby, 'realised he couldn't get at the reliquary and waited until Martha showed up.'

'But what was Martha doing up at that time in the morning?' asked Ben. 'She was fully clothed, wasn't she?'

'Also how did the killer know she was going to turn up?' said Harry. 'Unless she was in league with him.'

Ian laughed. 'I knew I'd get you weaving fantastical theories. Unfortunately, we can't prove any of them, so we have to plod on with boring police work until we can uncover the truth. Or not, as the case may be.'

'Well,' said Libby, 'we had a visit this afternoon from Dominic's widow.'

'What?' Ian put his cup down sharply.

'Estelle Butcher? Is that her? She was informing us that it was all our fault and she was going to sue, or something.'

'The woman's a nightmare,' said Ian. 'We found her snooping round Butcher's house. She couldn't get in, but started shouting the odds when we told her she wasn't allowed to. We took her for questioning at the station, but she wouldn't say how she knew he was dead before we'd informed her, except that it was on the news.'

'Well, it was,' said Libby, 'but not until this morning. Did it make the papers?'

'We managed to scotch it until this morning. If he'd been a better known actor it would have leaked before then. And she was down there before the announcement.'

'So she knew something. About his murder? Is she the murderer?' said Peter.

'There's no evidence to suggest that, and, although her arrival is highly suspicious, we couldn't very well hold her any longer.'

'Is she the real Mrs Butcher?' asked Libby. 'Did you find evidence at Dominic's house?'

'No convenient marriage certificates or revelatory wills,' said Ian with a grin, 'but we checked, and Estelle Butcher does indeed appear to be married legally to Dominic Butcher. And the photo on the driving licence in her wallet is of her.'

'But they were living separately,' said Libby. 'She was trying to make it sound as though they were still a loving couple.'

'There was no evidence of that, either,' said Ian, 'but she's definitely trying to hide something.'

'Or find something,' said Harry. 'And hide what it is.'

Ian looked at Harry in surprise, while Peter said admiringly, 'He's on the ball tonight, isn't he?'

'Perhaps simply remove any evidence of their permanent separation,' suggested Ben. 'After all, to be the widow of a moderately famous actor would have a certain cachet in some people's eyes.'

'And, despite what Ian says, if he's made a will leaving everything elsewhere rather than to her, she might be keen to get her hands on that,' said Libby.

'I doubt she'd want to,' said Ian. 'All Butcher left were debts. The house here was rented.'

'What about the family house?' asked Libby. 'Is the lovely Estelle living in it?'

'Yes, and, for once, he seems to have done the right thing, because the mortgage is paid off on his death.'

'That's a motive if ever there was one,' said Libby,

remembering her own post-divorce period when keeping up payments on the large family home had been a nightmare.

'It seems unlikely that she would have arranged to meet him at the dead of night in deserted monastery ruins to do it, though,' said Ian. 'Or that he would agree to meet her then.'

'That's the problem, isn't it,' said Libby, frowning. 'Why was he there? I mean, it's logical for Martha, or Cornelia or whoever she is, to be there. She was very protective of that reliquary, and I can quite believe that she got up early to check on it. Probably did that every morning, and don't forget it was due to be removed that day, so it was one of her last chances to look at it.'

'So why was Dominic there?' said Harry, returning them to the first problem. 'Have the fuzz got any idea, Ian?'

'What a sweet, outmoded expression, petal,' said Peter. 'I don't believe they're called fuzz these days, are they Ian?'

'Much worse,' said Ian. 'And the only idea we've got is that he was planning to steal the reliquary. He had a variety of impressive hardware under that habit.'

'So someone stopped him by bopping him on the head,' said Libby. 'And then hung about for a couple of hours before doing the same to Martha. Doesn't make sense.'

'You said Martha was very protective of the reliquary,' said Ian. 'Would she have been liable to try and steal it if she thought it was in danger?'

They all looked at him in surprise.

'In danger of what, though?' asked Peter. 'Of being stolen? That doesn't make any sense, either.'

'But might she have thought she could keep it safe rather than see it sold to the highest bidder?' said Harry.

'That figures.'

'That means, then, that it was someone else who was watching over the reliquary,' said Ben, 'to make sure it went back to the auctioneers, or Mrs – what was her name?'

'Chappell,' said Ian. 'Yes. Which, of course, means that we looked at the security guard very carefully indeed. But he is simply an employee of the security company and has been for years, with no connection to Marshall, Chappell or the auctioneers.'

'But that is the way you're thinking?' said Ben.

'It's one avenue,' said Ian with a smile.

'Oh, we're not going to get anything out of him,' said Libby. 'He's just come to pick our brains.'

Ian laughed. 'Well, you do occasionally spot something we don't.'

'Have you found anything to link Bernard Evans's murder to this one?' asked Peter.

'Not yet, but that's not to say I won't. I'm looking into the Beaumonts at present.'

'Alastair?' said Libby, surprised.

'No, the family. Remembering what he told both you and me, that the thing boomerangs backwards and forwards, usually illegally, it occurred to me that it was a member of the family who killed Evans and took it, deciding it would be better back in the family vault and bringing luck back to the glorious Beaumonts.'

'Only Alastair says it never does. But he'd have been around in the seventies – he'd know if the reliquary came home?' said Libby.

'He says it didn't, to his knowledge. But I'm now looking into the known extended family at that time, to see if there were any black sheep.'

'Because, of course,' said Libby hesitantly, 'it might

have been a family member who didn't want to keep the reliquary, but didn't see why the *proceeds* should go out of the family.'

Ian gave her the look of a teacher with a favourite pupil. 'Well done, Lib.'

'Ah!' said Ben. 'That makes sense of all the other times it was nicked. Someone in the family got indignant about outsiders making money from it.'

'That's all very well,' said Harry, 'but it *wasn't* nicked this time, so does that mean that Marshall or Chappell or whoever is a distant Beaumont?'

'The person looking after the reliquary saving the proceeds for the beautiful Beaumonts once again, you mean?' said Peter.

'All very complicated,' said Ian, 'and all lines which are being followed up. It's an immensely complicated investigation, so you're welcome to poke around a little, as long as you don't tread on our toes or antagonise witnesses.'

'That's very handsome of you, Ian,' said Libby, 'and did I tell you about Andrew and Bartholomew Tollybar?'

She related the whole search for the will and Andrew's willingness to help.

'So whether Jolly Tolly's will gets us any further, I've no idea, but we might know where it went next and who purloined the papers.'

'And there's a possibility that whoever did told his or her children and it's that line of the family that are the black sheep,' said Ben.

'A whole flock of the bloody things, by the sound of it,' said Harry.

Ian looked interested. 'It's certainly another theory. You will keep me posted about anything Andrew turns up, won't you?' He stood up. 'I must go. The security guard will let you into the Monastery and will give you the keys to your shed. There's no need for you to go into the Abbey, is there?'

'Only to see Sister Catherine, but you never know when they'll be praying,' said Libby. 'But I shall try to see her. I feel responsible for the whole thing, somehow.'

Chapter Sixteen

Fran drove over from Nethergate the following morning to join the small band of Oast House Theatre members who were to remove the costumes, lights and other paraphernalia from the Monastery.

To their surprise, ten minutes after the security guard let them in, Sister Catherine unlocked the atrium doors and hurried outside.

'Oh, Libby,' she said, catching Libby's hands in her own. Libby dropped the costumes she was holding. 'I'm so sorry this should have happened. We blame ourselves, you know. If we hadn't found out about that – that – *thing*, this wouldn't have happened.'

'It's more my fault than yours,' said Libby. 'If I hadn't told Peter, he wouldn't have written the play –'

'I've told you,' said Ben coming up behind them with his arms full of lighting cable, 'that train of thought is useless and unproductive. If you go back to first causes you'd be blaming Adam and Eve.'

'But that's what the bible teaches us,' said Sister Catherine with a smile. 'The whole problem of the human race!'

'Wrong analogy,' grinned Ben. 'The roots of causality.'

'Have you heard how Martha is?' asked Libby.

'Still unconscious, although I believe she's now in what they call a medically induced coma. I wish she could tell us what happened.' Sister Catherine twisted her hands together. 'If only we hadn't had that thing here …'

'That, unfortunately,' said Libby, picking up the costumes, 'was down to the police. They thought it might drag someone out of the woodwork. It worked only too well.'

'I just wish we'd never even heard of the thing,' said Sister Catherine. 'After all, it's really nothing to do with us. At least it's gone now.'

They all turned to look into the empty atrium.

'The police removed the plinth as well, then?' said Libby.

'As soon as the reliquary went,' Sister Catherine nodded. 'Dear Martha was so proud of her responsibility towards it.'

'Apparently her name wasn't Martha?'

'No. When she came here she was recovering from a rather unpleasant marriage, and she said she wanted nothing more to do with her old life, so she adopted the name. She felt it was appropriate.'

'So you knew nothing of her life as Cornelia Fletcher?' said Ben.

'Nothing.' Sister Catherine shook her head. 'I expect the police know more than we do. They went through all her belongings. I found that very distressing.'

'Most police investigations are unpleasant,' said Libby, 'especially when they involve murder.'

Sister Catherine sighed. 'That poor man. We pray for him.'

'But –?' began Libby, but Ben stopped her with a glare.

'We'll soon be out of your way,' he said. 'I shouldn't think you'd want any more plays here.'

'It's not up to us, but the Trust. The Abbey doesn't own the Monastery. It just happened to be a fortuitous –'. She stopped. 'Well, you know what I mean. Please come and say goodbye when you leave.' And she was gone in a swirl of black.

'I don't care what you say,' said Libby somewhat belligerently to Ben, 'I still feel guilty. Those poor nuns, and worse, poor Martha.'

'I know.' Ben patted her shoulder through the tangle of cables. 'Come on, the sooner we're out of their hair the better.'

Libby loaded her costumes into a hamper and went back to the gardener's shed for more.

'The police have been through these,' said Fran, looking up from a pile of habits.

'I expect they have,' said Libby. 'They'll have taken anything they thought suspicious.'

'That accounts for being one short.'

'Eh?'

'One habit short.'

'No, that would have been the one Dominic wore,' said Libby.

'I counted that,' said Fran, sitting back on her heels. 'We're still one short.'

They looked at one another for a moment.

'Has Ian given you a receipt for anything?' asked Fran.

'No. Oh, God.' Libby let out a long breath. 'We'll have to tell him.'

'When?'

'Now. I bet he'll want someone to come over.' Libby went to find her phone and found Ben instead. She explained and he called Ian's police number.

'Yes,' he said, ending the call. 'We're to leave the costumes, but we can carry on with the other stuff. Someone will be over as soon as possible. He sounded a tad cross.'

'I bet he did,' said Libby. 'So who took the other habit?'

'The murderer,' said Fran, appearing from behind a

screen of free-standing lights waiting to be loaded on to Bob's butcher's van.

'Stands to reason,' said Libby.

'What's going on?' Peter came up with his clipboard. They told him. 'Oh, bugger. The costume hire people are going to go mad.'

'Peter!' said three shocked voices.

'Well, they are. I had to tell them yesterday about the habit Dominic was found in – now to tell them another one's missing – it's going to be a hell of an insurance mix-up.'

'I don't see how we can be held responsible for them,' said Ben. 'They'll be covered by their own insurance, won't they?'

'No, it'll be down to us,' said Peter gloomily. 'I wish I'd never heard of the bloody reliquary.'

'That's what everyone's saying,' said Libby. 'Look out, here come the police. That was quick.'

In fact, it was DI Davies who was ushered through by the security guard. He looked round a little sheepishly and asked to be shown the evidence.

'We haven't got any evidence, exactly,' said Libby, 'just a lack of it, if you know what I mean.'

Davies asked them to unpack the costumes already in the hamper, counted through them, then went to the shed.

'And there's one short?' he said. 'Apart from that on the deceased?'

'Yes. That's why DCI Connell wanted them checked.'

Davies frowned. 'Right. I'd better call in.'

'He doesn't know what to do next,' whispered Libby, as they left him in the shed.

'I expect they'll impound the lot,' said Fran. 'Although I don't know what good that will do.'

But DI Davies returned to say the costumes could be

returned to the hire company, and a receipt would be issued for the robe worn by Dominic. He didn't seem inclined to say anything else, and in frustration they watched him go.

'Now they'll set up a search for the missing robe,' said Libby. 'And they'll start here, I bet. Poor Sister Catherine.'

When Libby and Fran went to the Abbey to say goodbye, Libby warned Sister Catherine what might happen.

'I know,' said the nun mournfully. 'Mr Connell just called to tell us. I can't tell you how awful it is. We've already had the police all over the Abbey, now they're coming again. Mother Abbess is beside herself. They're searching the nuns' quarters, and even the chapel. We'll have to be reconsecrated.'

'Oh, dear,' said Libby helplessly. 'I'm so sorry.'

Sister Catherine smiled sadly. 'We brought it on ourselves, Libby. Or at least, I did. I'm going to be doing penance for the rest of my life.'

'Do you think she will?' asked Fran, as they went back to their cars.

'I don't know.' Libby shook her head. 'But even if she isn't told to, she'll probably do it off her own bat.'

Back at the theatre it was a silent and sober party who unloaded the lights, props and costumes. Peter packed up the remaining habits and put them in his car.

'I'm going to drive them up now,' he said. 'No sense in hanging on to them any longer.'

'I'm going home,' said Fran. 'Why don't you two come to dinner tonight and stay over? Get away from it all for a bit.'

Libby called over to where Ben was uncoiling cables. He stuck up a thumb.

'We can go and have a drink at The Sloop first if the weather stays fine,' said Fran, 'so come about seven?'

132

Finally leaving the theatre shipshape, Ben went across to the Manor to see his mother and attend to anything in the estate office that might have cropped up in his absence.

Libby walked slowly down the drive trying to work out exactly what had happened on Saturday night. The single most inexplicable thing, in her view, was the time lapse between Dominic's murder and the attack on Martha. Almost as if they were unconnected.

The high street was quiet. The schools hadn't yet broken up for the summer, and only a few shoppers wandered between Nella and Joe's farm shop, the eight-til-late and Bob's butcher's shop. Libby waved through the window of The Pink Geranium at Harry and stopped for a word with Donna, who was approaching with her baby in a sling.

'Just going to collect the books,' she told Libby.

'He still hasn't replaced you,' said Libby. 'I think he's hoping you'll come back.'

Donna laughed. 'With a husband who works the unsociable hours mine does? He'll be lucky.'

Libby walked on. The village was its normal, peaceful self, as if nothing as vicious and unpredictable as murder had ever ruffled its surface. When she opened the door of number 17, Sidney shot out between her legs and she tripped down the step. All was as usual.

But it wasn't. Libby felt unsettled and vaguely depressed as she went to make herself a cup of tea and realised she'd missed lunch. As she waited for the kettle to boil, she acknowledged that this feeling was because Dominic Butcher's murder was so much closer to home than most of the others she had been involved with, for even when a body had been found in the Manor grounds it had been nothing to do with Libby, Ben or any of their friends. But Dominic had been cast in their play, they had all been there. Somewhere, there was culpability.

On the easel in the conservatory sat the most recent painting due for delivery to Guy's shop. As they were going there for dinner in the evening, Libby decided to put the finishing touches to it. But she couldn't concentrate, and, in the end, merely signed it and left it to dry.

Sitting under the cherry tree in the garden with a fresh cup of tea, she once more turned to the insoluble problem of the murder.

'You see,' she said to Sidney, who had returned to keep her company, 'unless the murderer was one of the nuns, someone else had to have hidden in the monastery ruins before they were locked up, or broken in, somehow. That means someone who knew Dominic was going to be there, or who was there for the same reason – to steal the reliquary. And if that was the case, why didn't they just go for it? That would make sense – and Martha could have been attacked when she came to protect it. Instead, there's a gap of nearly two hours –' She stopped.

Actually, apart from the evidence of the security guard who had found Martha at six o'clock, what did they have on the time of her attack? How did they know that Martha hadn't interrupted the burglary at the same time as the murder?

She stood up, racking her brain for anything Ian might have told her. She couldn't ring him up and ask him, but she was sure there must have been a reason for putting Martha's attack so much after Dominic's murder.

But there was another thing she'd forgotten to ask about. Why, when Martha was attacked, apparently trying to protect the reliquary, had the alarms not gone off?

Chapter Seventeen

'It was last night,' Libby said to Fran later, as they sat at a table in front of The Sloop waiting for Ben and Guy to bring drinks. 'Ian said Dominic's death had been put at earlier than four, which means the security guard missed him on his four o'clock round, but would have seen Martha, so there must have been a gap between the two attacks.'

'It's very odd,' said Fran staring out at the little harbour, where the two tourist boats, *The Dolphin* and *The Sparkler*, bobbed quietly at anchor. George and Bert, their respective owners, sat a little way off outside Mavis's Blue Anchor café, a blue haze of smoke curling round their heads.

'Do you think the killer waited for Martha purposely?' asked Libby.

'Must have done,' said Fran. 'Probably so that she could turn off the alarms and he could steal the reliquary. So he must have known all about her.'

'Then why didn't he steal it? And why didn't the alarms go off?'

'Martha must have come down to the atrium and turned the alarms off before she was attacked. And perhaps the killer heard the security guard coming and made off empty-handed.'

'I still wonder why she was down there to turn the alarms off so early,' said Libby.

'Just to have a last look, as she was so attached to it.'

'Yes, she did say it was a pity it couldn't stay there.'

Libby frowned. 'There's something wrong about it all.'

Fran gave her an old-fashioned look. 'You could say that.'

'And where does Estelle come in? She's a spanner in the works, well and truly. Just how did she know Dominic was dead?'

'I was thinking about that,' said Fran. 'I know Ian told you the police had kept a lid on it until yesterday morning as far as the media were concerned, but what about social media? They say you can pick up news as soon as it happens, well before any official announcements.'

Libby frowned. 'You mean someone put it out on one of the sites? But who?'

'Anyone could have. Not the nuns, of course, but one of the security guards, perhaps saying "we'll be in trouble over this", or a member of the company. No one told them not to, did they?'

'I suppose it's possible,' said Libby, 'but you have to be a friend or a follower or something before you can read people's updates. How would Estelle have known anyone connected with us?'

'These things spread, you know that. One person's hundred followers read it, their hundred read it and there you are. And Dominic's name was sufficiently well known for it to be picked up.'

'Wouldn't she have admitted that to Ian when he asked her?'

'She might have felt it was embarrassing, admitting she'd picked it up that way and come snooping down to see what she could get out of it,' said Fran. 'Oh, good, here are the drinks.'

The conversation turned away from the murder as they sat and contemplated the sunset over the sea. Along Harbour Street, Cliff Terrace and Victoria Place the fairy

136

lights strung between lampposts came on, and the cupola on top of the Alexandria, the recently restored theatre, glowed like an imitation moon.

'I was thinking,' said Libby, 'now we've started doing outreach theatre –'

'Doing what?' said Ben.

'All right, productions in other places –'

'Only one,' said Fran.

Libby let out an exasperated sigh. 'Let me finish! I was thinking that perhaps we could bring something down here to the Alexandria. They let other amateur groups hire it, don't they?'

'I think so,' said Guy, 'but at the moment they've got a series of one-nighters. They need to appeal to the holiday-makers.'

'I had an idea about an End Of The Pier show,' said Libby. 'A really old-fashioned one. After all, the people who come to Nethergate aren't the same sort who go to Brighton or Blackpool. They like the old-fashioned, traditional feel of the place. Don't you think it would work?'

'It might,' said Ben. 'Who's looking after the Alexandria now?'

'It's administered by a trust,' said Guy, 'but I can find out who to approach, if you like, although it would probably be next summer before you could do anything.'

'That's all right, next summer would be perfect,' said Libby. 'Thanks, Guy. Oh, and I've brought a new picture with me. It's in the boot.'

Fran had prepared sea bass and roasted vegetables, followed by her own version of Eton Mess.

'Lovely,' said Libby as she licked the last vestige of cream off her spoon. 'I'm too full to move.'

'Come on, Ben,' said Guy. 'We'll get coffee.'

Fran leant over and topped up Libby's wine glass.

'So do you think we're going to get anywhere at all with our own investigations?' she asked. 'Or do we give it up now?'

'I thought I might look up the social networking sites for mentions of Dominic,' said Libby. 'See if we can trace where Estelle's information came from.'

'Not tonight, though,' said Fran.

'No, of course not. The other thought I had was: suppose she knows all about Dominic's family background. We might be able to find out if he was a renegade Beaumont.'

'I expect Ian's got people on that already. He wouldn't need Estelle's information.'

'I still wish I could talk to her,' said Libby.

'But she was horrible to you,' said Fran. 'She wouldn't talk to you.'

'I wonder if I could get round that,' said Libby. 'Sympathise, or something.'

'Hypocritical,' said Fran. 'Anyway, you don't know where to find her.'

'She might have stayed somewhere near the village. Harry said she was scared of something, maybe something the police might find, so she might be keeping an eye on things.'

'I still don't think she would talk to you,' said Fran. 'I'd leave it alone, if I were you.'

'Coffee.' Guy put the cafetière on the table. 'And now you can stop talking about the murder.'

The following morning, after Guy and Ben had gone out to fetch croissants for breakfast, Fran and Libby sat down at the kitchen table and began their search of all the social media sites.

It soon became apparent that, as Fran suspected,

Dominic's murder had trickled through as early as ten o'clock on the morning he had been murdered, but where the news had originated they couldn't tell. They did a search for Estelle Butcher on the networking sites and found she had a presence on all of them. A lot of her information was protected, but it was still easy to see who she talked to and what about. However, there was nothing about Dominic.

It was just after breakfast when Libby's phone rang.

'Patti! Why aren't you at church?'

'I'm in Italy, remember?'

'Oh, yes. Why are you calling me from Italy?'

'Catherine just called. She'd forgotten too, but she wanted you to know – Martha's regained consciousness!'

'Well,' said Libby as she ended the call, 'that's that, then. Murder solved.'

Fran was frowning. 'I'm not sure ...'

Libby sat forward. She recognised that look. 'What is it?'

Fran shook her head. 'It's probably nothing.'

'What is? Come on, what did you see?'

'I don't know. There was a sudden brightness – like a sun flare. And then that suffocating darkness – you know? That I've had before.'

'Couldn't that be Martha remembering the bash on the head and then losing consciousness?'

'It could.' Fran sighed. 'I wish I could interpret these things better.'

'You haven't been having so many of your moments for the last couple of years, though, have you? Except when we rescued Rosie, of course.'

'That was an easy one,' said Fran. 'This is more difficult. If Martha had died I could have understood it.'

'But she didn't,' said Libby. 'So?'

'Perhaps it means she doesn't remember anything.'

'Of course. They say that after a bash on the head people don't remember.'

'Then again,' said Fran, 'it may not be about Martha at all. Just triggered by the mention of her regaining consciousness.'

'So we ignore it?'

'I don't see that we can do anything else,' said Fran. 'Presumably someone will be able to question Martha and we'll know. It just didn't feel right, somehow.'

All day, Libby waited to hear something about Martha. There was nothing on the news, national or local, and no phone call from Ian.

'Not that you could expect him to call,' said Ben, when he returned from the estate office in the late afternoon. 'I doubt if we'll hear any more until it's all wrapped up.'

Libby sighed. 'You're right. I just wonder what Fran's moment meant.'

'I doubt it's significant. You can just relax now.'

'Won't we have to go to the inquest?'

'Maybe, although it's more likely they'll call Peter to tell them about the play and why both the reliquary and Dominic were there. Do we know when it is?'

'No, Ian hasn't told us. If we were needed, I suppose we'd know. Oh, well, I suppose I can get down to planning the End Of The Pier Show now.'

'The what?'

'Remember? Yesterday – the Alexandria. I had a look at their website earlier. We'd have to hire it ourselves, but there's nothing like it there at the moment. So I emailed.'

'You did what? Without discussing it with me or Pete?'

'It was only an enquiry,' said Libby, feeling a bit red in the face. 'Just to see how much it would cost and all that sort of thing.'

'Well don't go and do anything stupid until we've had a committee meeting about it,' said Ben.

'Can't I at least plan a show in case?'

'Nothing to stop you,' said Ben, sounding disgruntled. Libby sighed.

She was just changing channels on the television to catch the local news when her mobile rang.

'Just thought you'd want to be updated,' said Ian. 'I knew you'd be chewing the woodwork by now.'

'We heard Martha regained consciousness from Sister Catherine,' said Libby. 'What –?

'Hold on. First – the inquest was adjourned this morning for further enquiries. One reason was that Mrs Fletcher had regained consciousness and there was a possibility that she would be able to talk to us. So far, she hasn't.'

'Oh, Ian! Why?'

'Partially because the doctors say she can't yet, but also because she hasn't said a word about anything so far. She merely seems distressed.'

'So is that the only progress? What about Estelle?'

'You know I can't give you any more information about the case, Lib. Just rest assured we're looking into her background.'

'We found out that Dominic's death had been leaked on the social media sites the same morning,' said Libby. 'We thought maybe that was how she heard of it.'

'The same thought had occurred to us, strangely,' said Ian, and Libby could hear the smile in his voice. 'We occasionally get there without you.'

'Oh, all right,' said Libby. 'Do you know who leaked it in the first place?'

'Too difficult to trace,' said Ian. 'But unlikely to have been the murderer.'

'No. But I do wonder what it is Estelle is so scared will

141

be discovered.'

'So do we, but I expect we'll find out. We're going back to Mr Butcher's house tomorrow, and we'll be looking at any other places connected with him.'

'How was he paying his bills?' wondered Libby. 'You said he left nothing but debts and didn't have a job.'

'And I shouldn't have said that much,' said Ian. 'I'll let you know progress if and when I'm able, but there's nothing more you can do.'

'Except carry on looking into Jolly Tolly,' said Libby.

'Who?'

Libby grinned. 'The will of Bartholomew Tollybar, of course.'

Chapter Eighteen

It was Friday before Libby heard any more about Martha's condition, when, once more, Patti called her from Italy.

'Will you call the Abbey?' asked Patti. 'Catherine seems not to be able to keep a telephone number in her head. She wants to tell you about Martha.'

So Libby called the Abbey and asked for Sister Catherine.

'Oh, Libby, I'm so glad you called. Now before I forget, I've got a pencil and I'll write down your number. I felt so silly phoning Patti in Italy.'

Libby told her both numbers. 'And now, what about Martha? Patti says you have some news.'

'Indeed, I do, although not entirely good news. I was allowed to go and see her yesterday, because she is, at last, speaking.'

'And what did she say?'

'Well, nothing really.' Libby could hear the puzzlement in Sister Catherine's voice. 'She kept saying she was sorry, and she couldn't remember anything. Well, that's not quite true. She says she remembers going down early to check that the reliquary was all right because it was going to be collected that morning, but nothing more. Apparently, that's quite normal. But she seems very agitated.'

'Because she can't remember, I expect,' said Libby. 'She felt it was her responsibility, didn't she. Does she know about Dominic yet?'

'Dominic –? Oh, the poor man who was murdered. No, I don't think so.'

'She'll feel even worse then,' said Libby. 'Poor woman. I wish I could see her. Do you think they'd let me?'

'I think you have to have permission from the police,' said Sister Catherine. 'You could ask your friend.'

'What do you reckon?' said Libby to Fran later. 'Shall I phone Ian?'

Fran, who had come to Steeple Martin to talk about Libby's End of The Pier show, was dubious. 'He might feel you're interfering.'

'But I was the one who saw her most,' objected Libby. 'We got really friendly.'

'Call his private mobile, then,' said Fran. 'Then he can answer if he chooses, or ignore you if he feels like it.'

Ian, however called back within half an hour.

'Yes, you may visit her, but check with the hospital. She's still very fragile, and she doesn't know about the murder yet. They had to leave her in a medically induced coma to let the brain swelling go down. At least I think that's right.'

'And is there any other news?'

Ian sighed. 'No, Libby. Oh – except that we've found the old man who left Bernard Evans the reliquary in the first place. His name, anyway.'

'You have? Gosh! Who was he?'

'A Ronald Barnes, who died childless at the age of ninety. We've got someone looking into the possibility that Bernard was a distant relative. If it doesn't impact on the enquiry, I'll let you know more when I have it.'

'So there we are,' said Libby, relating this to Fran as she made tea. 'Shall we see if we can trace Ronald Barnes?'

'You think we'd do better than the police?' laughed Fran. 'I hardly think so! Anyway, we've got Andrew

144

tracking down your Jolly Tolly, we don't need any more, do we?'

'Spose so.' Libby sat down at the kitchen table. 'I shall phone the hospital in a minute. Do you want to come, too?'

'No, one's enough. Just don't upset her.'

Libby was allowed to visit Martha the following afternoon. She was still in intensive care and attached to an alarming number of tubes and machines, but when a nurse showed Libby in, she opened her eyes and tried to smile.

'Don't talk if you don't want to,' said Libby, leaning to give her a kiss on the forehead. 'I brought grapes, but I don't suppose you're allowed them. I just wanted you to know we're all thinking of you.'

'The play?' whispered Martha.

'Yes, all of us connected with the play,' confirmed Libby.

Martha's smile faded and she frowned. 'It's still there?' she said.

'The play? Oh, the reliquary. No, that's gone back to the auction house, I believe, although it won't be sold yet. In fact, the police might have it, for all I know. I think they think you saved it from being stolen.'

Martha's expression lightened a fraction. 'I did? They didn't tell me that.'

'What – um – what did they tell you exactly?' asked Libby hesitantly.

'That I'd been hurt at the Abbey and did I remember anything. I couldn't at first, then they mentioned the play and the reliquary and gradually I began to remember a little. Just getting up early and going to –' She frowned. 'Where did I go?'

'The atrium?' suggested Libby nervously, hoping she didn't trigger a setback.

'Ah – the atrium.' Martha's eyes closed. 'And then ...'

her voice faded. 'No,' she said after a moment. 'Nothing. A bright light.'

'That's –' began Libby, and stopped. She daren't tell Martha that was what Fran had seen. And what did it mean, anyway?

The nurse opened the door and sent Libby a significant look.

'I've got to go, now, Martha.' She leant over to give her another kiss. Martha caught her arm.

'Will you come again, Libby? I'm only allowed to see Sister Catherine apart from you.'

'Yes, of course. But what about relatives?'

'I have none,' said Martha, and closed her eyes again.

'No relatives?' Libby asked Ian when she reported on her visit as requested.

'Apparently not. Her parents are dead, she said. There are only some distant relatives – second cousins, or something.'

'Second cousins aren't distant,' said Libby. 'That simply means that their parents were first cousins. I've got very close cousins and second cousins.'

'Well, it didn't sound as though Martha had,' said Ian, 'and I could hardly question her closely about it.'

'What about the husband?'

'She has no desire to see him, according to Sister Catherine, but we are, obviously, tracing him.'

'Could he be a suspect?' asked Libby.

'Unlikely,' said Ian. 'They've been estranged for some time. How would he have known about the reliquary?'

'Are you sure it's all about the reliquary?'

'It's hardly going to be about anything else, is it? If someone had a grudge against Mrs Fletcher they wouldn't break into the Abbey at dawn to have a go at her. Much more likely to attack her on the outside.'

'Yes,' said Libby reluctantly, 'and she does go out and about. She was going to come and see us. So may I go and see her again?'

'Yes, and let me know if she remembers anything else. I don't want to pester her.'

'And is there a guard? I didn't see one.'

'Despite what you see on the television, vulnerable patients aren't easy to get at, Libby. There is no way in to that ward except through various security measures. I'm sure you went through them.'

'Yes, I did,' said Libby. 'Oh, well. I just wouldn't like her to get attacked again.'

'You don't say?' Ian laughed. 'Go on with you. Enjoy your Saturday night.'

Sunday was damp. Libby, trudging up the Manor Drive towards Hetty's traditional rib of beef with Yorkshire pudding, was joined by Lenny and Flo, who carried a precious bottle from her late husband's cellar.

'You needn't have brought that, Flo. Hetty's got a good few left.'

'Special, this is gal. My Frank laid down a case for me birthday.'

'Oh, Flo! Is it your birthday?' Libby stopped and stared at Flo in horror.

Flo cackled. 'Yeah – and I'm not sayin' which one. Don't carry on about it these days, but we always have a bottle of this.' She patted the bottle.

Lenny winked. 'Knew what I was doin', didn't I?'

'Taking up again with Flo?' said Libby. 'I don't think it was your decision, Lenny.'

Ben, who had gone to the Manor earlier, opened the door to them.

'Happy birthday, Flo!' he said, giving her a kiss.

Libby looked at him accusingly. 'You knew. Why

didn't you tell me?'

'She doesn't like a fuss,' said Ben. 'Just happens that this year her birthday falls on a Sunday. Mum's done something special.'

'No roast?' Libby's face fell.

'Pudding.' Ben leant forward and whispered. 'Spotted Dick tied up in a cloth in the old iron stock pot.'

'Do they not mind being reminded of their hop picking days after all that trouble we had?' Libby frowned.

'Of course they don't. That's why they're here in Steeple Martin, isn't it?'

Peter joined them, and to their surprise, so did his younger brother James, both of whom had brought flowers. Flo pretended to be annoyed, but was obviously pleased, and quite delighted when the Spotted Dick made an appearance.

'So what's happenin' about the young fella that got killed?' she asked, after Hetty had produced coffee and Ben offered brandy.

'Not a lot, at the moment,' said Libby. 'Even the lady who was attacked has come round now, and doesn't remember a thing.'

'What lady?' asked James. Libby explained.

'So we've no idea who killed Dominic, who attacked Martha, if it was the same person or even why they were attacked,' said Peter.

'To steal that weird thing,' said Flo, who had been to one of the performances and peered disparagingly at the reliquary.

'But no one did. It was still there,' said Ben.

'That woman protected it,' said Lenny, after giving it some thought.

'That's what it looks like,' said Libby, 'but there seem to be at least two hours between the attacks.'

'How d'yer know?' asked Flo.

'The security guard's rounds. Four a.m. and six a.m.'

'Now, 'ang on,' said Lenny. 'Do yer mean he didn't see this Dominic on his first round?'

'Yes,' said Libby, Peter and Ben together.

'So, 'ow do yer know he was dead then?'

'Doctor's evidence,' said Ben. Lenny sniffed.

'And 'ow was 'e killed?' asked Flo.

'Blunt instrument, wasn't it?' said Peter.

'But what with? Have they found the murder weapon?'

'Pity it wasn't that thing,' said Flo. 'Horrible, it was. Dead fingers. Ugh.'

They all laughed.

'She had a point, though,' said Libby to Ben, as they strolled home through the drizzle a little later. 'It would almost have been right if he had been hit with the reliquary.'

'Which was still in its case,' said Ben.

'I wonder if it had any fingerprints on it?' mused Libby.

Ben sighed. 'I don't suppose you'll ever know, Lib. And don't go asking Ian.'

The light on the answerphone was flashing as Libby let them into number 17. As Ben headed for the kitchen and the kettle, she pressed the button.

'Libby, it's Andrew Wylie. I've had a good poke around and come up with some information, although I don't know how useful it will be. It won't solve your murders, anyway. Give me a ring when you can.'

'I'll leave it till tomorrow,' said Libby, following Ben into the kitchen. 'Let's have a murder-free night.'

'That doesn't sound like you,' said Ben. 'And anyway, he says it won't solve the murder – or is that why you're willing to leave it?'

Libby grinned. 'I just fancied having a night of

149

ordinariness and watching some Sunday evening telly.' She gave him a kiss on the cheek. 'Like normal couples do.'

'He called me, too,' said Fran the following morning when Libby rang her. 'I said I'd talk to you.'

'Does he want us to go and see him?'

'I think that would be best, don't you?'

'Rather than have him drag everything to you or me. When shall we say?'

'I could do this afternoon,' said Fran. 'Believe it or not, Chrissie and the baby are coming over this morning. It will give me an excuse to get rid of them.'

'Poor baby Montana,' giggled Libby. 'Have you got used to it, yet?'

'I keep calling her Monty, to Chrissie's annoyance, but I think that's what everyone will call her eventually. Go on, you call Andrew and text me the time he wants to meet.'

Andrew was quite happy to see them at any time, he said, but they settled on two thirty that afternoon.

'And we'll have tea,' he said. 'I have cake!'

'Really? Did you make it?'

'No, Rosie brought it back from Westmorland. It's Pepper Cake.'

'Oh, well, they say black pepper is good on strawberries, so why not in cake?'

Libby and Fran met outside the block of flats.

'How were Chrissie and Monty?'

'You'd think I'd never had three children the way she goes on,' said Fran, as they climbed the stairs. 'Or that I had two other grandchildren. And she's constantly moaning that she never goes out.'

'She wants a regular babysitter,' said Libby.

Fran sighed. 'I know. And lots of other grandparents care for their grandchildren all the time. I do feel guilty sometimes.'

'Well, don't,' said Libby, 'although I know that's easy for me to say when I haven't got any.'

Andrew welcomed them in and showed them to the table in the window where he had various documents laid out.

'The kettle's on,' he said, 'so sit down and have a look at what I've found out. I think you might be surprised.'

Chapter Nineteen

'First, the London Directories,' said Andrew, putting a document in front of them. 'I printed everything out I was allowed to.'

'And this is for our Barty?' said Libby.

'It is. Bartholomew Tollybar lived here,' he pointed, 'and appears to be a trader of some kind. So I looked up everyone else mentioned in his will, but it is Thomas Tollybar who I think is of the most interest.'

'Thomas?' said Fran.

'Remember your Barty's housekeeper? And her son? Well, his name is Thomas and he took the name Tollybar, so obviously he is Barty's son. He had a daughter, who had a son and a daughter, both of whom kept the "Tollybar" in their names. The son also had a daughter –'

'Hold on,' said Libby, 'this is getting complicated. This is the,' she counted on her fingers, 'the great granddaughter of Barty?'

'Great-great granddaughter,' corrected Andrew. 'She died in 1911, also leaving a daughter.'

'And this is interesting why?' asked Libby.

'Wait till I fetch the tea,' said Andrew, grinning.

'I don't understand this at all,' said Fran. 'Why are we interested in the Tollybar line?'

Libby shook her head. 'I'm quite glad I never decided to become a historian.'

Andrew returned with a tray, and offered cake.

'After we've got to the bottom of this, Andrew,' said

Fran firmly. 'We're getting totally confused.'

'Right, I'll make it simpler for you,' said Andrew, putting down the teapot. 'Let's go back to the Beaumonts.' He pulled another document towards him. 'After Tollybar bought the reliquary and bequeathed it to his housekeeper, it turned up briefly back at Maidenhaye – I took the chance of calling Alastair Beaumont and he confirmed this – but said it disappears from the records almost immediately, so everyone always thought it was a mistake. Now, it so happens that at this point in history a third or fourth cousin of the direct line was packed off to India in disgrace, and it isn't a great leap of imagination to assume that the reliquary went with him.'

'That is a bit of a leap,' said Fran, frowning.

'Ah – not when you discover that just after the first World War an Australian soldier who had been recuperating in England turned up at Maidenhaye claiming to be a descendant of this particular member of the family saying he would love to see the famous relic his ancestor mentioned so often in family history.'

'Well!' Libby and Fran exchanged looks. 'That is progress,' said Libby.

'Alastair tells me this person has been added to the family tree rather arbitrarily, and they assumed there would be other descendants, but none have ever come forward. In a letter, Alastair's grandfather says this person, whose name is Albert Glover, seems to want to know more about the reliquary "than is seemly". He and the rest of the family deduce that it did go to India, and perhaps thence to Australia with the black sheep who was banished, but has not passed to Albert's particular branch, but they have no way of tracing it or the family.'

'But why didn't Alastair tell us all this when we went to see him?' Libby burst out. 'It's essential knowledge.'

'I don't suppose he thought it was,' said Andrew, once more offering cake. 'It disappears as far as the family are concerned.'

'But we wanted to find out about the person who left it to Bernard Evans. That's the biggest clue to what's happened since. It was obviously a descendant of the black sheep! What was his name, by the way?'

'The black sheep?' Andrew pulled another document forward. 'The Hon John Jarvis, commonly known as Jack. Despoiled the playing fields of Eton, apparently, as well as a few young women.'

'Not very hon, then,' said Libby. 'So can we trace him in Australia?'

'Give me a chance, Libby! I think I've done pretty well to get this far!'

Libby was contrite. 'Sorry, Andrew, you certainly have. I was just a bit indignant that Alastair didn't tell us all this.'

'He didn't know a lot of it. He's grateful, too.'

'So, the Tollybar connection,' said Fran. 'You said we would see why that was important.'

'Right.' Andrew leant back in his chair and twinkled at them. 'You see, Bartholomew Tollybar's great-great-great granddaughter –'

'Is that the final one we got to before?' asked Libby.

'It is. May Tollybar Williams. She turns up at Maidenhaye just after World War One as well.'

'What?' said Libby and Fran together.

'I told you it was interesting,' said Andrew. 'More cake?'

'Surely the Beaumonts recognised the name? After all Alastair knew about Barty, his grandfather must have done, too.'

'But they didn't know her middle name,' said Andrew. 'Alastair's grandfather again.' He picked up another

154

document. 'He says "We have been lucky enough in these hard times to secure the services of a new lady's maid for my wife, May Williams. She seems to have attracted the attention of our soi-disant cousin, Albert." Which strikes me as interesting.'

'So how do you know it was the great-great-great granddaughter of our Barty?' said Libby.

'Because they got married.'

There was a stunned silence.

'I told you it was interesting,' said Andrew. 'So now you've got the renegade Beaumonts and the Tollybars united in a search for the reliquary.'

'You think that's what May was doing at Maidenhaye?' said Fran.

'I haven't got proof, but I think it's a fair assumption that the Tollybars also believed that the reliquary was family property and wanted it back. Presumably, both Albert and May believed Alastair's grandfather and realised that it was no longer in the family's possession. Their marriage seems to suggest a pooling of resources.'

'So,' said Libby with a frown, 'it wasn't them that left it to Ronald Barnes.'

'No,' said Andrew, 'but if Bad Jack Jarvis did go to Australia from India and Albert Glover is a genuine descendant, then there could well be others. If Jarvis had more than one child, they each had more than one – you see?'

'Yes, of course,' said Fran. 'So do we think Bernard was a descendant?'

'He could have been. We're all waiting for the details of his benefactor.'

'And then trace him backwards?' said Libby.

'Maybe,' said Andrew. 'Meanwhile, do you want me to go on digging?'

155

'Yes, please,' said Libby. 'But what about Bernard? Can't we just trace his family tree backwards?'

'I tried the direct line and it goes nowhere near the Jarvis line,' said Andrew. 'We'll have to rely on other sources.' He waved the teapot at them. 'More tea?'

'Lovely,' said Libby. 'And Andrew, I can't tell you how grateful we are. May I pass this on to the police?'

'To Ian, certainly,' said Andrew, 'though whether it will help him, I've no idea.'

'It may help with Bernard's murder, if not with Dominic's,' said Fran. 'We still have no idea about that, or why his wife Estelle has turned up.'

They left Andrew's flat just after half past four and stood looking out over Nethergate bay.

'I still can't believe Alastair Beaumont didn't know any of this,' said Libby. 'You can't help wondering if he was concealing it on purpose.'

'I doubt it. Andrew turned most of it up, and applied to Alastair for confirmation. I don't suppose Alastair had ever read his grandfather's letters.'

'But he's sorting out all of the archives in the muniment room, I told you. Cataloguing everything.'

'But didn't you say they were doing it from the earliest records? Perhaps he just hadn't got to Grandfather yet.'

'But.' Libby held up a finger. 'We actually looked at the family tree. Peter held one end of it.'

'So? It must have been huge.'

'It was. It was a family tree they'd had drawn up a few years ago, he said.'

'So, if Albert Glover, for instance, had just been pencilled in in Grandfather's time, he might not have appeared in the current one.'

'And Alastair did say they'd got so many off-shoots now they couldn't keep track.'

'Exactly what Andrew said – one child has two more, they each have two and there you are. The start of a whole new family tree.'

'So whole sections could be left off?' said Libby. 'I see what you mean. Complicated, isn't it?'

'It is a bit.' Fran smiled. 'What I do know, though, is that this reliquary must be fabulously valuable or there wouldn't be such competition for it.'

'Mmm.' Libby stared thoughtfully at the cupola on the Alexandria, just visible above the rooftops below. 'Unless it was the religious aspect that they were fighting for.'

'More likely to be the family luck and fortune,' said Fran. 'The religious aspect doesn't really come into it these days, does it?'

'It did with Martha,' said Libby, as they turned and made their way towards their cars.

'Because she was living a religious life,' said Fran. 'And even if she would have liked to see the reliquary staying in St Eldreda's, the Order didn't. They knew they had no claim on it, and they're faintly disapproving anyway.'

'It does seem a bit ironic,' said Libby. 'Martha is almost killed preventing the bloody thing being stolen when the nuns don't want it anyway.'

'That's one way of looking at it,' said Fran.

Rather than leave yet another message for Ian, Libby decided to send an email, which she did while a shepherd's pie browned in the oven. When she'd sent it, she clicked on her inbox and was surprised to find an email from the trustees of the Alexandria.

'You know we're having a meeting tonight about the Oast's next production,' Libby said over her shoulder to Ben.

'Yes?'

157

'Well, I've got something else to add to the agenda.'

'Yes?' said Ben again, more warily.

'The End of The Pier Show looks like it's on.'

It was still light when they walked to the theatre. Peter felt that meetings would be less likely to degenerate into purposeless chat if held there rather than one of their homes or the pub. When they arrived, he had pulled two of the little white tables together in the bar area, and Harry was behind the bar.

'Might as well have a drink, ducks,' he said, as Libby raised her eyebrow at him. 'And it's my night off. Whatdjer want?'

Libby and Ben both had red wine and took their seats.

'So, next production,' began Peter. 'We've got several bookings from other companies and a few one-nighters. There isn't room in the theatre to do anything else before we get to panto.'

'Maybe not,' said Libby, 'but look what I received today.' She laid the printed-out email on the table. Peter and Harry both craned to see it.

'A variety show?' Peter looked shocked.

'At the Alexandria,' said Libby. 'I sent them an email about next summer, but they're saying what about the end of August this year because they've had a booking cancelled.'

'It's practically the end of July now,' said Peter. 'We couldn't possibly!'

'You could, you know,' said Harry, leaning back in his chair. 'What about that Old Time Music Hall you did the other year. You did a whole seaside set in that. You've still got the costumes, haven't you, Lib?'

'Yes! Oh, Harry, what a good idea! And I wonder if we could find any of the stuff about Will's Wanderers and Dorinda Alexander?'

158

'Who were they?'

'The original Pierrot troupe and the founder of the Alexandria.'

'Oh, come on, Lib!' said Ben. 'That wouldn't be in the best of taste, would it?'

'Just because the Alexandria's had an unfortunate history since their time? It's all beautifully refurbished now, and those people were there at the beginning. I bet we'd be allowed to use it.'

'Wasn't it Dorinda who built it?' said Peter, looking less shocked and more interested.

'Yes, that's why it was called the Alexandria, after her. And,' continued Libby, 'now I come to think of it, Will's Wanderers didn't perform there, it was Dorinda's own new troupe, the Silver Serenaders, who all wore silvery Pierrot costumes.'

'Seeing the age of the members of our company who might be taking part, that's very appropriate,' said Ben.

'We've still got the sketches and songs from the Music Hall,' said Peter slowly. 'If the cast are still around.'

'And not on holiday,' said Harry.

'The dates cover August Bank Holiday,' said Ben, pulling the email towards him.

'I'll ask everyone tomorrow,' said Libby, 'if you all agree?'

Peter and Ben looked at one another.

'She's done it again,' said Peter.

Harry laughed and raised his glass.

'Here's to Libby,' he said, 'and here's to the Silver Serenaders!'

Chapter Twenty

Concentrating on emailing, texting and calling performers who had taken part in the Old Time Music Hall the following morning, Libby had almost forgotten her email to Ian.

'Libby?'

'Ian!'

'Yes – were you expecting someone else? You've been engaged on both phones all morning.'

'Sorry – yes. I'm organising a show for the Alexandria all in a bit of a rush.'

'The Alexandria?' Ian sounded surprised.

'Yes – it's being run by trustees now, and fully refurbished. We've been asked to do an End Of The Pier Show for the last week in August.'

'Will you have time?'

'I think so. We're rehashing a Music Hall we did a year or so back.'

'Well, it'll keep you out of mischief,' said Ian, 'but I just wanted to say thank you for the email. It's extremely helpful, and I've already called Andrew. I've agreed to defray some of the expenses if he continues his researches, which he says you want him to do anyway.'

'Does that mean he won't be able to share the results with us if you're paying him?'

'We'll only be paying expenses, and you commissioned him first,' said Ian.

'I wouldn't call it a commission,' said Libby. 'He just

160

offered to help.'

'Well, it's very useful. And he's going to try and trace a common family member between Ronald Barnes, Bernard Evans and this – what was his name? Mad Jack?'

'The Honourable John Jarvis,' said Libby, 'or Bad Jack Jarvis.'

'Yes. It would explain why Bernard had it, but not who killed him.' Ian sighed. 'I must go. Good luck with the show.'

After informing Fran about the phone call and her expected role in the new show, Libby went on organising. She dug out the programme for the Music Hall, her file of music and sketch scripts and set about putting the show together. She was lucky to have contacts within the world of entertainment who were happy to supply both memories, song lyrics and precious scripts, and spent a happy day deeply involved in her task. Sidney tried to help by spreading the papers all over the table and the sitting room floor, which of course made them easier to find.

Peter joined her in the afternoon, and together they worked out the final details and Libby set the printer to work on a fairly final script and lyrics. Most people who had been in the original Music Hall were happy to appear, the only ones she'd been unable to get in touch with being those on holiday. The panto stalwarts were delighted, Music Hall, concert party and pantomime being so closely related, and Hetty had volunteered to go into the costume store and dig out not only the Music Hall costumes, including those for the seaside set, but those panto costumes she thought might "come in".

'I know what it is, of course,' said Libby, handing Peter a mug of tea. 'It's light relief after Dominic's death.'

'Possibly.' Peter nodded and took a sheaf of printed paper from the printer. 'Let's hope this one doesn't end in

161

disaster.'

'Oh, Pete, it wasn't your fault!' Libby hugged his shoulders. 'Please don't think it.'

'You thought it was your fault,' said Peter, 'and considering the Alexandria's recent history and how you were involved –'

'Oh, stop it. You're too superstitious and pessimistic by half.'

He shrugged. 'Maybe.'

Libby regarded him suspiciously. 'Hmm. Anyway, nearly everyone's coming to a first meeting tonight, so we can get off to a flying start.'

'Did you say you'd managed to get an MD?'

'I didn't say because I haven't,' said Libby. 'Biggest stumbling block so far.'

'Fairly essential, I'd have thought,' said Peter. 'Where are the usuals?'

'Either away now or will be away, or have other commitments,' sighed Libby.

'I don't suppose you thought of Terry's sister?'

'Bloody hell, Pete, no I didn't!' Libby leapt to her feet and grabbed her basket, which had once more replaced the more conservative handbags her nearest and dearest tried to foist on her. Finding a notebook, she began to leaf through it.

'Don't you keep numbers in your phone?' asked Peter.

'Of course I do, but not random ones, and I prefer to have everything written down in case the phone gets lost or stolen.'

'That's sensible, except that your phone's so archaic no one would *want* to steal it.'

'Anyway,' said Libby, shutting the book and reaching for the offending phone, 'I haven't got her number and I can't remember her name. I shall have to rely on Terry

162

again.'

Terry Baker, married to Jane of the *Nethergate Mercury*, had introduced his talented sister to the Oast House Theatre company for the party held for Hetty's birthday a few years ago. She not only played the piano, she sang, and had an enviable repertoire of old songs, including many of the London songs that were Hetty's favourites. And sure enough, as reported by Terry an hour later, she would only be too delighted to help, as she had just finished filming a series for television and had six weeks off.

'It seems a bit mean to make her work in her time off,' said Libby. 'How old's her baby now?'

'Nearly five,' said Terry. 'And her old man's moved in with her now, so he can baby-sit.'

'Your father?' Libby frowned.

Terry laughed. 'Her – whatd'yercallit – partner. Boyfriend. Young Robbie's dad.'

'Oh, right,' said Libby, relieved. 'I'll let her have all the music when it's settled. Will she want any other musicians?'

'Don't ask me!' said Terry. 'I've given you her number, you talk to her about it.'

By the time Libby began her meeting at the theatre, she had spoken to Susannah Baker, who not only had much of the sheet music Libby needed, but her own costume, as she did regular seasons with a professional London company doing their Music Hall with guest artistes.

'You wouldn't believe how many really quite famous people enjoy dressing up and singing comic songs,' she told Libby. 'Did you ever do it when you were a pro?'

'Yes, quite often. I loved it,' said Libby. 'I was always sad that females couldn't become chairmen!'

'I know,' said Susannah. 'I suppose you wouldn't

possibly have room for me to do a number at the piano? There's a nice one about a piano teacher called "Twiddly Bits" which I've done before.'

'Oh, lovely!' said Libby. 'I'll put you somewhere in the second half, if that's OK, as it will come as a surprise for the audience. And will you need other musicians?'

'A drummer, perhaps,' said Susannah. 'I know someone who will do it, I think.'

Libby announced this to the company, and handed out the rough programme she and Peter had decided on.

'I know it's going to be a lot of work to be ready in 5 weeks, but you can rehearse solos on your own most of the time. The main rehearsals will be for chorus sets and set pieces,' she said. 'Susannah would prefer Wednesdays and Thursdays as rehearsal nights until the week before the show, when she's happy to come every night. Is that all right with everyone?'

When the company had signified their assent, someone at the back put up a hand.

'Do we know any more about Dominic?'

Libby sighed and glanced over at Ben and Peter.

'I'm afraid not,' she said, 'but you remember Martha, who got attacked at the same time? Well, you'll be pleased to know she's come round and I've been to see her. Sadly, she doesn't remember a thing about it, which isn't unusual, apparently.'

'Shall we buy a card and some flowers?' suggested someone.

'They won't allow flowers in the ICU,' said somebody else. 'But we could get a card. Are we meeting tomorrow, Libby? I'll get a card and we can all sign it.'

After this was agreed, Libby asked them all to sing through some of the better known seaside songs they had used in the Music Hall, then let them go.

'Can you remember the routines we used in the seaside set?' she asked Peter and Ben as they walked back down the drive.

'We will between us,' said Ben. 'Can we get one of our choreographers to come along?'

'Already done,' said Libby. 'All set for tomorrow.'

The following evening, the piano was moved on to the stage – 'We must ask about their piano,' said Libby – Susannah was introduced and the first rehearsal began. Libby was gratified to hear the songs being sung with gusto and nearly all the right words, and the choreographer was pleased that only a few people went right instead of left in most of the routines.

In the break, Libby went over to Susannah. 'Everything OK?'

'Fine. These are routines you've done before, are they? They only need brushing up.'

'Yes, I just pinched them wholesale from our Music Hall. I've added a few more seaside elements and we've got a finale of some more seaside songs where we can wear more elegant costumes. We'll need to rehearse that more thoroughly. What about your drummer?'

'Yes, David's fine. He doesn't need to be here until the end though, does he?'

'No, but it will be nice if he can put in a few of the comic boom-tishes, especially for the solos.'

'Oh, he'll do that, don't worry! He's a pro, too.'

'Oh, lord – he doesn't expect paying, does he?'

Susannah laughed. 'No, he's going to do it for the love of it, too. Anyway, he said he was going to be down in this part of the world for a while.'

'Oh, he isn't local?'

'No, he's a Londoner. I don't know what his connections are down here, but it's lucky for us.'

The huge card for Martha was produced and duly signed, and Libby decided to leave it at the theatre until she knew when she would be able to see Martha, rather than cart it to the pub for the traditional Wednesday drink.

'Funny not to have Patti and Anne here,' said Libby, sinking into a chair in the snug. 'We've got quite a lot to tell them.'

'You have,' said Peter, putting glasses on the table.

'You don't think they'll think we're callous putting something as light-hearted as this show on so soon after Dominic?'

'Of course not,' said Ben. 'I think Patti will be sensible and see it, as you've said, as a good way to get over it.'

'Good,' said Libby, 'but it still feels odd to have more or less given up on the case.'

'Ian hasn't, and there's nothing else you can do, is there?' said Peter. 'All you can do is wait for Andrew's researches to turn something else up, and Ian's waiting for the same thing.'

'I doubt if that's all he's doing,' said Libby. 'I expect there's all sorts of enquiries to be made. Into Estelle, for a start. There's something not right there.'

'Well, if that's the case, Ian or his minions will find it,' said Ben. 'And, you've said yourself, the police always get there in the end, with or without you.'

The following day, Libby rang the hospital to see if she could visit Martha, and, given permission, arrived at the ICU just after lunch. Martha, now off nearly all her machines and drips, had been moved to a side room. She was sitting up, and smiled wanly as Libby came in.

'I'm almost ready for a main ward, but the police want to keep me here,' she said. 'It's very lonely.'

'Well, here's something to read,' said Libby, producing the outsize card. 'All the cast signed it. And I brought you a couple of books, although I don't really know your taste, but Sister Catherine approved these.'

After Martha had read all the signatures on the card and exclaimed delightedly over the books, Libby asked how she was feeling.

'Oh, much better. I still can't remember anything, though. Mr Connell came to see me yesterday, and although he said he just wanted to see how I was, I know he was hoping I'd begun to remember.'

'Don't worry,' said Libby. 'I'm sure he'll find out who did this. He's very tenacious.'

'Don't you and your friend sometimes – well, investigate?'

Libby laughed. 'Sometimes. That's what led to this whole debacle. My friend Patti asking me to look into the provenance of the reliquary on behalf of Sister Catherine. And look where that's landed us.'

'You don't blame yourself, surely?' Martha looked shocked.

'It's hard not to,' said Libby. 'If I hadn't told my friend Peter about it, he wouldn't have wanted to write the play ...See? It's dominoes.'

Martha looked distressed. 'Yes, I see, but that probably means I was the reason Dominic was killed.'

Chapter Twenty-one

'What?' Libby gasped.

Martha turned brimming eyes towards her. 'If I hadn't gone down to check on St Eldreda that one last time – the murderer must have been disturbed and killed Dominic.'

'How on earth do you make that out?' asked Libby, relieved. 'Dominic was dead hours before you were attacked.'

'He was?' Now Martha looked bewildered. 'Not at the same time?'

'No, they've proved that.'

'Oh.' Martha looked down at her hands. 'Oh. I see.'

'So you haven't any reason to feel guilty.'

Martha looked up, frowning. 'But I don't understand. Was Dominic trying to steal the relic? If so, whoever killed him wanted to save it.'

'Maybe, but then he attacked you.'

'I don't understand that, either. It made sense when I thought I'd interrupted a murder, but if Dominic was killed earlier, why was the murderer still around?'

'That's what no one seems to be able to work out.' Libby patted Martha's hand. 'So don't you worry about it, there are enough policemen doing that.'

She went on to tell Martha about the new Oast House Theatre project and the Alexandria.

'Perhaps I'll be out in time to see it?' said Martha wistfully. 'I'd like that.'

'Patti will bring you, I'm sure,' said Libby. 'And now, I

must go. We've got another rehearsal tonight, and I need to feed Ben before we go.'

Martha gave a tremulous smile. 'I quite miss having a man to feed,' she said.

'You often miss things that in real life became quite tedious,' said Libby. 'And to be fair, he feeds me almost as much as I feed him.'

Martha had put her finger on the inconsistencies in the case, mused Libby as she drove home. Despite all the investigations into the provenance of the reliquary and Bernard Evans's murder, the most urgent problem was Dominic's murder and the attack on Martha which, frankly, made no sense.

Martha having not been taken to the nearest hospital due to the severity of her injuries, the drive home was long enough for Libby to meditate on the case from start to finish and come to no conclusions at all. It was with relief, then, that she drove into Steeple Martin and saw the familiar white cone of the Oast House Theatre above the rooftops of the high street and felt able to concentrate on the forthcoming rehearsal.

Several of the solo performers had brought their music for Susannah. Fran had arrived, as she was in one of the set pieces with Libby as part of the congregation in the wonderfully Victorian "Those Bells Shall not Ring Out!" They were also both in "If I Were not Upon the Stage", another familiar music hall piece, where Libby had changed the "jobs" from the traditional chimney sweep and policeman to those more suitable for a seaside entertainment.

'I went to see Martha today,' she told Fran as they sat in the auditorium waiting for their turn to go on stage. 'She's a lot better. But puzzled. She didn't know Dominic had died so much earlier than her attack.'

'I suppose Ian is trying not to worry her.'

'Yes. He went to see her yesterday and she said it was just to see how she was, but he obviously wants her to remember something.'

'And she can't?'

Libby shook her head. 'She seems terribly fragile. I do hope this doesn't leave her with some kind of permanent effect.'

'Don't start feeling guilty again,' said Fran, 'and listen. I had a thought. We still don't know about that phone call saying the beneficiary was coming on the last night, do we?'

Libby sat up straight. 'Gosh! No, we don't. I did tell Ian – I wonder if he's got any further with it?'

'And he told you not to try and get in touch with her, didn't he? What was her name?'

'Chappell. Mrs Chappell. And, remember, we heard that she was going to come to a performance, but in the end she never came. Or, if she did, she didn't let us know. If that call on the last night *was* bogus, whoever tried it on was taking a risk unless he or she *knew* Mrs Chappell hadn't been.'

'I can't believe it was a serious try-on,' said Fran. 'I think it was probably more to test the security arrangements.'

'Test the –?'

'See if there were arrangements. To see, maybe, how easy it was going to be to get in.'

Libby wrinkled her brow. 'But Dominic knew how to get in – he was already in. If, that is, he really was intending to steal the bloody thing.'

'But there was someone else there, wasn't there?' said Fran. 'And I can't get anything on him. I've tried and tried, but all I get is that bright light associated with Martha,

170

which is obviously her being hit on the head.'

'Well, to be fair, you don't usually get a clear picture of the murderer, do you?' said Libby. 'Eh up – we're on.'

'I wish we could ask Ian,' sighed Fran, as they made their way down the aisle and on to the stage.

'So do I,' said Libby. 'I feel locked out somehow, even though we started the case off.'

'Don't start that again,' muttered Fran, taking her place on stage. 'Come and be a member of the congregation and concentrate on something else.'

Libby found a missed call on her mobile at the end of rehearsal.

'It's from Ian,' she told Fran. 'He's got something to tell us.'

'Text back that you're at rehearsal. He might decide to come down to the pub.'

Libby did so. 'I didn't know we were going to the pub tonight,' she said, putting the phone away.

'We are now,' said Fran with a grin. 'Go on, go and tell Ben and Peter.'

Fran's hunch was right, and Ian was waiting for them in the pub, a cup of coffee before him.

'We are honoured,' said Libby, sitting down next to him. 'You've got something to tell us?'

Ian frowned. 'Yes, but not brilliant news, I'm afraid.'

'Well, what is it?' asked Fran. 'Something about the reliquary stand?'

Ian and Libby both turned surprised glances on her.

'It's that bright light,' she muttered. 'Sorry.'

'No, you're absolutely right,' said Ian. 'It's ironic, really.'

'What's ironic?' asked Peter, as he and Ben deposited drinks on the table.

Ian gave a wry smile. 'What hit Martha. It was,

171

effectively, the reliquary. The stand,' said Ian. 'It's confirmed that she was pushed and hit her head on it.'

'Hasn't it taken rather a long time to find that out?' said Ben.

'No, we knew, you remember, but Forensics were puzzled. They did more tests.'

'What a shame she can't remember what happened,' said Libby. 'I bet she'll be devastated that it was her precious St Eldreda who bashed her.'

'Strictly, it wasn't,' said Peter.

'She'll see it like that,' said Fran.

'She was so protective of the reliquary,' said Libby. 'I bet that's why she was attacked.'

'Has she said anything to you?' asked Ian. 'I know you went to see her again today.'

'You do?' Libby raised her eyebrows.

'Of course. She's being watched. You know that.'

'Hmm. Well, she said she remembers going down to see St Eldreda – her words – for the last time and that's all. She assumed she'd interrupted Dominic's murder.'

'And you told her otherwise,' said Ian with a resigned expression.

'Wasn't I supposed to?'

'The less we lead her, the more her memories will be genuine. Oh, well, it can't be helped. There is one other thing you need to know.'

'What?'

'Her husband has apparently turned up.'

'Her husband?' said Libby and Fran together.

'Mr Fletcher, yes. I've no idea how he knew what had happened, but he turned up at the hospital. He was refused entry, of course.'

'Does Martha know?'

'No, and she's not to.'

'If her real name was in the papers that's how he'd know,' said Fran. 'And we know how quickly information about Dominic got out there. Look at how fast Estelle was on the scene.'

'Anyway, why do we need to know?' asked Libby. 'If Martha's not to know it would have been better not to tell us, seeing how unreliable I am.' She sniffed and everyone laughed.

'Because there's every chance he'll try and see other people. There was a phone call to the Abbey which we assume to have been him.'

'Phone calls!' said Libby, holding up a finger. 'That's what we were going to ask you. What happened about that phone call I told you about saying the beneficiary was coming on the last night?'

'We haven't traced that call,' said Ian, 'but Mrs Chappell never did come, although she intended to. Her daughter-in-law went into labour on your first night and she rushed off to Aberdeen.'

'It was a fairly ridiculous try-on if it was one,' said Ben. 'Whoever it was must have known it would never been handed over just like that.'

'A warning, then?' suggested Peter. 'Who took the phone call?'

'I don't know, but it was Martha who told me. She was our liaison with the Abbey. I think she said it was Sister Catherine.'

'I daren't ask her,' said Ian. 'The doctors are on my back every time I go near her.'

'When will she come out?' asked Fran.

'Not until she no longer needs specialist nursing,' said Ian. 'Once she's off all drips and monitoring equipment she'll go back to the Abbey. They're used to looking after the sick.'

173

'They won't let anyone in there, either, will they?' said Fran.

'Do you think someone might try?' Ian narrowed his eyes at her.

'Yes.' Fran lowered her own eyes and picked up her drink.

'Someone's worried that she'll remember,' said Libby. 'That means someone who's been around the whole time.'

'Not necessarily,' said Ian. 'Don't forget that whoever killed Dominic could have been a complete outsider.'

'A partner in crime? Otherwise, who would know? I can't see Dominic telling anyone else, can you?' said Peter.

'Estelle, then,' suggested Libby. 'We don't know that they were completely estranged, do we?'

'It certainly looked like it,' said Ian. 'There was no evidence of any contact between them at his place, except some fairly heavy solicitors' letters. We've gone over the whole place again, especially since the break-in.'

'Break-in?' said four voices.

'Attempted break-in, I should say.' Ian grinned round at them all. 'Sorry we didn't keep you informed.'

'Oh, stop it.' Libby slapped his arm. 'Come on, when was it?'

'Thursday night. There were padlocks on all the doors and the windows had been sealed, so whoever it was only made a very half-hearted attempt. But it was enough to make us think there was something in there that someone wanted to get at.'

'And that presumably points at Estelle,' said Libby.

'Or the partner in crime suggested by Peter,' said Ian.

'Dominic was in debt, you said, didn't you?' said Ben. 'So there's nothing in his place worth stealing.'

'It's incriminating evidence they're after,' said Libby.

'But what incriminating evidence?' said Fran. 'A letter

174

from someone? Email accounts? What?'

'We've looked at all those,' said Ian. 'Most of the contacts either on his computer or in his address book are connected with television. It's as if he had no family at all.'

'Isn't Estelle's name there?' said Peter.

'No. Which makes us think he had cut everybody from his former life out – except his show business contacts.'

'But you've got his birth certificate? You know where he came from?' said Libby.

'Yes, Libby, don't worry. And his marriage to Estelle. That's her real name, by the way.'

'Why does all that matter, anyway?' asked Ben. 'It's poor old Bernard Evans whose background we wanted to trace.'

'And we are,' said Ian. 'It's all costing a fortune. Superintendent Bertram's very pleased she handed over to our division.'

'Can we do anything?' asked Libby. 'That won't interfere, of course.'

'Of course,' said Ian. 'Never let it be said!'

'I think you've got enough to do organising the End Of The Pier Show,' said Peter. 'I'm sure Ian will tell you if there's anything you need to know.'

'Like tonight,' said Libby. 'You think Martha's husband might try and get to her through us?'

'It's possible, although I have no idea why. Just be on your guard. One thing – from the phone call received at the Abbey and his approach at the hospital, it looks as if he doesn't know her name is now Martha. He might not even know she was an oblate.'

'Then why did he call the Abbey?' asked Peter.

'It mentions the Abbey in the media. Not that there's been much, but as you found out, social media is the very devil. No one can control it.'

175

'OK, we'll be vigilant,' said Libby. 'Now – who wants another drink?'

For Libby, Friday and Saturday were taken up with organising the new show. She visited the Alexandria and admired its restored Edwardian glory, and received permission to look through the boxes and files left by the original owner, Dorinda Alexander. There were a few old costumes, too, all housed at the Nethergate Museum, and although Libby had seen them all in far less formal surroundings a few years ago, she was delighted to be able to go through them all, and was even allowed to photocopy some of the programmes and other documents.

'To think,' she said ruefully to the librarian, who was helping her with the photocopier, 'I could have taken all this lot home with me at one time, as a gift.'

'Really?' The librarian looked interested, but Libby decided it probably wasn't politic to go into the story and just smiled again, benignly.

'We're doing an old style End of The Pier Show at the Alexandria at the end of August,' she said. 'I do hope you'll come and see it.'

The Alexandria management had promised posters by the beginning of the following week, so Libby arranged to collect some as soon as she received the phone call. Then, leaving the car where it was, in a reserved spot in the Alexandria car park, she climbed up to Cliff Terrace and Peel House.

Jane answered the door holding Imogen's hand.

'Hello! This is a nice surprise,' she said. 'Do you want something, or is this a social visit?'

'Oh, dear! Do I only see you when I want something?'

Jane laughed, leading the way into the sitting room. 'Of course not, but I'm happy to be a source of information for Sarjeant Investigations Limited.'

'Well, not this time,' said Libby. 'I was at the Alexandria, so I thought I'd see if you were in.'

'What were you there for?' asked Jane. 'Oh – of course – the show Susannah's playing for. Looking forward to that.'

'Not only playing, she's doing a number on her own, too.'

'Oh, good. She's terrific. Well, you know that, don't you? Actually,' Jane sat down and leant forward. 'I think I shall do a feature about it. After all, Susannah's quite well known – been on TV and that sort of thing – and you and Fran are, too.'

'Notorious,' said Libby.

'Well, people know you around here, and the Oast's got a wonderful reputation. It would make a lovely piece, don't you think?'

'It would and it would be terrific publicity, thanks, Jane.'

'Come on then, let's go and make some tea. Imogen – juice?'

Imogen took Libby's hand. 'Doose,' she agreed.

Chapter Twenty-two

After a lazy Sunday, Libby attacked her rather neglected housework on Monday morning, made a sandwich and took it to the theatre to begin sorting through the costumes Hetty had selected. Halfway through the afternoon, she sat back on her heels and puffed out a long breath. Dust swirled in the working lights above the stage like so much fairy dust and got up her nose.

Pushing back a lock of hair, she fished in her pocket for her mobile and, after a moment's thought, found Andrew's number.

'Libby,' he answered in a whisper, 'I'm in the library. I'll call you back.'

Libby got to her feet and picked up some of the costumes to carry them through to the rail in the dressing room. Although they had all been cleaned before being put away, some smelt musty, and she put these aside to give them a good airing. She was just going back for a second load when the phone rang.

'Sorry about that Libby, I've had to come up to the British Library.'

'What for?' asked Libby, surprised.

'I do have other projects,' said Andrew, sounding faintly put out. 'Not just yours.'

'Oh, sorry,' said Libby, contrite. 'I thought …'

'I know, I know,' said Andrew. 'Unfortunately, I've not been able to spend all my time on the Tollybar/Beaumont project, but I'm trying to find out if they had children.'

'Who did?'

'May and Albert Glover, remember? It's not easy tracing downwards, much easier going upwards. Unfortunately the names are all quite common. You wouldn't believe how many May and Albert Glovers there were back in the early twenties. And of course, I can't get at the census records for 1921 yet.'

'Oh? Why not?'

'They haven't yet been opened – the hundred-year rule, you know.'

'Oh, I see,' said Libby, who didn't.

'However, I think I've found a connection between Bernard Evans and the person who left him the reliquary.'

'You have? What was his name again?'

'Ronald Barnes. He never married, but he had siblings. Bernard is the great-great-great nephew. Apparently, there is a letter which went to Bernard with the reliquary which Ian is trying to have unearthed from the police files. It was obviously never followed up at the time.'

'So what we have to do now is prove a link between Bad Jack Jarvis and Ronald Barnes?'

'But why, Libby? Why is that important?'

'Because there's a link back to the Beaumonts. All this business of them wanting the reliquary back – I'm sure it's a motive.'

'I must say I don't see Alastair Beaumont as a murderer,' said Andrew dubiously.

'Neither do I. It's got to be one of those domino lines.'

'Domino –?'

'You know – what you said the other day. One person has two children, they each have two, then they have two each –'

'Yes, yes, I see. You could be right, but I'm damned if I see what good it's going to do.'

'I'm not sure either,' said Libby, frowning, 'but Ian wanted you to carry on, didn't he? So there has to be a reason. And only a Beaumont or a Tollybar would know about the reliquary.'

'So are you suggesting that whoever killed Bernard Evans and Dominic Butcher was a Beaumont or a Tollybar?'

'Not the same one,' said Libby, 'but yes.'

'And that's the purpose of all this delving into family history.'

'Well, of course it is. We have to find out who knew enough about the reliquary to want to steal it. And we now know that Ronald Barnes did, and so did Albert Glover. Now, if we can prove that they are related –'

'They would both be putative descendants of Bad Jack Jarvis. Yes, I get it.'

'But that doesn't get us anywhere with the current generation,' said Libby gloomily. 'Did Bernard Evans have any children?'

'I don't know,' said Andrew. 'Ian must have that in the old case files.' He sighed. 'When I've finished what I'm doing now I'll get back on to Albert and May's children. If any.'

Libby switched off the phone and stood staring at the still swirling dust motes. Things were now so complicated in her head that she'd begun to lose sight of the starting point of the case.

'Which was,' she said out loud, her voice echoing in the empty auditorium, 'finding out where the reliquary had come from. Which we now know.'

'Only we don't.' Peter's voice came back at her making her jump. She put up a hand to shield her eyes.

'Where are you?'

'Here.' He strolled through the auditorium doors and

180

down towards the stage. 'You were talking to yourself, were you?'

'I'd just been talking to Andrew.' Libby gathered up another armful of clothes. 'You can help me take these to the dressing room, if you like.'

Peter picked up the rest. 'As I was saying – you don't know where the reliquary came from.'

'Yes, we do, from Mr Marshall.'

'The whole point, Libby, is where did he get it from?'

'Oh, bugger, of course. Presumably the killer of Bernard. It's annoying, isn't it? It just pops up here and there, waves at us and disappears again.'

'So Andrew's trying to do what?'

'That's what he was asking. I think we've all rather lost the plot. Basically find out who might have known about the bloody thing from family connections.' Libby hooked the last hanger on to the rail.'

'It could be nothing to do with that, you know.'

'I know. It could just be a random act. Someone finding out how valuable it is and knocking Dominic on the head. But you see, that's the puzzle. Dominic found out about it from us and from the play. If he'd stolen it, it would have been a random act to solve his debt problems. But someone killed him and *didn't* take the reliquary.'

'But meant to and Martha stopped them. That could still be random.' Peter led the way to the workshop, where he filled and switched on the kettle. 'Come on, I want to find that seaside backcloth we had for the Music Hall.'

'Someone who'd heard about it? Someone like Estelle, perhaps?' said Libby, pulling out a selection of rolled canvasses.

'Eh?' Peter was getting out rather stained mugs. 'Oh, you're back on that are you? Yes, well, Estelle could have heard about it, or anybody connected with the play. And

181

then, it *was* on the TV and in the paper. It could have been anybody. I think your delving into family history might be a red herring, Lib.'

'There's still the problem of how he got in, and the time difference between Dominic's death and Martha's attack.'

'We-ell,' said Peter, thoughtfully stirring the mugs, 'how about the murderer hearing the guard coming on his rounds just after he's killed Dominic and leaving it a good long time before he goes back and is then disturbed by the guard again? Are they sure Martha was attacked only just before the guard found her?'

'Fairly sure, and she herself says she got up and went to check on the thing at about a quarter to six before Matins. That's two hours at least between the attacks.'

'I give up, then. But I still say it could be random. Come on, concentrate on finding this scenery. We've got to check measurements, and send somebody over to have a look at their lighting rig, don't forget.'

Libby valiantly put the whole Monastery case to the back of her mind over the next two days and, as Peter had suggested, concentrated on the new show. On Tuesday evening the soloists, perforce unaccompanied, gathered at the theatre to try out their pieces in front of each other, to see if they remembered them well enough. On Wednesday morning Patti telephoned to say she and Anne were back in the county and would see them at the pub that evening if they were free.

'Yes, but we're rehearsing again,' said Libby. 'Mad, isn't it?'

'We're going to The Pink Geranium for dinner as usual, so we'll see you afterwards. I expect you've got lots to tell us, haven't you?'

'Some,' said Libby cautiously. 'Bet you've got more!'

'Oh, we were very quiet,' said Patti, 'but it was

182

glorious.'

Libby was early at the theatre, switching the coffee machine on in the bar and arranging chairs on the stage to represent the minimal set for the first ensemble piece. Susannah arrived and was immediately surrounded by members of the cast to talk about their individual songs, but eventually, Peter, who was overseeing rehearsals as he wasn't taking part, was able to instil some sort of order and they began the first seaside set.

Susannah made them go through it twice, and Libby reminded them of some of the moves they had used in the Music Hall. It was at this point that she became aware of a man sitting alongside Susannah and following the music. When she decreed a coffee break, Libby went over to them.

'Libby, this is David,' she said. 'Your new drummer.'

David gave her a delightful smile and held out his hand.

'I'm pleased to meet you,' he said.

'Me too,' said Libby with a grin. 'So pleased Susannah persuaded you to join us. I hope it won't be too much of an imposition.'

'Not at all. I expect she told you I'm down here on a bit of a break anyway, and I would have got bored with nothing to do.'

'But that's what you're supposed to do on a break,' said Libby. 'Are you staying in Nethergate?'

'Just outside. I was lucky to get a holiday let at short notice.'

'It's the recession,' said Libby. 'A lot were left empty this year. Can I get you a coffee?'

'We'll get our own, Libby,' said Susannah. 'Come on, David.'

'Drummer?' asked Fran, as Libby joined her.

'Yes. He seems nice. How old would you say he is?'

'Too young for you, Libby. Early forties?'

'I'd say so. He's staying just outside Nethergate.'

'I wonder why,' said Fran, her eyes resting thoughtfully on the back of David's glossy brown head.

'Why?' Libby's eyebrows went up. 'He needed a break, he said.'

'And he's working for us?'

'He said he was bored.'

'Hmm,' said Fran.

'Why are you being so suspicious?' said Libby testily. 'Don't look a gift horse in the mouth.'

'I hope he doesn't come to the pub with us afterwards.'

'He won't if no one asks him,' said Libby. 'Come on, let's get some coffee now the queue's died down.'

The rest of the rehearsal went as well as could be expected, and, to Fran's relief, David and Susannah left together.

'David's giving me a lift,' she said, 'and I want to get back as early as possible.'

'Of course,' said Fran, as she watched them go, 'she's got a baby, hasn't she?'

'Not a baby any more, Uncle Terry tells me. Five, or nearly. And that baby's father and she are now living together, so all happy families.'

'I guessed she and David weren't a couple.'

'Really? How?' Libby led the way out of the theatre.

'They just didn't seem like it. I suppose if they're both professionals they'll have worked together.'

'That's how Susannah knew about him being down here and why she asked him.'

'Oh, she asked him, did she? Not the other way round?'

'What are you on about?' said an exasperated Libby.

184

'You've taken a proper dislike to him, haven't you?'

But Fran would only shake her head.

Patti and Anne were waiting for them in the pub, and, after hugs of greeting, Patti went to fetch drinks at the bar, where Ben interrupted her and took over.

'Tell us all about it, then,' said Libby. 'And have you got pictures?'

'Loads of pictures, but they're all still in the camera. I'll put them on the computer and then you can see them. Gorgeous place.'

'And hugely me-friendly,' said Anne, indicating her wheelchair. 'And we actually managed to paint some pictures.'

The conversation was still on the painting holiday when Peter looked up.

'Hello, Ian. Is this a social call?'

'More or less.' Ian smiled a tired smile. 'I'd like a coffee and a chat. Hello, everyone.'

Ben got up and went to fetch a coffee.

'You look tired,' said Libby. 'Has it been a long day?'

'It has. It started with Martha being let out of hospital.'

'Really? Is she back at the Abbey?'

'Not so loud,' said Ian. 'You never know who's listening.'

'There's only people from the theatre within earshot, Ian, and they know all about Martha anyway,' said Fran.

'Well, let's keep it that way,' said Ian. 'No newcomers for your show?'

'Susannah – but she's Terry Baker's sister, you remember? So as she's Jane from the *Mercury*'s sister-in-law she'd know all about it, too. I expect.'

'And then, of course,' said Fran, fixing her eyes on Ian,

'there's our new drummer. David.'

'I knew it.' Ian shook his head. 'And you've guessed who he is, haven't you Fran?'

'What?' said a bewildered Libby. 'Who?'

'David Fletcher,' said Fran. 'Martha's husband.'

Chapter Twenty-three

'How did you know that?' demanded Libby.

'I don't know,' said Fran helplessly. 'I just knew there was something wrong about him. Then as soon as Ian mentioned Martha it was there, as a fact.'

'She *was* suspicious,' Libby confirmed, 'and I couldn't understand it. Susannah brought him along because she's worked with him before. He seemed nice.'

'He's a professional musician and he's suddenly accepted a free gig in a small, little-known theatre for – what is it? A week? With rehearsals?' Ian looked sceptical.

'Susannah said he was down here anyway, and he said he'd needed a break.' Libby nodded gloomily. 'I see. But how was I to know?'

'You weren't. But he obviously does,' said Ian. 'As far as we know, he still doesn't know Martha lives permanently in the Abbey or that she's an oblate and changed her name. The only contact Mrs Fletcher says they've had over the past couple of years is through her solicitors, whom she strictly forbade to give her address.'

'Well, how did he know about her being involved here?' asked Patti. 'Sorry to interrupt.'

Ian smiled at her. 'You aren't, Miss Pearson.'

'Please call me Patti. Pearson makes me uncomfortable.'

'Patti, then. The reason he knew was the media using her real name, which, of course was in the police statements. Not at first, because we didn't release it.'

'But what does he want?' asked Libby. 'Is he a suspect?'

'I doubt it,' said Ben, 'or he wouldn't have turned up looking for her.'

'Do you think he thinks she's going to die and he'll inherit something?'

'Could be, Libby, but we can't be sure. At the moment we want to keep him away, so please everyone, don't say anything to him.' Ian sipped at his coffee. 'This is hot.'

'We won't,' said Patti. 'We're not likely to meet him.'

'And none of us will,' promised Libby. 'We can avoid him most of the time.'

'Just watch for him trying to start up conversations with the company,' said Ian, 'and don't tell any of them that Martha's out.'

'We can warn them all not to say anything to anyone,' said Peter. 'They'll understand if we say the police investigation could be compromised.'

'Fine,' said Ian. 'And now tell me what else has been going on.'

Libby told him what Andrew had said that afternoon, and Peter repeated his random theory. Ian smiled wearily again.

'I wish it was, Peter, but someone had to know about the reliquary and how to get in to the Monastery. I know it was on the TV news and in the local press, but there was no clue given as to the value of the item. Which means we have to find out who knew. We've ruled all of you lot out, you'll be pleased to know.'

Libby looked affronted and the others laughed.

'You were rather too obvious, you know,' said Ian.

'I suppose we were,' said Libby. 'Fancy being a suspect!'

'I don't, thanks,' said Fran. 'And now, I really must get

going. Oh, Ian. What about Jane and Terry Baker? Shall we tell them?'

'You'd better, I think, but tell him not to tell his sister. She'd be bound to react to Fletcher differently if she knew.'

'Well, there's a turn-up for the books,' said Libby, as she and Ben walked home. 'I wonder why he's here? Martha didn't sound as though there was any love lost between them, although of course she didn't tell me anything about him'

'Perhaps it was the life-style?' suggested Ben. 'You know, professional musician, always travelling, suspect fidelity, perhaps?'

'Maybe, and if she was already a particularly religious sort that wouldn't go down well. But why did she marry him in the first place?'

'It's a puzzle,' said Ben. 'And I expect Ian will get to the bottom of it. Meanwhile, we have to keep quiet about the whole thing.'

'I wonder if he'll come with Susannah tomorrow,' said Libby. 'I think, in case, we'd better tell Susannah she isn't needed until eight thirty, then we'll have a chance to tell everyone to keep mum.'

Libby spent Thursday envisaging ever more unlikely scenarios concerning David Fletcher and Martha, whom she still couldn't think of as Cornelia, so that by the time the company were assembled at the theatre in the evening she had built him into a comic-book villain in her head.

'This is just a piece of advice I've been asked to pass on by the police investigating Dominic's murder,' Peter began, as they all settled into seats in the auditorium. 'No one is to mention anything about the attack on Martha, or even mention her name to anybody outside the company, and that, unfortunately, includes our new MD, Susannah, and her drummer, David. This is because the police are keeping details of her attack under wraps for the usual reasons.'

'So if anyone knows about the facts, it means they probably did it?' suggested someone at the back. 'That's what they do on TV.'

'Something like that, I guess,' said Peter. 'You'll be pleased to know that none of us are suspects –' general laughter '– but we must all take this very seriously. Speak to no one about it, and particularly if someone starts asking questions.'

'Sometimes it could just be morbid curiosity,' said Libby, 'like slowing down at the scene of an accident, but you never know.'

'It's like the war, isn't it?' said someone else. 'Be like Dad – keep Mum!'

'Walls have ears,' said Ben. 'And now, let's get on with blocking the Bells number.'

When Susannah and David arrived, Libby couldn't help staring at David, and noticed that several members of the company were doing the same. She caught as many eyes as she could and scowled mightily at them.

The Bells scene was finally set quite twenty minutes after Susannah had arrived, when Libby asked her to play it for them and see if the movements all worked to music.

'I see why you asked us to come late,' she said to Libby, as they made their way to the foyer for coffee in the break. 'All that setting – don't you get bored?'

'Yes, but it must be the same for you,' said Libby. 'All that rehearsing and practising.'

'But I'm not normally an accompanist, so I don't have to fit in with anyone else unless it's a band or an orchestra. And to be fair, the bands I play with are so well rehearsed and have worked together so often, they hardly need to rehearse. In fact, I frequently have the music emailed to me, possibly with a recording, and learn it before I get to the gig. Then we go through it at the sound check.'

'Is that all?' said Libby, awed.

Susannah laughed. 'You'll find a lot of vocalists do it that way, too. Especially those that work in a specific genre.'

'Well, I never knew,' said Libby. 'I was in provincial rep when there was such a thing, so I never came across it.'

'David's the same,' said Susannah, putting her money into the coffee machine. 'I know people don't think drummers need to read music, but they do. And David's a classical percussionist, among other things.'

'Blimey.' Libby allowed her gaze to travel to David who was deep in conversation with Peter. Safe there, she thought. 'So what's he down here doing a free gig for us for?'

'I'm not actually sure,' said Susannah. 'I told you, I don't know what his connection to the area is, but there obviously is one or he wouldn't be here.'

'He might have just fancied Nethergate for a holiday,' said Libby. 'Some people do.'

'I don't think so.' Susannah frowned. 'He told me he had to be in the area for some time. What he's doing about work I've no idea.'

'How did you know he was here?'

'Oh, he rang me. Told me what I've just told you, and said he didn't know the area and was there anything I could tell him about it. Which struck me as a bit odd, but then I mentioned that I was doing your show and he immediately said did I want a drummer.'

'Didn't you think that was odd, too?'

'A bit. But then, musicians *are* odd. They tend not to live conventional lives, or even if they do, they don't have

191

conventional hours.'

'Must be difficult with a child, then.'

'It is, but now Emlyn's moved back in with me things are a lot easier.'

So, thought Libby, as she strolled towards David and Peter, he did invite himself in. Very suspicious.

Peter barely acknowledged her presence and carried on speaking:

'... and with the advent of the internet and social media dissipating news faster than we can get it out there, there are worries that we're going to become completely redundant.'

David was looking a little glazed.

'Can I get you off your hobby horse, Pete, so we can start again?' Libby smiled at David and put her arm through Peter's, guiding him away.

'Well done,' she whispered. 'Was he asking?'

'He was trying,' muttered Peter. 'Tell you later.'

No one wanted to go to the pub that evening, so Peter, Ben and Libby settled for a drink in the foyer bar. Libby told them what Susannah had told her.

'Well, he was definitely trying to get something out of me,' said Peter. 'Although if we hadn't been warned about it I probably wouldn't have noticed.'

'What did he say?' asked Ben.

'Started off by saying weren't we the company who'd performed in the old Monastery when that person got murdered. Now, that's just the kind of thing all sorts of people have said over the last few weeks, and quite normal, but, as I said, once you've been warned ...'

'So what did you say?' said Libby.

'Just yes, it was awful, and I hoped the police would catch the killer.'

'What then?'

'He said wasn't someone else attacked and I said I didn't know much about it, we weren't actually there and our production had finished. I think that surprised him.'

'You made it sound as though we'd gone for good?' said Ben. 'Excellent.'

'If he took it that way, I can't help it!' said Peter, with a grin.

'So did he ask anything else?' said Libby.

'No, he just said wasn't it awful something like that should happen in a Monastery of all places, and I managed to turn the conversation into –'

'A rant on the current state of the publishing industry,' Libby finished for him. 'It was brilliant.'

'Did you think to call Jane and Terry and warn them?' asked Ben.

'Bugger, no I didn't, said Libby. 'I'll pop down there tomorrow. Easier than over the phone.'

'That's just an excuse to go and have an ice cream on the Harbour wall with Fran,' said Peter.

Libby grinned. 'Might even see if the *Sparkler* or the *Dolphin* are going out and have a trip round the bay.'

'All right for some,' said Peter with a theatrical sigh.

'You could come too, if you wanted. You choose your own hours.'

'Not at the moment. There are too many things going on in the world,' said Peter. 'I need to be in close touch.'

'They're not going to start sending you off to war zones again, are they?' asked Ben, looking worried. 'I thought you'd given all that up.'

'I have. But there are other sorts of crises, as you well know. And the public can't always rely on the social networking sites.'

'I still rely on the BBC,' said Libby, 'although even they get things wrong sometimes.'

Libby drove down to Nethergate the following morning and parked as near as she could to Peel House. After knocking on the front door for a few moments, she heard the door to the basement flat open.

'Is that you, Mrs Sarjeant?'

Jane's mother was peering up at her, holding Imogen by the hand.

'Hello, Mrs Maurice. Yes, it's me. Is Jane at work?'

'Yes, she had to go in this morning. She'll be back just after one.'

'Fine, I'll pop back. Will you tell her?'

Mrs Maurice said she would, and Libby crossed the road to look down on Victoria Place and its beautifully planted, regimented flower beds. She decided it would be rather nice to sit there on one of the benches and gaze at the sea.

She wandered down, found an empty bench and sat down, breathing in an invigorating dose of ozone.

'Hello,' said a voice. 'Fancy finding you here.'

And David Fletcher sat down beside her.

Chapter Twenty-four

'You startled me!' Libby fought down an irrational panic. She was sitting in a public place, for goodness' sake. And David Fletcher was hardly dangerous.

'Sorry, I didn't mean to.'

'No, of course not.' Libby tried a smile. 'I just didn't expect to see you.'

'Oh, I come in to Nethergate every day to shop or eat. The cottage I'm renting is a little way out of town so there's nothing nearer.'

'Was there nothing available in town?' asked Libby.

'Oh, yes, but not as peaceful.'

'So you sacrificed amenities for peace?'

'You could put it like that. So what are you doing here?'

'Visiting friends,' said Libby.

'Oh?'

'Yes,' said Libby, smiling determinedly. 'And I must go now, or I'll be late.'

'Oh, I was hoping I might persuade you to have lunch with me.'

'Sorry,' said Libby, desperately hoping he would not decide to walk with her. However, the hope was doomed. He stood up with her and walked beside her to the end of Victoria Place.

'I was talking to Peter about your murder last night,' he said.

Libby's heart sank. 'My murder?'

'The chap who was murdered in your last production.'

'Oh, he wasn't,' said Libby, remembering what Peter had said the night before. 'If you mean the person who was killed in the Monastery, that was after our play. We'd gone by then, thank goodness.'

'Oh.' David looked disappointed.

'Why are you interested?' Libby turned to look directly at him. 'We know very little about it, and even less about the man who was murdered.'

'I thought he was a member of your company.'

'Only for that production. None of us knew him. Why do you want to know?' Libby took a deep breath. 'Did you know him?'

David now looked horrified. 'No – no, of course not! I was just interested.'

'Well, I must say we aren't,' Libby lied. 'It's quite different when you find yourself questioned in a murder case, even when you had nothing to do with it.'

'No, of course, I understand. I'm sorry. I was being the worst sort of ghoul, wasn't I?' He smiled.

'I understand, too,' said Libby. 'People do find this sort of thing interesting, but it's quite different when you're mixed up in it, as I said.'

'Yes, you've been involved with several murder cases, haven't you?'

Oh, bugger, thought Libby. Aloud, she said 'Yes, a few, quite by accident. And now you must excuse me – I'm late already.'

And, sure enough, she could see Jane approaching Cliff Terrace out of the corner of her eye, although she didn't want David to see exactly who she was meeting.

'Right. I'll see you next week, then.' David held out a hand. Libby took it.

'See you then,' she said and turned away to follow Jane, hoping David wouldn't watch her. However, by the time she reached the top of the steps to Jane's mother's flat and could legitimately turn round, he'd gone, so letting out the breath she didn't know she'd been holding, she went down the steps and knocked on the door.

Ten minutes later she was sitting in Jane's kitchen while Jane made large ham sandwiches.

'Imogen's had her lunch with Mum,' she said, handing over a plate, 'but she likes to sit with me while I eat mine.' She sat down at the table. 'What's this all about, then?'

Libby explained the situation, including her meeting with David that morning.

'Ian doesn't think he's a suspect, as far as I know, but he's obviously after something. He's tried questioning me and Peter now, and virtually invited himself into our production.'

'So what do you want us to do? Question Susannah about him?'

'No, no! You mustn't do that! Just don't talk about the murder, and especially Martha, to anyone.'

'It's a bit late for that, isn't it?' said Jane doubtfully. 'It's been in the papers – even the nationals – and on local TV. Campbell made sure of that.'

'But there hasn't been much about Martha, and Ian wants it to stay that way. The police only released her proper name, so he doesn't know about the Martha bit.'

Jane frowned. 'Why has he come down here with all flags flying under his real name, then? If Martha was Mrs Fletcher, surely he'd realise that someone would put two and two together?'

'Maybe, but it's a common name, and don't forget he knew Susannah was here and he was likely to meet her.'

'Made a point of it, in fact,' said Jane. 'Coffee?'

'Yes, please. Actually, of course, the fact that none of us have referred to the coincidence must make him realise we know nothing about her.'

'Double bluff?' said Jane.

'Well, yes. And few of the details of the attack on Martha have been released, even the time difference between that and the murder.'

'I didn't know about that,' said Jane.

'And you don't now,' said Libby. 'Just pretend you know nothing. I don't suppose Susannah will say anything unless he asks directly, and she won't know anything herself, but might think to ask you. That would be perfectly legitimate, wouldn't it?'

'So we say we know nothing more than was in my report.' Jane put mugs on the table. 'Hot, Imogen.'

Imogen slid off her chair, nodding. 'Hot,' she said and wandered off.

'That's it. Mind you, I can't remember what you said.'

'Not a lot, and this week even less.'

'Not much to say, really, is there?'

'And I suppose that's Ian's problem.'

'It is rather. He's desperately trying to find a link between Martha or Dominic and someone who knew the true value of the reliquary. Peter thinks it's a random attack, but neither you nor Campbell made much of its value, so a random thief wouldn't think it was worth stealing – just a bit of old finger.'

'That's true.' Jane tapped her mug with a fingernail. 'It really looks like an unsolvable case, doesn't it? No fingerprints or anything.'

'No murder weapon, either, except for Martha's.'

'Martha's?'

'She was pushed on to the stand, hit her head on the corner.'

'What, and the murderer saw what he'd done and scarpered?'

'Or heard the security guard coming.'

'But where did he scarper to? They didn't find anyone anywhere in the grounds, did they?'

'No,' said Libby, 'but to be fair, the security guard was too preoccupied with Martha and calling in to do an immediate search. It was more how he got in.'

'Dominic could have let him in,' suggested Jane.

'And then there was a falling out between thieves? Yes, it's been considered, but how did Dominic let him in?'

'How close a check was made after you'd all left?'

'Not close enough, obviously, as Dominic remained hidden.'

'There you are then. It could easily be a member of the audience.'

'In cahoots with Dominic? Or on his own?'

'Oh, in cahoots,' said Jane, 'or he wouldn't know where to go or where to hide.'

'It's definitely a thought,' said Libby.

'I expect Ian's thought of it, or one of his minions has.'

'He hasn't asked for audience details,' said Libby, 'and because almost all the tickets were sold by credit or debit card we could give them to him.'

'There's something about the data protection act,' warned Jane, 'although maybe that doesn't apply to the police.'

'Oh, well, I'll tell him I've warned you and mention what you've said. It's up to him, then.'

'He asked you to warn us, then?' Jane looked interested. 'Does he think this David's dangerous, then?'

'No, I'm pretty sure he doesn't, but he's worried about him.'

'We shall be on our guard, then. In fact, Susannah and Emlyn are coming to supper tonight, so it's a good job you told me. I just hope Terry doesn't say the wrong thing.'

'He won't. He doesn't say much anyway,' said Libby, standing up. 'Thanks for the sandwich and coffee. I promised to pop in on Fran to update her so I'd better go.'

Libby made a detour to the Alexandria to see what ticket sales were like, and admire the posters. Then she made her way along Harbour Street and waved to Guy in his shop before knocking on the door of Coastguard Cottage.

She and Fran walked back to Lizzie's ice-cream booth while Libby related the day's events.

'I think Jane could be right, you know,' said Fran, licking rum and raisin drips from the cone. 'A member of the audience.'

'Perhaps even the one who pretended to be the beneficiary on the phone?'

'Don't get ahead of yourself, Lib. But an audience member subsequently hidden by Dominic makes perfect sense.'

'Yes, it does. But as Jane said, I expect Ian's thought of that. I will tell him about David Fletcher accosting me today and just drop that in, though.' She looked over to the little harbour. 'I did wonder about a boat trip today, but neither of them are there.'

'Next trips are five o'clock and five fifteen,' said Fran, 'so the holidaymakers can get home in time for supper.'

'Too late for me,' said Libby. 'I'd better get home and do something spectacular for supper. I seem to have been neglecting my inner domestic goddess recently.'

'It's having Harry round the corner,' said Fran. 'Too easy to pop down there for something delicious.'

'We've been limiting ourselves recently,' said Libby, finishing the last of her ice cream. 'Special occasions only. Or at least only once a week.'

'Saturday night special,' said Fran. 'Are you going

tomorrow?'

'We could. Would you like to come? And I'll ask Pete, who'd probably be there, anyway.'

'Great. Can we stay over?'

'Of course. You'll have to get back on Sunday morning, won't you? Because of the shop.'

'Unless Sophie can be persuaded to open up for us. Did Adam tell you she's moving to London?'

No!' Libby stood stock still in amazement. 'I bet that means he's going with her.'

'No idea,' said Fran. 'Anyway, we can talk about it tomorrow. You go and cook something delicious for Ben and ring me if tomorrow's on.'

On Saturday morning Libby tentatively rang Adam.

'Hello, Ma. What can I do for you?'

'I hadn't heard from you for a bit, so I thought I'd see how you were.'

Adam laughed. 'Aha! Fran's been talking, has she?'

'She told me Sophie's going to London, that's all.'

'And you want to know if I'm going with her?'

Libby made a face at herself in the mirror. 'Well, yes.'

'Bel and Dom both live in London,' said Adam.

'I know.'

'But where would I get a job like mine?'

Libby let out a small breath. 'They must have gardeners in London.'

'Yes, they do. Fancy landscapers at even fancier prices. And I'd have to get taken on by one of them – not easy. No, Ma, I'm staying here. Mog wants to keep me on, and we're part of Lewis's maintenance team at Creekmarsh. Besides, helping out in the caff will keep me out of mischief, and I'll be back living in the village most of the time.'

'But what about Sophie? You're not –?'

'Splitting up? No, but we're both young, and although we managed a long-distance relationship when Sophie was at uni, it's not ideal. We'll just see what happens. And my brother and sister are both up there if she needs any support, or I need to go up and stay overnight.'

'Do Bel and Dom know this?' Libby asked, wondering if her elder children approved of Adam's cavalier plans.

'Of course they do. We don't always tell you everything, Ma! And I'll see you tonight – I'm working.'

'Adam's staying in the village,' she told Ben, who was sorting out paint tins in the conservatory, which had been partially rebuilt earlier in the year.

'That's good,' he said. 'He can finish off replanting the garden.'

'He's not staying for our convenience,' said Libby. 'He loves his job and being on Lewis Osbourne-Walker's team at Creekmarsh Place. Which makes me think the attachment between him and Sophie isn't as strong as it was.'

'They've both changed over the past few years,' said Ben. 'Adam's much more grown up, and I expect Sophie is, too.'

'At least I might see him more than Fran does, now,' said Libby. 'That's a bit mean and ungracious, isn't it?'

Ben put down his paint pot and came to give her a hug. 'No, it isn't. You're his mum, and he's still your baby.'

Libby had reported her encounter with David to Ian's official mobile number, but by the time Fran and Guy had arrived to park their car and dump their overnight bags, nothing had been heard from him, officially or unofficially.

As usual, Harry had booked them in to The Pink Geranium at nine o'clock, the latest time he took bookings, in order that he could join them at the end of their meal.

'G&T?' Ben asked Fran.

202

'Is there any wine open?' Fran sat down next to Libby on the sofa.

'Red,' said Libby holding up a glass. 'So did you ask Sophie about Adam?'

Fran looked at her friend warily. 'Er – yes.'

'It's all right.' Libby patted her arm. 'I talked to Adam. Everything's fine and he's staying here. He'll see us tonight.'

'Good.' Fran accepted her glass and leant back. The cane sofa creaked alarmingly. 'Have you heard from Ian?'

'No. I think we've rather ground to a halt, haven't we?'

'Again,' said Fran.

The Pink Geranium was packed, as usual on a Saturday night, and they found Peter waiting for them on the sofa in the left-hand window, a bottle of red wine and five glasses in front of him.

'And here we are again, folks,' he said as he poured wine for them all. 'A murder to talk about, Ad to wait on us and Harry to cook for us. *Plus ça change, plus c'est la même chose.*'

'We're not going to talk about the murder,' said Libby firmly. 'Fran and I think we've done all we can, and Ian's not keeping in touch with us, so that's that.'

Ben and Guy exchanged glances. Peter smiled, leant back in his corner of the sofa and languidly lifted his glass. '*Bonne chance.*'

Adam, looking cheerful, appeared to take their order, and suffered the pats on the back and kisses thought appropriate to acknowledge his decision to stay in Steeple Martin.

'Hub of the universe,' said Peter. 'I've always said so. That's why we persuaded the old trout to come and live here.'

'You did it out of the kindness of your hearts so I would

have a ready-made support network, you know you did,' said Libby.

'And now look what's happened,' said Peter. 'I knew it was a mistake.' He ducked as a menu was aimed at his head.

The food, as always, was excellent, and after an indulgent dessert had been consumed by them all except Peter, Harry joined them.

'So the caretaker'll be back on a more permanent basis,' he said, nodding at Adam. 'And you'll lose yours, Guy.'

'But we won't let Chrissie or Lucy know, or they'll be there all the time cadging free holidays,' said Fran, who didn't have the best relationship with her children, except for Jeremy, living in America.

'So update us on the murder, petal,' Harry said to Libby.

'Nothing to report. It's given up on us,' said Libby.

'Or Ian has,' said Harry.

'Either way, nothing to report,' said Libby.

'In that case, how about coming over to Creekmarsh with Ad and me in the morning to raid the veg beds? Anyone?' Harry looked round the table. 'Lewis has said we ought to harvest anything we can or it'll go to waste.'

'I'll come,' said Libby.

'We can't, we've got the shop,' said Fran.

'Busman's holiday,' said Ben.

'Right, missis,' said Harry. 'Report here at ten complete with gardening gloves. You'll be back in time for lunch with Hetty.'

'Sorry, Ma,' said Adam, when he came to kiss her goodnight. 'You know what he's like.'

'I do,' said Libby, 'and I shall enjoy it. I haven't been to Creekmarsh for ages. Not since that party last year.'

'It's an opening day,' warned Adam, 'so you might

204

have to avoid punters.'

'No worries,' said his mother, patting his cheek.

Fran and Guy gave Libby a lift to The Pink Geranium in the morning on their way home. She waved them off and went inside to find Adam and Harry already busy assembling large amounts of plastic bags, secateurs and string.

'Come along then, troops,' said Harry. 'I've got to get back here for the lunchtime rush.'

It was a blessedly sunny day, and by the time they'd driven up the long shady drive to the front door of Creekmarsh Place, there was a healthy crowd queuing for tickets to see the grounds, mainly famous for being owned by a television personality, the cheeky-chappie builder and handyman Lewis Osbourne-Walker. Sadly for the crowd, he was rarely in evidence at the weekends.

Adam led them to the walled vegetable garden and set them to their tasks.

'The punters can come in here, but they're only allowed to keep to the path in the middle,' he said. 'They shouldn't bother you.'

Half an hour later, Libby, stood up straight to stretch her aching back and gasped.

Heads together at the entrance to the vegetable garden were David Fletcher and Estelle Butcher.

Chapter Twenty-five

Libby scrambled out of the vegetable garden and stumbled over to the greenhouse, where Harry was gathering baskets full of tomatoes.

'Dominic's wife,' she whispered, 'with Martha's husband! They mustn't see me!'

Puzzled but obliging, Harry stepped in front of her as she fished out her mobile and rang Ian's official number. When she was asked to leave a message, she did so, then tried his personal number.

'Can you keep them there?' asked Ian, sounding as if he was already on the move.

'I don't know how,' said Libby. 'I can't let them see me, or they'd bolt. They obviously met here thinking no one would see them. And Estelle's met Harry, so he can't do it.'

'What about Adam?' Libby heard a car door slam.

'If I can find him,' said Libby. 'Go on, we'll do our best.'

She rang off and tried to ring Adam, who obviously hadn't taken his mobile into the garden with him.

'I'm going to try and track them,' said Libby. 'If I make my way down this wall, I can come up behind them.' She peered over Harry's shoulder. 'Yes, look, they're walking very slowly down the middle path. I'll work my way through the beans and potatoes and try and keep them in sight. If I see Ad, I'll wave.'

Luckily the rows of bean sticks that bordered the central

path provided a little cover as Libby proceeded slowly, pretending to check each plant. She couldn't hear what David and Estelle were saying, but it was obvious that this was not the first time they had met.

As they came up to the exit gate from the vegetable garden, Libby was surprised to see Adam appear there pushing an oversized wheelbarrow which he proceeded to get stuck in the gateway. Libby looked over to the greenhouse and saw Harry put up a thumb.

Adam was now arguing with David and Estelle, who looked furious. Without warning, she turned on her heel and marched back the way she had come, David following reluctantly behind her. Adam was doing his best by calling: 'Hey, you can't go out that way!' but the pair continued to the end and left through the entrance gate, Libby sidling cautiously after them.

But she was too late. By the time she emerged, neither was in sight. She turned and saw Adam coming out behind her.

'Can you get back to the car park and see if they've gone?' she said. 'I'll go this way.'

Pushing the wrong way through happily ambling visitors, Libby swore under her breath. She reached the car park in time to see Adam scowling down the drive.

'Two cars,' he said, 'leaving as I got here. And look – here's Ian.'

Adam led the way into the big kitchen of the house, where Lewis's mother Edie held sway. Today, however, it was empty.

'Tell me what happened,' said Ian, as Harry entered looking bewildered.

Libby explained.

'And I can't even begin to think why they were together,' she said. 'I mean, the estranged husband and wife of the two victims. It doesn't make sense.'

'Put that way, it does,' said Ian. 'We've been wondering about a connection between Butcher and Martha, and now there seems to be one.'

'David and Estelle were having an affair? Is that why they broke up with Martha and Dominic?' said Libby.

'I wouldn't think so. Martha left David long before Estelle and Dominic split up.' Ian rubbed a hand over his face. 'I wonder where they've gone.'

'Back to David's cottage?'

Ian shook his head. 'Are you sure neither of them saw you?'

'Pretty sure. I stayed in the greenhouse,' said Harry, 'and managed to get hold of Ad who tried to hold them up with his massive wheelbarrow.'

'It didn't work, though,' said Adam. 'Sorry, Ian. Mind you, I don't even know the story behind all this, so I'm not sure why I was trying to stop them.'

'I'll tell you later, love,' said Libby. 'So, what now, Ian?'

'I'm putting a tail on Fletcher. Estelle Butcher hasn't been seen at either her London address or the hotel she was staying in when she was last down here, so I can't tail her. But if you're sure about them not having seen you – and they don't know Adam – they might try and get in touch with you again. There's obviously something they either want or need to hide.'

'Can't you ask Martha?' said Harry. 'She'd know.'

'She might not,' said Ian. 'She's very fragile still, and her memory hasn't come back.'

Libby sighed with frustration. 'There must be something we can do.'

'The police will, Libby,' said Ian with a slight smile. 'All you can do is keep your eyes open and if you see either of them again, separately or together, let me know.' He stood up. 'Good try, though, and it's certainly given us another lead.'

'Well,' said Harry, when Ian had gone. 'I'll have to get going if my punters are going to get any lunch. Are you staying here, Ad?'

'No, I'm having lunch at Hetty's.' Adam stood up. 'I'll just go and let Edie know we've been in.'

On the drive back, Libby explained the entire story of the murder and the attack on Martha to Adam.

'And this is the ex-husband of the woman who was attacked and the ex-wife of the man who was murdered?' asked Adam. Libby nodded. 'Well, I just wish he wasn't called Dominic.'

'I didn't like that when I first met him,' said Libby. 'He wasn't a particularly likeable sort, was he Harry?'

'I really only knew him as a customer,' said Harry. 'Embarrassingly chatty with other diners.'

'Oh.' Adam pulled down the corners of his mouth. 'So we don't think either of them will show up in the village?'

'Estelle won't – at least, I shouldn't think so – but David might.'

'So I ought to keep out of sight if they do?'

'So they don't connect you with the rest of us? I wonder if that's what Ian meant? Perhaps it would be useful.'

'How much do they know about your set-up? I mean, the theatre and everything?'

'Not much. Estelle only found out about it when she heard of Dominic's death, the same with David.'

'Do we know how David knew about his wife being attacked?' asked Harry.

'She was in the paper under her real name. When David came down here and found Susannah was working with us he must have thought his troubles were over,' said Libby.

'But what troubles?' asked Adam. 'You haven't explained that.'

'No, because we don't know. I got the impression from Martha that she was through with all men and had been out of touch with her ex. Ian confirmed that, so what David wants is anyone's guess.'

'And now they're in cahoots,' said Harry. 'Very Spies-are-us. Makes you wonder, lovies, doesn't it?'

'Well, yes,' said Libby.

'I mean – do we know absolutely posi*tiv*ely that Estelle knew nothing about what was going on with Dominic before his death?'

'No, not provably,' said Libby. 'Ian said there was no contact obvious in his house. Not even an address. Only a couple of solicitors' letters, I think.'

'Hmm,' said Harry. 'I reckon you should take a look round it.'

'Harry! How could we do that?'

'New Barton Lane, isn't it? You could go and have a bracing Sunday afternoon walk after lunch.'

'After one of Hetty's roasts? You must be joking!'

'All right – tomorrow. My day off. I shall take you hiking.'

'But we can't go into the house. What point would there be?'

Harry shrugged. 'Dunno. Just got a hunch.'

'Where does David live?' asked Adam.

'In a rented cottage near Nethergate. I don't know where, exactly.'

'That's a pity,' said Adam, as Harry parked the car outside The Pink Geranium. 'I could have gone and had a reconnoitre.'

'You keep out of it, sonny,' said Harry, swinging himself elegantly out of the car. 'I need my staff in one

210

piece, however part-time they are. Not to mention my tenant.'

'It doesn't matter about me, then?' said Libby, scrambling rather more inelegantly out of the back seat.

'Oh, you're always in trouble, you are. More lives than a cat.'

'Thanks.' Libby handed over the bags full of vegetables they'd managed to salvage after the unscheduled interrruption. 'I'll see you at Hetty's, Ad.'

'And I shall see you tomorrow complete with walking boots,' said Harry. 'They suit me.'

'All right,' said Libby. 'Let me know what time.'

'À la bonne heure, as my beloved might say,' said Harry.

His beloved was waiting for them, already ensconced at Hetty's huge pine table with a glass before him.

'What's all this I hear about cop chases and expeditions?' he asked, as soon as Libby appeared.

Hetty turned from the Aga and raised her eyebrows. 'What yer been up to now, gal?'

Ben groaned. 'I'll go and fetch the wine, shall I, Mum? I've heard this already.'

Libby sat down. 'Didn't Harry tell you?'

'He hasn't had time. He had to get straight on with opening the caff. He said you'd tell me. And Het wants to know, don't you Auntie?'

'Don't you Auntie me,' said Hetty, flicking him with a tea towel. 'Go on, gal.'

So Libby repeated the story, including Harry's decision to take her spying on Dominic's old house.

'I don't understand what good that will do,' said Peter, leaning back and crossing elegant ankles.

'Neither do I. He says he has a hunch. And as I've never seen where Dominic lived, I'd quite like to.'

211

'Why?' Peter's eyebrows disappeared into his blond hair, which as usual, hung over his forehead.

'Nosy, I suppose,' said Libby. 'Hello, Ad.'

Adam went to kiss Hetty's cheek and she gave him an affectionate push.

'Filled everyone in, Ma?' he said.

'Yes, and now I think we should talk about something else,' said Libby, or Ben will get cross.'

'Yes, he will,' said Ben, returning with two bottles. 'Just pour this out and let's get on with the real business of the day.'

On Monday morning, Libby dealt with three queries about the End Of The Pier Show, two from performers and one from the Alexandria, and, on a sudden inspiration, called Susannah to ask for hers and David Fletcher's addresses as they needed them for insurance.

'It's something to do with not being covered if you're not a member of the company,' she said vaguely. 'I don't understand it, but better safe than sorry.'

'Isn't that covered by public liability insurance?' said Susannah.

'Is it? Peter and Ben deal with all that stuff – I'm clueless.'

'Oh, that's OK,' said Susannah. 'As you say, better safe than sorry.'

Harry rang a little later.

'Guess what I've got!' she told him gleefully. 'David Fletcher's address.'

'You weren't thinking of walking all the way over there, were you?'

'No, but I can drive over there at some point. Or Ad can.'

'Leave your darling boy out of it. You already have a posse, no need for a junior branch.'

'All right, all right. When are we going for our walk?'

'After lunch, I thought, if the rain holds off.'

'Do you know where it is?'

'Yes, Pete had it. I shall call by in my hiking gear with my knapsack on my back at two o'clock. Be ready!'

Libby dug out some old trainers bought with the intention of taking up jogging, which had never happened, put chicken and vegetables in the slow cooker and made herself a sandwich. By two o'clock she had also found an old plastic poncho in case of rain, and felt quite proud of herself. Harry, she discovered, really had turned himself into a hiker.

'Rambler, really, petal,' he said, looking down at himself. 'Up until a few years ago, before you arrived to set the place talking, I did a lot of this.'

'Proper walking boots and socks and everything,' said Libby, admiring him. 'Who'd have thought it?'

'Not you, obviously. Now, come on.'

Chapter Twenty-six

They walked to the end of Allhallow's Lane and turned left, away from the village, into New Barton Lane. After passing the New Farm cottages on their right, the houses petered out.

'Are there more houses down here?' Libby asked, looking round at the flat fields, colourless under a heavy grey sky.

'Over there, see?' Harry pointed to his left, where there was a stand of trees.

'How do we get there? Tramp across a field?'

'Gawd, but you're thick. A lane, stupid.'

Sure enough, a few yards further on a lane hardly worthy of the name turned off to the left.

'More like a farm track,' said Libby, peering at the tyre ruts.

'Exactly,' said Harry. 'That's what it is. There's a public footpath and a bridleway along here, although you'd never know it. The farmer wasn't any too happy about it.'

'They often aren't,' said Libby. 'Is it still a farm?'

'No. The people who bought it turned the farm buildings into cottages for holiday lets. Never took off, though. I suppose that's why Dominic got one.'

As they reached a bend in the lane the trees appeared, and, beneath them, a large brick farmhouse with a Kentish Peg roof to the right, and on their left a cluster of converted stables and barns. One, looking more like a prefab than anything else, had blue-and-white police tape fluttering across the front door.

'That's it,' said Libby, coming to a halt. 'Bleak-looking, isn't it?'

'I wonder why he didn't have one of the prettier ones,' said Harry.

'I expect it was the cheapest. Oh, and look! It's got a garage.'

The attached garage also had police tape across the door.

'Did the police find his car?' asked Harry, trying to peer through a crack at the side of the metal door.

'I don't know. I suppose it would have been in the car park at the Abbey. That's where we always parked.'

'If it was, wouldn't the alarm have been raised earlier?'

'Oh.' Libby stopped and stared at him. 'Of course. He must have hidden it somewhere else.'

'Unless his accomplice was to have taken him home. Or pretended he was going to.'

'Oh, I wish Martha could remember a bit more,' said Libby.

'Perhaps she doesn't want to, dear.' Harry went up to one of the front windows and peered in. 'Can't see a thing. Shall we knock?'

'What for? There's no one there. They seem to have even removed the police guard.'

'Still,' said Harry, and gave the front door a sharp knock.

Much to their surprise, they heard a noise inside. Holding their breath, they waited, but no one came. Libby motioned Harry back and they retreated round the side of the garage.

'A cat? Did he have a cat?' whispered Libby.

'How do I know? Anyway, the police would have taken a cat to the RSPCA.'

'Mice?'

'Don't be a prat. No, that was a person.'

'Why didn't he come out to see what we were doing prowling around? He must have heard us talking.'

'Because he, or perhaps she, is not supposed to be there,' said Harry. 'My knock must have made her jump, or she wouldn't have given herself away like that.'

'Not the police then?'

'Be your age! I don't know where you got your brains from, woman. My guess is the fragrant Estelle.'

'Makes sense,' said Libby. 'What shall we do?'

'Tell Ian, of course. Why, do you think we should mount a commando raid ourselves?'

'He is going to be so fed up with me,' said Libby.

'What, when you've supplied him with valuable information two days running?'

'Because I've been blundering round his investigation.'

'Rubbish. You were very kindly accompanying me on a walk on my day off. You didn't know he lived here, did you?'

'No, but I knew it was off New Barton Lane. Ian would never believe I'd stumbled on the place by accident.'

'What about yesterday? That was a genuine accident, wasn't it?'

'Well, yes.'

'There you are then,' said Harry. 'I'm going to ring up now, before she can make a run for it.'

'*You* are?'

'Yeah, me. After all, I quaite fancy the lovely Chief h'Inspector. Give me the number.'

Libby handed over her mobile. 'They're both under "Ian",' she said. 'I'm going to keep a look out in case she breaks free.'

But there was no movement from the house.

'Back door,' said Harry's voice in her ear, making her jump. 'I'll go and look.'

He was back in a moment. 'Boarded up,' he whispered. 'Ian says to walk away as though we're leaving. Someone will drive along the lane in an unmarked car after us. They don't want to alert her.'

'Does Ian think it is Estelle, then?' asked Libby, as they made their way back to the farm track.

'Possible. Come on, the track goes beyond the farm and joins up with another lane further on.'

On pushing further up the track, Libby realised how difficult it was to listen for sounds of escape from behind, when your ears were full of the sound of your own breathing, the squelch of mud beneath your feet and the rustle of waterproof clothing. What she did hear, after a while, was the sound of a car engine.

Harry turned round. 'I think it's the police.'

They stood back to let the car pass, but as it drew level the passenger window slid down and the red-haired head of Sergeant Maiden stuck out.

'Hello, Mrs S! Just looking around. House back there, isn't it?'

'Yes. Are you going to have a look?'

'I expect so. Don't want to alarm anyone, though, do we. You going to go along home?'

'Eventually,' said Libby, 'if Harry can find his way. You don't want us walking back past the house, do you?'

'Rather not, if you don't mind,' said Sergeant Maiden. 'I expect the Chief Inspector will be in touch.'

'I'm sure he will,' grunted Libby, as she watched the car pull into a farm gateway.

'Reckon they're going to stage a raid?' said Harry, as they walked on past.

'No,' said Libby. 'I do wish we knew who was inside.'

'It can only be Estelle, can't it?'

'Possibly with David. Perhaps they're both in there looking for something.'

They tramped on up the lane until it forked.

'Which way now?' asked Libby.

Harry grinned at her. 'Oh, ye of little faith! We go right here, back on ourselves and we rejoin New Barton Lane. Then we can go home.'

'Glory be,' muttered Libby, as they set off down the right-hand fork.

This lane was better surfaced and didn't seem quite as long as the one going through the old farmstead.

'That's because it doesn't twist and turn as much,' said Harry. 'Here we are – New Barton Lane.'

'And not even very far from where we left it,' said Libby with relief.

'Come on, then, keep up,' said Harry, looking back over his shoulder at her. 'You're not fit, that's your trouble.'

'I didn't think you were, either,' grumbled Libby. 'I'm not going out with you again.'

'Promises, promises,' carolled Harry, as he strode ahead.

Libby's feet knees and back were protesting violently by the time she reached home. She made a cup of tea and took it upstairs to drink in a hot bath, but just as she was about to step into it, the phone rang. Shivering, she answered the bedroom phone.

'You're at home, then?'

'Yes, Ian, I've just got in and I was about to get in the bath.'

'Oh.' Ian sounded disconcerted. 'How long will you be?'

'Why?'

'I wanted to talk to you.'

'Now?'

'I'm in Canterbury. I'm just about to leave to come to Steeple Martin.'

'I'll be out by the time you get here,' said a resigned Libby.

She thought she heard someone knocking at the front door ten minutes later, but decided it couldn't possibly be Ian yet. By the time she'd climbed out of the bath and wrapped her damp hair in a towel, the knocking had stopped and she swore under her breath.

Ian arrived about fifteen minutes later, by which time she was wearing her most disreputable painting trousers and a very baggy sweater. She blushed when she saw Sergeant Maiden standing behind Ian on the doorstep.

'Sorry,' she said, 'I've just had a bath.'

'I know,' said Ian. 'What I'm wondering is – did you happen to leave a downstairs window or door open while you were up there?'

Fear clutched Libby's stomach. 'I don't think so, why?'

'We saw someone disappearing into the wood at the end of the lane.'

Libby frowned. 'He could have come from anywhere.'

'He or she came from behind your terrace of houses. Has your back hedge been thoroughly repaired?'

'Not entirely,' said Libby.

'Then let's go and have a look at it,' said Ian, and led the way through the house to the garden.

'Someone's pushed through,' he said, pointing at a gap in the hedge. 'How long that been there?'

'It hasn't,' said Libby. 'We were only out here the other day.' She looked at Ian. 'I did actually hear someone knocking while I was in the bath, but by the time I'd got out it had stopped.'

Sergeant Maiden nodded. 'Fits,' he said.

219

'But you said you saw someone as you arrived.'

'I don't think we did, we just said we saw someone. Actually a good five to ten minutes before we knocked on your door. We went to see if we could find it.' Ian led the way back into the sitting room.

'So what did you want to talk about?' asked Libby, sitting on the sofa.

'What exactly happened when you went on your supposed walk today.'

Libby sighed. 'I told Harry you'd be angry with me.'

'Now, why should you think that?' Ian raised one eyebrow.

'Because you usually are,' said Libby, crossly. 'And this walk wasn't my idea. Harry wanted to do something with his day off.'

'And that involved poking around Butcher's house?'

'No! I didn't even know where it was. Peter had the address.'

'So why did Harry want to have a look?'

'Nosiness, I expect,' said Libby. 'Anyway, as we walked past it we stopped, and …'

'And?'

'Well, Harry knocked. And then we heard a noise. I thought it might be a cat.'

'That had let itself in? No.'

'Well, you sent someone out,' said Libby. 'You must have thought it was worth investigating.'

Ian sighed and looked at Sergeant Maiden. 'We did, and you were right. However, by the time Sergeant Maiden got there, just after he saw you, whoever it was had gone.'

'But how? The back door was boarded up, and didn't you say there were padlocks? We didn't hear anything and there were certainly no cars except your one.' She looked at the sergeant.

'We don't know. Nor do we know how she – if it was Mrs Butcher – got there.'

'Dominic's car,' said Libby frowning. 'We were wondering about that. It couldn't have been left in the Abbey car park or it would have roused suspicion.'

'It wasn't. We found it about half a mile away, with some clothes in it. It looks like a carefully prepared getaway.'

'Which makes it even likelier that he was intending to steal the reliquary?'

Ian nodded. Libby sighed again. 'I'm going to make more tea. Would you like some?'

As usual, the big kettle was simmering on the Rayburn, so it took next to no time for Libby to reappear in the sitting room with a tea tray.

'Go on, then, what did you find in that house?'

'It looks as though someone had stayed there overnight, and certainly a search had been made.'

'Do you think that's where Estelle went when she left Creekmarsh yesterday?'

'If she did, what's she done with her car?'

'She could have left it somewhere and Fletcher could have given her a lift to Butcher's house,' suggested Maiden. Libby nodded agreement.

'But if she ran away after we'd been there,' said Libby, 'why would she come knocking on my door?'

'No idea,' said Ian, 'but you remember I did say someone might try and find out if you knew anything?'

'You meant David.'

'Yes, but the same applies to Mrs Butcher.'

'But I don't know anything.'

'Now you've been up to the house, she must think you do. You're sure she didn't see you yesterday?'

'No. The only time we've met was at Peter and Harry's.

What did she want, do you think?'

'At the house?' Ian shook his head. 'There's nothing in there that relates to her at all, except solicitor's letters.'

'But she's frightened.' Libby frowned. 'She's scared something will be found that will incriminate her, yet you don't think she killed Dominic?'

'The unbreakable cast-iron alibi,' said Ian. 'So she's scared of something else.'

'And is it the same thing that David Fletcher's scared of?'

'Is he scared?' asked Ian. 'I didn't think so.'

'No, actually, neither do I – he just wants to find something. And I think what he wants to find is Martha.'

'So we keep mum,' sad Libby. 'And what about if Estelle turns up here?'

'You tell her nothing and get in touch with us,' said Ian. 'By 999 if necessary.'

'Do you think she's dangerous?' said Libby, nervously.

'It depends on what she's looking for or scared of,' said Ian, standing up. 'We'll be off, and, Libby, no more poking around.'

'No, Chief Inspector,' said Libby, and saw Maiden give her a wink.

She related the whole saga to Ben when he arrived from the Manor half an hour later.

'Young Harry's a menace,' was his comment, as he held up a gin bottle. 'Drink before dinner?'

'Yes, please, I need one.' Libby curled up in the corner of the sofa. 'I'm worried about Estelle turning up here. How did she know where I lived?'

'Would Dominic have had your address?'

'No, I don't think so. I don't think he even had this phone number.'

Ben handed her a glass and sat down beside her. 'I

wouldn't worry about it. After all, she didn't try and break in, did she?'

'No. I wonder where she's gone now?'

'She'll be aware the police are on to her, so as far away as possible, I should think,' said Ben. 'What's for dinner?'

The sun came out again on Tuesday. Libby was once again trying to work on some small paintings for Guy's gallery-cum-shop when Andrew rang.

'I've got a bit more news,' he said. 'Fran said she can come round after lunch. Can you?'

'Delighted,' said Libby. 'About two-ish?'

Fran was already installed in a chair by the window when Libby arrived.

'Sit down, Libby, and I'll bring in the tea,' said Andrew.

'Do you know what this is about?' Libby asked when he'd gone into the kitchen.

'No – he just said he'd got some news. I meant to ask if he'd told Ian yet, but I haven't had a chance.'

'I'll ask him now,' said Libby as he came back into the room. 'Andrew, have you told Ian or anyone at the police station this news?'

'Not yet,' said Andrew, looking surprised. 'I know your Mr Connell told me to keep going and that he would defray any costs, but I don't know if he would want what I've found out. So I thought I'd – ah – run it by you first.' He looked pleased with the colloquialism.

'Now,' he continued as he poured out tea. 'Where had we got to?'

'Albert Glover and May Tollybar got married. Oh – and Ronald -what was his name?'

'Barnes. It's Albert and May – who was May Williams if you remember – I'm concerned with. You know I wanted to find out if they had children? Well, they did.'

'They did?'

223

'They had three children, Caroline, Jessica and Robert.'

'Who would also be Glovers?' said Fran.

'Who would also be Glovers. And we're assuming, descended from Bad Jack Jarvis.'

'So they're all Tollybars crossed with Beaumonts?' said Libby. 'Where does that get us?'

'Well,' said Andrew, 'so far, I've only traced Robert's family. He married and had a daughter called Maureen.' He looked at each of them in turn and twinkled. 'And she had a daughter called – Estelle!'

Chapter Twenty-seven

'She didn't!' Libby gasped. '*Our* Estelle?'

'Estelle Butcher née Wilcox, yes.'

'That might account for a lot,' said Fran. 'I think you should tell Ian immediately, Andrew.'

'Oh, do you?' His face fell. 'I thought it might be quite nice to do a bit more investigating on our own first.'

Libby and Fran exchanged looks.

'We can carry on investigating, Andrew, but you really must tell Ian. You see, she's disappeared.'

Libby explained what had happened on Sunday and subsequently on Monday afternoon.

'Hmm,' said Andrew, frowning. 'This must mean she knows about the reliquary.'

'In the light of who she is, it could well be that Dominic got information about it from her in the first place,' said Fran.

'Do you think that's what she's been trying to conceal?' said Libby.

'Could it be,' said Andrew slowly, 'that this Dominic had heard about it from his wife while they were still married, then, when finding out it was coming to the Abbey he told her, and they plotted together to steal it?'

'That's got to be it,' said Libby, 'but Ian said there was no sign of any contact between them at the house.'

'But Estelle thought there would be, and that's what she's been looking for,' said Fran. 'Go on, Andrew, you must call the police.'

'Oh, very well.' Andrew sighed and got up to fetch his phone. 'What's the number?'

Fran quoted Ian's official number, and the waited while Andrew punched it in.

'Oh, Mr Connell! I didn't expect you to answer so quickly. Yes, that's why I'm calling. The ladies thought I should.' Andrew's eyes flicked to Libby and Fran. 'Yes, they're here with me now. Well, it's like this …'

Andrew repeated his story, then spelt out a few details.

'Yes, Chief Inspector, I'll carry on, certainly, if you think there is anything else to find. Of course, of course. Ronald Barnes. Yes, do.' He switched off the phone.

'He sounded very interested. Quite sharp, I thought.'

'Yes, he would,' said Libby. 'And he wants you to look at Ronald Barnes?'

'And see if there any living descendants of either apart from Estelle.'

'Ah! A sort of race for the treasure?'

Andrew pulled down his mouth. 'Quite. It sounds like a bad *Boy's Own* adventure, doesn't it?'

'If it wasn't for people being killed it would be quite exciting,' said Libby. 'I used to love those comics when I was a girl.'

'You were supposed to love the girly ones, all boarding school and ballet classes,' said Fran.

'Oh, I loved them, too, especially the pony ones. So where will you go next, Andrew?'

'I'll have a look at the Glovers' other children, and I'll trace old Albert back and see if there's a definite connection with Bad Jack, and see if the same applies to Ronald Barnes.' He rubbed his forehead. 'This reliquary seems to have caused an awful lot of trouble.'

'Right from its earliest days, yes,' said Fran, 'and it's carrying on now.'

'I wonder what its actual value is? Was it in the auction catalogue?'

'No, there wasn't even a reserve price quoted,' said Libby. 'Incalculable, I expect. It's got huge gem stones set in a pure gold casket. Welsh gold, I expect.'

'But it seems to be its value as a sort of talisman – a good luck charm – to the families that causes all the problems. Alastair Beaumont told you that, didn't he, Lib?'

Libby nodded. 'But whenever it disappears – or gets stolen – that's always for money. And Dominic needed money.'

'And somebody needed money when they stole it from poor old Bernard Evans. I wonder if that was a member of the family?'

'Which family, though?' said Libby. 'The Beaumonts or the Tollybars?'

'Good Lord, you make it sound so complicated!' said Andrew. 'More tea, anyone?'

When they left Andrew's flat, they went to lean on the wall and look out over the roofs of Nethergate and the bay beyond.

'Opens up a whole new can of worms, doesn't it?' said Libby.

'Odd, really, that tracing the family and the story behind the reliquary should have brought us to this point,' said Fran. 'All goes back to family. And if you think about it, that's been the case in some of our investigations.'

'Yours included,' agreed Libby. 'Awful things, families.'

'Andrew didn't say if Estelle had any siblings.'

'No, but he would have mentioned them if she had. He said he was going to check on Albert and May's other children. Albert and May would be Estelle's great-grandparents, wouldn't they?'

'Mm.' Fran nodded, squinting at the sun on the sea. 'Didn't you have the urge in there to say, well, come on, get on with it? There's loads he could do online, isn't there?'

'I expect so, but we don't want to deprive him of his trips to Kew and the British Library, do we?' said Libby. 'I just hope he comes up with another bombshell soon.'

'Didn't you say you'd managed to get David Fletcher's address?' Fran suddenly straightened up and turned back towards the road. 'We could go there now.'

'Now?' Libby looked flustered. 'But Ian's told me not to go poking around any more. That's definitely poking around.'

'He didn't tell me. Come on, we'll go in my car,' said Fran.

'Could I park mine somewhere else?' asked Libby, following her across the road. 'Andrew will wonder why mine's still here if he sees it.'

'It is quite conspicuous,' said Fran. 'OK, we'll see if there's a space on Harbour Street.'

Finding a space took far longer than Fran wanted, and she was extremely impatient by the time Libby joined her.

'OK. OK, not my fault,' said Libby, buckling her seat belt. 'And this is your idea, remember, not mine for once.'

Fran drove out of Nethergate along the road that would eventually lead to Creekmarsh, and turned off towards the village of Heronsbourne.

'Here,' she said, pointing at a row of whitewashed cottages. 'I bet they're all holiday lets.'

'A bit isolated,' said Libby. 'Heronsbourne's another couple of miles up the road, and it isn't that close to Nethergate.'

'I don't suppose people mind these days, as long as they've got a car,' said Fran. 'And they do look pretty.'

'All right,' said Libby, 'we've seen it. What do we do now?'

'I don't know,' said Fran, helplessly. 'I'm not sure why I wanted to come.'

Libby looked at her shrewdly. 'That was your brain again. There must be a reason. You must have seen something.'

'No, I'm sure I didn't. I just felt it was urgent to come out here.'

'In that case,' sighed Libby, 'we'd better go and see if everything's all right, hadn't we?'

'What number is it?' asked Fran as they approached the row of cottages.

'Four. On the end farthest from the road,' said Libby.

'Where do they park?' asked Fran looking round. 'This is only a footpath.'

'There must be somewhere round the back.' Libby walked to the end of the row, where the cottages came up against a stand of trees. 'Yes, look.'

Behind the cottages a space had been cleared, and in it stood three cars.

'Are any of those David's?' whispered Fran.

'I've no idea, I've never seen his car.'

'Estelle's?'

'Same. Never seen it.'

Fran stood in front of the end cottage, irresolute. 'Dare we knock?'

'I've already been told off once for interfering at a property,' said Libby. 'I don't want to risk it again.'

'Couldn't you have some message about rehearsal?'

'I'd have phoned him, hardly come all the way out here. It's not even on the way to anywhere.'

'We could be going to visit George at The Red Lion.'

'That's not an adequate excuse for being here,' said

229

Libby. 'No, I think we shall have to leave it and hope you weren't foretelling another murder.'

Fran looked agonised. 'Don't say that!'

Libby stared at her for a moment. 'I know,' she said. 'I'll ring him.'

'Have you got his number?'

'Yes, I put it in the phone that first night he came to rehearsal. He won't know I'll be calling from outside his house. Come on, we'll do it from the car.'

Back in Fran's car, Libby found her mobile and selected David's number. It was answered almost immediately.

'Yes?'

'Oh, David,' said Libby, realising she hadn't thought of a reason for calling.

'Libby?'

'Yes, it's me. Um – are you picking Susannah up tomorrow for rehearsal?'

'Yes, I am, why?'

'I wonder if you could possibly come a little early?' said Libby, with sudden inspiration. 'A couple of the soloists would like to rehearse with you. You know, for odd effects.'

'Swanee Whistle?' asked David with amusement.

'That sort of thing, yes,' said Libby. 'Have you got one?'

'It's in every drummer's essential kit,' laughed David. 'What time do you want us?'

'Seven thirty if that's all right,' said Libby, wracking her brains for some way to find out where he was. 'I've got to check with Susannah first because of baby-sitting and so on, so I'll ask her to confirm with you.'

'Don't worry about that,' said David, 'I'm just about to go over there, so I'll ask her.'

'Oh – thank you,' said Libby. 'Er – yes. Thank you.'

'Pleasure,' said David, sounding puzzled, as well he might. 'I'll see you tomorrow then.'

'Indeed, yes, tomorrow,' said Libby. 'Have a nice time at Susannah's.'

'Oh, she just wants to go through some of the music on our own,' said David. 'And I shall stay to supper afterwards. Do you know Emlyn?

'No, I'm afraid not.'

'Nice chap. I expect you'll meet him at the show.'

'I expect I will,' said Libby faintly. 'Bye for now, then.' She switched off the phone.

'Now for goodness' sake don't forget to summon a couple of soloists early tomorrow,' said Fran. 'What was that all about?'

Libby explained, keeping a watchful eye on the cottages.

'There's a car coming out on to the lane,' said Fran, looking in her mirror. 'Do you think that's him?'

'Heads down,' said Libby. 'The trouble with your car is that it's noticeable.'

They both hunched down in their seats, Libby only risking a look as the silver-grey car swished past them.

'Yes, that was him,' she said, sitting up straight. 'Now what?'

'Shall we go and have a look?' said Fran.

'Really?' said Libby, pulling a face. 'What if he comes back?'

'Why would he do that?'

'He might have forgotten his music or something.'

'Oh, for goodness' sake,' said Fran, opening her door. 'I'll go. You stay here.'

Libby watched as her friend crossed the road, walked to the end of the row of cottages and peered in through the window of number four. After a moment, she left the window and walked round the side of the cottage and out of sight. Libby fidgeted and worried, and had just decided she'd better go and find out what had happened when Fran reappeared.

'You were ages!' complained Libby. 'What did you find?'

'I'm not sure,' said Fran with a frown. 'Well, I am sure, but I'm not sure what it means.'

'Oh, come on! What did you see?'

Fran fastened her seat belt and started the engine. 'A basket of washing,' she said.

'A basket –? Well, what's wrong with that? Where was it?'

'In a sort of porch at the back. There's a washing line in the back garden, and it looks as though this washing had been taken off it.'

'So? Maybe he thought it would rain before he came back?'

'Whenever have you known a man do that? They usually forget all about it and let it stay out all night.'

'That's true,' acknowledged Libby, 'at least, the ones I've known do. But I don't suppose they're all the same.'

'The washing in that basket was folded,' said Fran. 'And on top was a bra and a pair of tights. David Fletcher is not alone in that house.'

Chapter Twenty-eight

'Estelle?' said Libby.

Fran shrugged and turned left on to the Nethergate Road. 'It would explain where she was.'

'On the other hand,' said Libby, 'it could simply be that he's brought a girlfriend down here for a spot of non-connubial bliss.'

'Could be,' said Fran. 'I take it you don't want to tell Ian about it?'

'No, I don't!' said Libby. 'I'm not getting into more trouble.'

Fran gave her an amused smile. 'That's not like you.'

'I don't know why everyone thinks I'm such an idiot,' said Libby self-righteously. 'I'm perfectly normal and well-behaved.'

'You make yourself sound like a puppy,' said Fran.

Libby pondered on the twin subjects of Estelle's ancestry and David's living arrangements as she drove home. She decided that Fran's theory of Dominic knowing about the reliquary and therefore getting in touch with his ex-wife when he found out it was going to be at the Abbey was sound, but David's connection with Estelle, particularly if she was hiding out in his cottage with him was a complete mystery. Unless – she swerved slightly as a thought struck her. Unless David and Estelle were related.

She thought back to Andrew's revelations. He was going to look into the rest of Albert and May Glover's descendants. Estelle didn't appear to have any siblings, but she could have cousins. And those cousins could well know about the reliquary and feel they had a right to it. Excited, she pulled the car into the side of the road and found her mobile.

'Fran, what about cousins?'

'What?' Libby could hear clattering in the background and assumed Fran was preparing dinner. 'What are you talking about?'

'Cousins. Could David be a descendant, too? A cousin or something?'

'Hell, I don't know! And where are you?'

'Going home. I'm almost opposite the turning to the Tyne Chapel. I just thought it could explain everything.'

'Go home, Libby,' said Fran wearily. 'I'm sure Andrew will find out if David has any connections to the family. And at the moment I'm more worried about why I felt it was so urgent to go to that cottage.'

'OK, sorry,' said Libby. 'I'll see you tomorrow evening.'

'I'll come early,' said Fran.

Libby cast a glance to her left, where, across the fields and at the top of a small hill, stood the infamous Tyne Chapel. She shuddered, put the car into gear and set off for home.

She found Ben chopping vegetables in the kitchen and relayed the events of the afternoon while making herself a cup of tea.

He threw the contents of his chopping board into a sizzling pan and frowned.

'Not like you to want to stay on the side of the law,' he said, 'but you can't help but be worried about Fran.'

'What, her feeling that it was urgent?'

'Exactly. Look how many times those feelings of hers have been right.'

'We can hardly go to Ian with that sort of information,' said Libby. 'But I'm going to ring Andrew and find out if he can look David Fletcher up and see if he has a connection to the family.'

While Libby rang Andrew, Ben finished his stir-fry and dished it up. 'TV dinner?' he suggested when she came back into the kitchen. 'The news will be on.'

They took their plates into the sitting room and settled down to watch the news just as Libby's mobile rang.

'Where are you?' asked Ian peremptorily.

'Eating my supper,' said Libby, with a mouthful of bean sprouts.

'Oh.' There was a pause. 'Sorry – I don't know why, but I thought you might be out somewhere.'

'What is it, Ian?'

'Since we heard from Andrew earlier we've been searching for Estelle Butcher and she's completely vanished from the face of the earth. We even went to Fletcher's cottage in case she was there, but there was no one there at all.'

'David's at Susannah's rehearsing and having supper,' said Libby. 'I spoke to him this afternoon. Did you go round to the back of the cottage?'

'What? What do you mean, the back? I sent a couple of officers out there, I assumed they knew what they were doing. Why do you ask? Oh, no. Don't tell me you went?'

'No,' said Libby hastily, hoping she wasn't about to get Fran into trouble. 'But Fran had one of her feelings so we went out there. And Fran went to look round. I stayed in the car,' she added virtuously.

'And? What then?'

'Fran saw a basket of laundry with women's clothes in it. At the back of the house.'

'Good God!' exploded Ian. 'Why didn't you tell me?'

'That's rich!' Libby was indignant. 'Think what you would have said if we just phoned up and said we saw women's clothing at David's cottage. It's only because you can't find Estelle and you know there's a link between them that you're angry.'

'Sorry.' There was a pause. 'So, anything else?'

'No. Except that I asked Andrew if David Fletcher could be another member of the Beaumont-Tollybar family. He's going to look into it. Listen, Ian, you won't go and drag David out of Susannah's house, will you? The poor girl has nothing to do with any of this.'

'After what you've told me, Libby, I can hardly wait around until he decides to go home. I shall ring him and ask him to meet me at his cottage.'

'I suppose that will do,' said Libby. 'I hope you don't find anything sinister.'

'Like Estelle Butcher's body, you mean?' said Ian. 'So do I.'

'Oh, bugger,' said Libby, as she ended the call. 'I'd better warn Fran.'

'Send her a text, then you can at least eat a bit of your supper while it's hot,' said Ben.

But Fran, of course, wasn't content with a text, and called back immediately.

Libby sighed, put down her fork and explained.

'Well, at least he's looking into it. I shall be prepared for a telling-off,' said Fran.

'Come off it, he never tells you off.'

'We'll see,' said Fran, and left Libby to eat her rapidly cooling supper.

All evening Libby waited for Ian to call and tell her what had happened, but both phones remained silent.

'I doubt if he feels he needs to let you know,' said Ben. 'You aren't on the "need to know" list, even if you did give

236

him the information.'

'I feel used,' said Libby.

Ben kissed her cheek. 'Never mind, love. Would you like a hot chocolate or a whisky?'

'What do you think?' Libby punched him on the arm.

Wednesday limped by twice as slowly as it should. Libby heard from neither Ian, David or Susannah. She called Fran at lunchtime, who hadn't heard either.

'Not even the telling-off?' said Libby.

'No, nothing. I'll call if I do, otherwise I'll see you at half past seven. You did phone some of the others, didn't you?'

'Oh, hell, I forgot. I'll do it now. Do you think I need to, though? David might have been locked up by now.'

'I'd do it, in case. Susannah might turn up on her own.'

Duly summoned, several soloists, mainly the comedy performers, turned up just before half past seven. Libby sat on the edge of the stage anxiously staring at the auditorium doors. At exactly seven thirty, they swung open and Susannah came in, chatting brightly to David. Libby exchanged glances with Fran and stood up.

'This really good of you,' she said, 'I hope it wasn't any trouble, Susannah?'

'Not at all. I'm enjoying this, you know.'

'Thank you, too, David, and for bringing Susannah.' Libby swallowed nervously, hoping she sounded normal.

'Pleasure. As I told you, we did a bit of rehearsing yesterday and she and Emlyn gave me supper, so the least I can do is give her a lift.'

'Even if supper was curtailed somewhat?' said Susannah with a laugh.

Libby's insides clenched. 'Oh?'

'The police rang me,' said David, taking the covers off the drum kit. 'There was an intruder at the cottage I'm renting. I had to go and check.'

'And was there?' asked Fran, who had come up beside Libby.

'No. They made me open up and check all through, but nothing.'

'So who reported it?' asked Libby.

'No idea. Someone had been seen prowling around the outside and in the back garden,' he said cheerfully. 'Nothing to steal, anyway.'

'That was kind of Ian,' muttered Libby, as she and Fran moved to seats in the auditorium.

'Kind?'

'I asked him not to pull Ian out of Susannah's and involve her. And he didn't.'

'Quite clever, really,' agreed Fran. 'And they got the chance to check the inside of the cottage.' She shook her head. 'And I don't get any sense of impending doom hanging around him.'

'No. He seems very cheerful. Perhaps we were wrong.'

'About him and Estelle being in cahoots?'

'Well, yes, in a way. After all, he could have simply linked up with her because her husband had been killed at the same time as the attack on his wife.'

'Ex in both cases, and how could he have linked up with her?'

'Oh, I don't know! I'm talking rubbish, aren't I?'

'I don't know,' sighed Fran. 'After misreading the signs yesterday, I don't know what to think.'

Libby turned to look at her friend. 'You felt it was urgent to go there right at that moment, didn't you. It could easily be that something was happening then, but it was gone before we arrived.'

'David killed Estelle and got rid of the body in about fifteen minutes? Not very likely.'

Libby frowned. 'You still think it was to do with Estelle?'

'It's the only thing that made any sense.' Fran turned her attention to the stage. 'Look, he's really fitting in up there.'

David was following Bob the Butcher's performance of a comic song intently, putting in sound effects at the appropriate moments.

Libby shook her head. 'I can't believe he's mixed up in anything.'

'No.' Fran sighed again. 'If only I could get rid of this niggle in my head, I'd like to forget all about it.'

'I know what you mean,' said Libby, 'but don't forget Andrew's still trying to find out about the families for us.'

'And for Ian.' She laughed. 'How many times have we said we'll bow out of one of Ian's cases and then been tempted back in?'

'A lot. Because we're nosy. At least, I am,' said Libby, standing up. 'Come on, let's go and do our stuff.'

At the end of the rehearsal, Susannah called over to Libby.

'Don't you all go for a drink after rehearsal? I'm sure Jane told me.'

'Yes,' said Libby warily.

'Can we join you? I've got a late pass.'

'Of course,' said Libby.

'The more the merrier,' said Ben. 'I expect Harry will come in if he's finished at the restaurant. You remember Harry? Peter's partner?'

'How could I forget,' laughed Susannah.

'We'll see you down there,' said Libby. 'Most of the others go, too. We've just got to lock up.'

With a wave, David and Susannah left. Peter, Ben, Fran and Libby looked at each other.

239

'Is he still trying to find things out?' asked Peter. 'Do we still need to be careful?'

'I think so,' said Fran. 'After all, we know now there's some kind of link with Dominic's wife.'

'But he still doesn't know anything about Martha,' said Ben. 'Only that she was attacked. But not who she is.'

'We think so, but does Estelle know? Would she have told him?'

'Estelle only knows about Dominic, nothing else,' said Libby. 'And whatever it is she was trying to find.'

'We'll just have to keep quiet, then,' said Peter.

'Oh, my God!' said Libby. 'Patti and Anne will be at the pub!'

'And they know all about it,' said Fran.

'But he wouldn't talk to them, would he?' said Peter.

'You never know,' said Libby. 'We'd better get down there and warn them.'

Chapter Twenty-nine

Libby's heart sank as she walked into the pub and saw David and Susannah at the same table as Patti and Anne, deep in conversation.

Anne looked up with a wide smile on her face. 'Libby, isn't this amazing? Susannah and I used to be in the same choir when we were at school!'

'Really?' said Libby weakly. 'Did you know one another well?'

'Oh, yes,' said Susannah, smiling fondly at Anne. 'Best friends, although we didn't go to the same school, just the same choir, but the choir was quite well known, and we used to go abroad and tour the country, so we spent most of the school holidays together.'

Ben appeared with drinks and bent to kiss Patti's cheek.

'How was the holiday?' he asked.

'Wonderful,' sighed Patti. 'But very hot.'

'Where did you go?' asked David.

Patti launched into a description of the villa, the estate and the food which kept the conversation away from dangerous areas, while Susannah and Anne caught up on each other's lives.

'And you met Patti when you were at uni?' asked Susannah, when they'd almost come up to date.

'Before she did her theology course, yes,' said Anne.

'Theology?' Susannah's eyebrows rose, and David turned his head.

'Yes.' Anne grinned mischievously. 'My Patti's a

vicar.'

Libby shot a warning look across the table to where Peter was sitting next to Patti.

'A vicar!' David looked at Patti. 'Wow! I don't think I've ever met a lady vicar before.'

Suddenly, there was tension round the table. Susannah and Anne were obviously oblivious, but Libby could see the signs in everyone else. Fran, who was sitting between Peter and Ben, caught her eye and gave a minute shrug.

'So, were you involved in the play at the Monastery?' David asked.

'Er – not directly,' said Patti, looking across at Libby with a plea in her eyes. 'Was I, Libby?'

'No,' said Libby, thinking frantically. 'Only that you told us the story that formed the basis of it.'

'And I was very grateful,' said Peter, taking over smoothly. 'I haven't written a play for the theatre for years and it was a great opportunity.'

'So none of you were actually involved with the Monastery beforehand?' said David.

'No,' said Ben, watching David's face. 'And of course, the Monastery is a ruin. It just happens to be attached to an Abbey.'

Libby held her breath.

'Oh, yes, the Abbey. That was where someone was attacked wasn't it?'

'I believe so,' said Peter, 'but as I've said before, we'd finished by then.'

'But it was one of your actors who was murdered?'

'Sadly, yes,' said Libby, 'but we know very little about either him or the murder.'

Susannah had clearly picked up on the atmosphere and pushed her chair back.

'I'm sorry to be a party pooper, folks, but I don't want

to push my luck and stay out too late. Do you mind, David?'

'No, of course not.' David swallowed the last of his drink and stood up. 'Good to meet you, ladies,' he said to Patti and Anne, and smiled round at the rest of them. 'See you tomorrow.'

Silence fell as they watched him leave with Susannah.

'What was all that about?' asked Patti, as the door closed behind them.

A collective breath was let out.

'He's the ex-husband of Martha,' said Libby. 'And he's in touch with the ex-wife of Dominic.'

Patti looked horrified. 'Oh, my God! Did I say anything wrong?'

'No, because you very sensibly realised there was an issue and passed it to Libby,' said Fran. 'And we don't know why he's so interested, just that he tried to see Martha in hospital and has made enquiries about her under her real name of Cornelia Fletcher. He doesn't know about her new name or occupation.'

'Complicated,' said Anne. 'So in future, we don't talk about the Abbey, the Monastery or Catherine?'

'Not when he's around,' said Libby. 'Ian's looking into it.'

'He'll get to the bottom of it,' said Patti. 'As long as you give him a hand.'

Ben and Peter laughed. 'He doesn't have an option,' said Peter.

Everyone left soon after that, and Ben and Libby strolled back up the high street arm in arm.

'He was really pushing tonight, wasn't he?' said Libby. 'What is it that he's after?'

'It couldn't be the reliquary itself, could it?' said Ben, rather diffidently.

'But it wasn't stolen!'

'Was it ever stated in the press that it wasn't stolen?'

Libby stopped dead, her mouth open. Ben grinned. 'Come on, let's go back and look it up.'

Libby woke up the laptop when they got back to the cottage, while Ben poured them both large whiskies.

'Look,' she said, scrolling down, 'hundreds of bloody reports.'

'Try the BBC ones first,' said Ben, 'then the nationals.'

Side by side at the little table in the window they began to read through the reports.

'No mention in the first couple of days,' said Ben. 'Go on a bit.'

But after the first few days, the media's interest waned. The police were giving out no new information – 'Well, there wasn't any to give, was there?' commented Libby – and even an in-depth piece in one of the Sunday broadsheets the following week, gave nothing more.

'The most it says is "during a burglary" and for Martha "attempting to prevent the theft of this valuable item",' said Ben.

'It never says it was stolen, but it doesn't say it wasn't,' said Libby, sitting back in her chair. 'If you weren't dissecting it like us, you could well think it had been stolen.'

'I wonder if Ian did that on purpose? Or his Superintendent, or press officer or whoever decides what's to be released,' said Ben.

'He should have told us,' said Libby indignantly.

'Why should he?'

'Well, we might have let slip it was safe back at the auction house.'

'At first, he didn't know David and Estelle were going to crawl out of the woodwork, did he?'

'True, but he must have hoped something would.' Libby shut the laptop. 'So now we've got to be even more careful of what we say.'

Ben stood up and stretched. 'I for one would quite like not to have to think about any of it for a good long time.'

Libby woke very early the next morning and sat straight up in bed.

'I've thought of something else,' she said to a bewildered and befuddled Ben. 'No, don't get up. I'll go and make myself some tea.'

'Bring me a cup,' muttered Ben and went back under the duvet.

Downstairs, Libby put the kettle on and fed Sidney. It was the missing robe. They'd all forgotten that. And could that be what Estelle was looking for? She warmed the teapot, spooned in tea leaves and poured on the boiling water.

If that was what it was, and it made sense, perhaps she had met Dominic, or been concealed by him in the other robe. Which she'd left behind somewhere and was now trying to find? No. She shook her head, poured out the two mugs of tea and took them upstairs.

'So what is it you thought of?' asked Ben, struggling to an upright position.

'The missing robe,' said Libby. 'I was just thinking perhaps that was what Estelle was looking for.'

'But it wouldn't be at Dominic's house,' said Ben. 'He was dead. He couldn't have taken it back there.'

'No. But it is still missing. Suppose Estelle is looking – or was looking – for the evidence that connects the two of them with the attempted theft, and suppose she took the robe?'

'Suppose she escaped wearing it?' said Ben. 'But how did she escape?'

'I reckon that was easy,' said Libby. 'I think whoever the murderer is, he hid from the security man when he did his rounds at six, or whenever it was, and sneaked down near his office, hid again, and got out after he'd let the police and ambulance in.'

'And threw away the robe?'

'Or hid it. Dustbins, maybe.'

'Do they have industrial dustbins at the Abbey?' asked Ben.

'I expect so, in which case they were probably emptied very soon after the Sunday.'

'The police may not have let them empty the dustbins,' said Ben. 'They often don't, do they?'

'That's true, and they'd have found the robe before we knew it was missing.' Libby sighed. 'I just woke up thinking about that robe, and realised that we haven't even thought about it since Pete took the others back up to London.'

'Ian will have,' said Ben. 'Forget about it. It isn't our problem.'

'Well, David is if he's still trying to ferret information out of us.'

'Perhaps you'll find something else out today,' said Ben. 'Now, give us a cuddle and then I'll go and cook you a proper breakfast as a treat.'

When Ben had left for the Manor, Libby was restless. She wandered into the conservatory and peered disconsolately at the painting on the easel, then out at the damp garden. Summer really hadn't taken off this year, she thought, although as a lot of the garden had been destroyed in a fire just before last Christmas, it was hardly surprising that it wasn't looking its best. That reminded her of the gap in the hedge, and she went outside to have a look at it.

'I wonder if it was Estelle?' she murmured to Sidney,

who had decided to accompany her. 'And if it was, what did she want? And where did she go from here?'

She stood looking up at the trees which pressed closely to the back gardens of Allhallow's Lane and led on to the Manor estate land.

'Ian and Sergeant Maiden saw a figure escaping into the woods which they thought was Estelle,' said Libby to Sidney. 'I wonder why they thought that. And why they were sure it was her on the run from Dominic's house? There's something they weren't telling me, isn't there, Sidney?'

She began to walk along the edge of the woods, Sidney trotting happily beside her, his tail in the air, pleased to have this entirely unexpected outing with his human.

'Mustn't be too long, though,' she said to him. 'I've left the back door unlocked.'

They came to where Allhallow's Lane petered out and a track led across the estate land. Occasionally, Ben would drive the four by four this way. You could get to the bridge where Peter had once fallen into the ditch, and to the "new" Hoppers' Huts, which had been built to replace the original ones, and were now being let experimentally as self-catering units. At least, they were hoping to, thought Libby, with a sigh.

Sidney wandered back to the woods, leaving Libby to walk along the track by herself. The ground, not as muddy as it would be in the autumn and winter, was still not pleasant, due to the unseasonal weather the country had been suffering, and Libby wasn't wearing the right shoes, but she carried on, just to see if she could work out where Estelle might have been going.

'She could have cut through here and gone down the Manor drive,' said Libby out loud, 'but where from there?'

Perhaps she had left her car in the village before going

to Dominic's house and came this way back to retrieve it. And then there was the puzzle of how she had got in to Dominic's house – and out again. Libby frowned at her feet and, looking up, realised she was almost at the Hoppers' Huts.

And one of them was occupied.

Chapter Thirty

Libby's heart was thumping. The little window next to the front door in the end hut was open, although there was no sound from within. She dithered. She didn't have her phone with her, so couldn't call Ben, and her sensible side realised that going and challenging whoever was in there would be stupid.

Had the person inside seen her? Did he or she know there was someone outside? She stood, rooted to the spot, not knowing whether to retrace her steps as quickly as possible and call Ben from home, or go on to the Manor and hope he was in the office.

Finally deciding it would be faster to go home, she began to walk quickly back down the track. Perhaps, after all, Ben had sent cleaners in, or maybe they'd had a last-minute booking she knew nothing about? Not convinced by either, she almost fell through the hedge, where there had once been a gate, ran across the garden into the house and grabbed her phone.

'What's the matter?' said Ben. 'Have you been running?'

'Yes. Ben, there's someone in one of the Hoppers' Huts.'

'What? There can't be!'

'The window's open on the end one. I was too scared to knock.'

'I'll go over now.'

'Not on your own! Ben, you can't!'

'All right, all right. I'll rustle up someone to come with me.'

'Pete – get Pete.'

'I'll see. Now – I'm going. Stay with the phone, I might need you to phone the police.'

Libby stood for a moment, thinking, then went and found the old trainers again, put her phone in her pocket and left the house again, this time locking up and leaving through the front door.

As she once more approached the huts, she saw the four by four bouncing along over the ruts coming from the other direction. She also saw, to her dismay, that the window was now closed.

'He must have seen me,' she said disconsolately as Peter and Ben came up to her.

'I'll go and have a look,' said Ben. Peter followed him up to the front door. Ben put the key in the lock and looked over his shoulder. 'Unlocked,' he said and pushed the door wide.

After waiting a moment to see if anything rushed out at them, Libby approached cautiously and peered inside.

'Someone's been here,' said Ben. 'Camping out, by the look of it.'

'Any take-away cartons?' asked Libby, remembering a previous occasion when someone had occupied one of the huts without their knowledge.

'No, but the bin hasn't been emptied,' said Peter. 'Call the police.'

'Proper police?' asked Libby. 'I mean – 999, like Ian said?'

Ben sighed. 'I suppose so. I'll do it.'

Peter and Libby surveyed the tiny space while he made the call. 'I suppose we mustn't touch anything,' said Libby. 'Evidence.'

'She must have gone as soon as you were out of sight, the same as last Monday at Dominic's place. The incredible vanishing Estelle.'

'We don't know it is Estelle,' said Libby.

'Who else could it be? Not David – we know he's safely ensconced in his cottage.'

'He could have driven back here after dropping Susannah off.'

'What for?' said Peter. 'To keep an eye on you?'

'Oh, I don't know, then.' Libby went up behind Ben, who had been studying the front door. 'How did she get in?'

'No idea. Doesn't look as though the lock's been damaged.' He looked up. 'Police.'

A patrol car was making heavy weather of the track. It came to a standstill just behind Ben's four by four and two disgruntled-looking officers got out. Ben explained the situation.

'Had a murder here a year or so back, didn't you?' said one, pulling on gloves to go and inspect the hut.

'Yes,' said Libby.

The policeman eyed her suspiciously. 'And you are?'

Ben made introductions and explained that Libby had been the one who made the discovery of the hut's occupation.

The other officer was assiduously jotting things down in his notebook, then went across to his colleague and held a low-voiced discussion.

'Reporting this further up the line, sir,' said the original officer, coming back to Ben. 'Understand there's another murder investigation going on.' He looked suspiciously from Ben to Libby, who had to quench a desire to laugh.

'We'll just have a look round while we wait for a member of DCI Connell's team to take over,' said the other

251

officer. 'If you'd like to – er – go home?'

'I'm going back to work,' said Ben. 'DCI Connell has my number.'

'And mine,' said Peter and Libby together.

'Can I come back with you?' Libby asked Ben.

'Come on, we'll all go back to the Manor and Hetty can make us coffee,' said Ben.

Hetty looked surprised to see them, but immediately set about making coffee.

'Bright officer, that,' said Ben.

'Eh?' said Libby.

'Picking up that this could be relevant to Ian's investigation,' said Peter.

'The other one only remembered the last murder we had here,' grumbled Libby. 'I think he thought it had something to do with me.'

'Guilty conscience,' said Ben. 'I wonder who they'll send over?'

'Will they want to see us?' said Libby.

'Of course they will. I suppose, unless anyone's got anything else on, we might as well wait for them here,' said Ben. 'Is that all right, Mum?'

'Course. Want some lunch, do yer?'

Peter's face brightened at the thought of a non-vegetarian lunch.

'That would be lovely, thank you, Hetty,' said Libby. 'Can I do anything?'

'Soup's made.' said Hetty. 'No need.'

Eventually, they were all surprised to see Inspector Davies being ushered in, looking as sheepish as ever.

'Forensics are there, now,' he told them, after asking them to repeat what they'd told the officer earlier. 'Whoever it was left in a hurry, presumably after seeing you, Mrs Sarjeant, and there's plenty of evidence in the bin, although the bed had been protected by something.'

'Sleeping bag?' suggested Libby.

'Possibly,' said Davies. 'As I say, we can't tell. I'm sure DCI Connell will be in touch in due course, and I don't need to tell you not to enter the premises. Oh, and could I have any sets of keys you have.'

'Of course.' Ben went to fetch them from the office.

'Is that it, then?' asked Libby, as Davies wrote out a receipt. 'Nothing else?'

'Not at the moment, madam,' he said, smiling – sheepishly – and, on silent feet, left the room.

'Soup?' said Hetty.

Libby fetched soup plates, while Ben brought out newly baked bread and Peter collected spoons.

'So?' said Libby, when they were seated. 'What do we think?'

'Estelle, it's got to be,' said Peter.

'But why?' said Ben.

'Because she's up to no good,' said Libby.

'But what sort of no good?' said Peter. 'She's not the murderer.'

'How do we know? She could have been inside the missing robe to avoid blood spatters,' said Libby. 'It makes sense, you know. If she and Dominic planned to steal the reliquary, he could have got her in to the audience, then hidden them both until we'd all gone, when they would wait for Martha to come down and open up the atrium doors to let them in.'

'That means Martha would have to have been in it, too,' said Peter.

'Well, no, they could have threatened her, wearing the robes so she wouldn't recognise them. They probably didn't mean to kill her,' said Libby.

'But Dominic was killed earlier,' said Ben, 'so where

253

does that leave Estelle?'

With a collective sigh, they turned to their soup.

'We're rehearsing again tonight, aren't we?' said Peter later, as he and Libby walked down the Manor drive.

'Soloists only,' said Libby, 'as we all know the chorus numbers back to front. I'm going to call Susannah and say we don't need David.'

'But then she won't have a lift.'

'She came on her own before,' said Libby. 'I don't suppose she'll mind.'

'Is this something to do with David?' Susannah asked shrewdly, when Libby called her.

'No – we just don't really need him for the soloists.'

'But you did before, to rehearse his sound effects and infills,' said Susannah.

'Well, he's done that,' said Libby, feeling uncomfortable.

'Come on, Libby. I don't know you very well, but even I can tell there's something about David that bothers you. And not just you, the others, too.'

Libby sighed. 'Look, Susannah, please don't say anything about this anywhere, especially not to David, but it turns out he's got a connection to the murder in the Monastery. The police have asked us not to say anything, but the fact that he leapt at the chance of coming into the show, means he's trying to find something out. Do you see?'

'I do,' said Susannah slowly. 'I told you, didn't I, that I was surprised at his eagerness. And I didn't know why he was down here in the first place. I wish you'd told me when I first said I'd bring him.'

'But no one knew who he was, then. It was only after the first time he came that we found out from the police.'

'Is he dangerous?'

'We don't think so. He certainly wasn't around when the murder happened.'

'So what's his connection to the case, then?'

'I'd rather not tell you that, Susannah, if you don't mind. He's just connected to someone else who's …'

'Connected to the case,' Susannah finished for her. 'OK, Libby, I get it, and I'll call him and tell him he's not needed tonight. But what if he's says he'd like to come anyway?'

'In that case we can hardly stop him,' said Libby. 'It's just that it's proving a bit of a strain for us having him around, even though he's a very good drummer.'

Susannah gave a short laugh. 'It's going to be a bit of a strain for me, now, too. Still, I asked. My own fault. You do manage to get yourselves mixed up in stuff, don't you?'

'I know,' sighed Libby. 'And honestly, I don't know how it happens. Certainly this time the only thing I did wrong was to tell Peter about the story of the reliquary.'

'Oh, well, don't they say each person is the author of his own downfall, or something like that? Your actor who was murdered must have had a reason to be murdered.'

'That's true,' murmured Libby. 'I hadn't thought about it like that.'

'See you later, then,' said Susannah. 'Minus David.'

Libby had barely time to go into the kitchen to put the kettle on when the phone rang again.

'Libby, it's Andrew. I've found out a bit more about the Glover family.'

'Oh, good – what is it?'

'Can you and Fran come over?

Libby glanced at the clock. 'Not now, Andrew. Can't you tell me over the phone?'

Andrew sighed. 'All right, but it's easier when I can show you properly.'

'Try,' said Libby.

'I told you your Estelle Butcher was the great-granddaughter of the Glovers?'

'Yes. Wilcox? Was that her name?'

'Her parents were Maureen and Barry Wilcox. Maureen was the daughter of Robert Glover, May and Albert's son.'

'So the first generation of the Tollybar/Beaumont alliance?'

'That's right,' said Andrew. 'And remember I said there were other children?'

'Robert's siblings?'

'Just so. And one of them was Jessica. So I started looking for her marriage certificate.'

'And?' prompted Libby, by now aware that Andrew would hang this out, and that she had deprived him of an afternoon's socialising. He sighed again.

'I couldn't find a marriage certificate for her, so eventually I looked for her death certificate. And when I found it, the person who had given the information – you know that has to be on a death certificate?'

'Yes?'

'Was one Edgar Glover, son.'

'Goodness! So she had a child out of wedlock? That was scandalous back then, wasn't it?'

'It certainly was. It also gave me a point to start looking for her and Edgar, and I discovered that she had ended up in the least salubrious part of the East End of London, and Edgar had been in prison at least twice. I don't know if it's of any relevance, but one of his former cell mates was a solicitor's clerk.'

Libby's mind leapt ahead. 'A solicitor's clerk? Who might have known about Bernard's visit to the Abbey?

And why?'

'Ah yes! And Edgar was a member of the family,' agreed Andrew. 'Sounds likely, doesn't it?

Chapter Thirty-one

Libby wasn't surprised when, as she and Ben were eating a hasty supper before leaving for the theatre, Ian called.

'Andrew told me what he found out,' he said. 'Why he has to tell you before calling me, I don't know.'

'He's not used to being a police informant,' said Libby.

'He isn't an informant! He's an expert witness.'

'Was it right, though? Did Edgar's cell mate provide him with the information about Bernard and the reliquary?'

'It looks like it. The man was certainly working for the solicitor whom Bernard had appointed. In fact, it was the same solicitor who had worked for old Ronald Barnes, and you'll be pleased to know that Andrew has also proved the link between Barnes and the Beaumonts. He, too, is a descendant of Jarvis.'

'So we *are* getting on,' said Libby. 'Does it get us anywhere, though?'

'Us, Libby?'

'Oh, Ian, you wouldn't be calling me otherwise!'

'All right, all right. But it does look possible that Estelle knew her Uncle Edgar –'

'Well, of course she did, but he's actually her first cousin once removed.' interrupted Libby.

'Let's call him "Uncle" for now. Anyway, she needn't necessarily have known him, if Jessica and he were black sheep. But if she did, she might well have known if he stole the reliquary and murdered Bernard.'

'He'd never have told a child though. How old is he

now? He must still be alive?'

'Drank himself to death on a Caribbean island, apparently, having come into money in his twenties.'

'There you are!' said Libby. 'Proof!'

'Possible, anyway,' said Ian.

'What about Estelle's mum – Maureen, was it? Isn't she still alive?'

'Cancer, ten years ago. And her father Barry, was much older than his wife and is now in a home.'

'Oh, poor Estelle,' said Libby. 'She must think the world's against her.'

'I don't see why.' Libby could hear the frown in Ian's voice. 'It happens all the time.'

Unsympathetic Calvinist, thought Libby.

'So where do we go from here?' she said aloud.

'*We* don't go anywhere, Libby. I'm keeping you informed out of courtesy, and just in case Estelle should make contact with you.'

'I don't see why she should,' said Libby. 'I doubt if she's going to offer us rent for the Hoppers' Hut. Oh, and Susannah Baker knows David Fletcher has a connection to the murder.'

'I told you not to say anything.'

'I know, but she worked it out for herself. He was so pointedly asking questions last night that he was making everyone uncomfortable. So she asked me. I didn't tell her who he was or what connection he had, though.'

'Can't you get rid of him?'

'Not easy,' said Libby, 'although we have done for tonight.'

Later, after rehearsal, which finished earlier than usual, Susannah asked if they were going for a drink.

'Not tonight, but we could have one here, if you like,' said Libby. 'Why?'

259

'I just wanted to talk to you. Or those of you who are involved in – this – er –'

'Business?' suggested Libby. 'Yes, OK, we can open the bar. But wait until all the others have gone.'

Peter opened the bar, while Ben, Libby, Fran and Susannah sat down at the little white tables.

'I just wanted to say that I've always found David to be a really nice guy,' Susannah began, 'and I can't believe he'd be involved in anything – well, criminal.'

'What do you know about him?' asked Peter, bringing wine and glasses to the table. 'I'm making coffee for you and Fran, by the way.'

'Thanks,' said Susannah, 'very kind of you. Well, now, David. He's classically trained, did I tell you that?'

They all shook their heads.

'He trained at the Guildhall and the Northern,' Susannah went on, 'and it was there he met up with some other musicians who were very much into big band music. He started playing with them and gradually got into that particular club of big band players. Most of the bands you might have heard of in that genre have the same musicians. He also got into pit playing –'

'What playing?' asked Peter.

'The pit,' explained Libby. 'For musicals and stuff.'

'His wife liked that better because he was in one place for a time, rather than all over the country and the continent.'

'His wife?' said Fran, while the others sat frozen.

'Yes. I never knew her, he kept her rather in the background.' Susannah frowned. 'I wondered if she was ill or something, he was always having to rush off home.'

'Jealous?' suggested Ben.

'Him or her? Oh, I can see why any spouse not in the business would be jealous,' said Susannah.

'So can I,' said Fran. 'Mine was.'

'Yours?' Susannah looked surprised.

'Oh, not Guy. My first husband,' said Fran. 'Anyway getting back to David …'

'That's just it. He seemed concerned about his wife. Or that's how it seemed. He seemed a nice guy.'

'And you never saw any evidence of him playing around?' asked Libby.

'Not personally. There are always rumours.'

'Yes,' said Libby and Fran together, nodding sagely.

'Well, that's all I wanted to say, really,' said Susannah. 'I don't know how he's connected with this murder, but I'm sure he's done nothing wrong.'

'I hope not,' sighed Libby. 'But he's been seen recently with –'

'Libby!' said three voices.

'Someone,' she continued with dignity, 'who has a close connection with the murder. So we have to be vigilant.'

'I see.' Susannah looked down into her coffee mug. 'I wish I hadn't asked him in, now.'

'Don't worry about it,' said Libby. 'It's nobody's fault.'

'Suppose he's arrested before the show? Or even during it?' said Susannah.

'As long as it's before the show, we can carry on without him,' said Libby. 'And I think we'd know if his arrest was imminent.'

'Oh, yes, your connections with the police,' said Susannah with a smile. 'That makes us all feel a bit safer, I suppose.'

'I wouldn't count on it,' said Peter darkly.

Susannah took her leave shortly after this, and the others finished their wine. 'I should have offered to drive her,' said Fran. 'I never thought.'

'You didn't know I'd asked David not to come,' said

Libby. 'So what do we think?'

'What do you mean?' asked Peter.

'I honestly thought when she asked to talk to us she was going to pull out,' said Libby. 'She admitted this afternoon that knowing David was connected to the case was going to put a strain on her.'

'It wouldn't have surprised me in the least,' said Fran. 'But she hasn't.'

'Because she's a professional.' Ben picked up the empty glasses and mugs. 'Even though she's not getting paid, she wouldn't let us down.'

'Did you tell Peter about Andrew's latest find?' asked Fran, as Ben went round checking all the theatre doors.

'What's that?' asked Peter. Libby told him about Uncle Edgar and the solicitor's clerk.

'So,' said Peter, as they left the building, 'Estelle sits on Uncle Edgar's knee while he regales her with tales of derring do and murder, and later on she thinks she might as well do the same? Is that what we think?'

'It's a bit far-fetched,' said Ben.

'But there is the family link,' said Fran. 'Presumably, Edgar was one of those who wanted to use the reliquary for gain, and felt entitled to it.'

'I suppose Ian now has to find out if it was Edgar who sold it to Mr Marshall,' said Libby, 'but I'm sure the police have looked into that, and he would have used an intermediary.'

'I wonder if that solicitor's clerk was questioned at the time of Bernard's murder,' mused Fran.

'I expect he would have been, but all he had to do was deny knowing anything. After all, we think all he did was pass the information to Edgar.'

'However, my dears,' said Peter, as they came to the end of the drive, 'this is all pure speculation, however inviting it may seem. God speed, farewell and *bonne nuit*.'

'Oh, damn,' said Fran. 'Why did I walk down here with you? My car's at the top of the drive.'

'I'll walk back with you,' said Ben. 'It's dark up there.'

'I'll come, too,' said Libby, 'or I'll have to walk home on my own.'

Ben grinned at her. 'And you know how I love that!' He put an arm through hers and the other through Fran's. 'Come along, harem.'

The Manor and the theatre were in darkness as they approached, until the security light went on over the Manor's front door. Hetty's rooms were at the back of the house to avoid this disturbing her.

'What's that?' Libby stopped.

'What?' said Ben.

'Sssh!'

'Back of the theatre,' murmured Fran.

Ben's eyes widened. 'Stay here,' he whispered, and padded off round the side of the building.

The women remained still, and after a minute or two the light went off. Then: 'Libby!' Ben's voice sounded strange.

The light came on again as Libby and Fran ran round the side of the theatre and found Ben, sitting on the floor holding his head.

'I think you'd better call the police,' he said shakily. 'We've had another attempted break-in.'

'Your head!' said Libby, on her knees beside him, while Fran had her mobile out.

'Whoever it was was trying to get in through the scene dock doors. I surprised him and got hit for my pains. I don't know what with, but it felt like a ton weight.'

'Could you see who it was?' Libby had one arm round him, while the other held a tissue to his head where blood was seeping through.

'No,' said Ben. 'I think it was wearing the missing robe.'

Chapter Thirty-two

Despite his protests, Ben was taken to hospital. Libby went with him in the ambulance and wasn't in the least surprised to arrive in A and E and find Ian waiting for them. Neither was she surprised when they were whisked straight through the waiting area with its due complement of drunks.

When Ben was taken through to have an MRI scan, Ian fetched Libby a machine-made coffee, and one for himself.

'Better than the tea, I speak from experience,' he said. 'Now tell me exactly what happened.'

Libby, still feeling very wobbly, duly told her story.

'If only I hadn't heard that noise it wouldn't have happened,' she finished. 'Why do I go blundering –'

Ian laid a hand on her arm. 'Stop that, Libby. For once, you weren't blundering in, and Ben had a duty to investigate if someone was trying to break into the theatre.'

'But you always say not to,' said Libby. 'We could have ignored it, or just called the police.'

'And said what? You heard a noise at night? With fields backing up to the building? I can imagine what the control would have thought of that, not to mention the patrol which was sent to investigate.'

Libby sighed, took a sip of coffee and made a face.

'Under the current circumstances, having only this morning discovered a break-in on your premises –'

'Not exactly on –'

'You know what I mean,' said Ian severely. 'It's natural

to wonder what was going on. Didn't you suspect, even briefly, that it was the same person who had been in the hut? Honestly?'

'Yes, of course we did,' admitted Libby. 'If we'd have called 999 with that story, would it have been any different?'

'I suppose it might,' said Ian, 'but what I'm getting at is – it's not your fault. Nor is it Ben's.'

Libby nodded, but her expression was doubtful. 'Did they find anything?'

'It doesn't look like it. There were marks on the door as if someone had been trying to get the padlock off.'

'There weren't any marks on the door of the hut.'

'No, but there are no padlocks on those doors. It could be that whoever it was expected it to be as easy to get into the theatre.'

'But why? If it is Estelle, why is she haunting us?'

'I don't think you, particularly, I think it's just hiding places.'

Libby shook her head. 'I still don't see why. Or how she got into Dominic's house when you'd had it locked down tight.'

Ian smiled. 'I think I've already told you once in this case, Lib, I don't always tell you everything.'

Libby looked up at him in surprise. 'You mean you *let* her get in?'

'And you and Harry rather spoiled it.'

Libby felt the warmth spreading up her neck and into her cheeks. 'We weren't to know!'

'You weren't supposed to be there, either.'

'All right, all right. Now you know why I said I was blundering –'

'Stop it.'

Libby sighed again. 'So the thinking is what? Estelle

broke into Dominic's house, was flushed out of there, found the hut and was discovered again and decided to see if she could take shelter in the theatre?'

'Makes sense, doesn't it?'

'It does, but I don't see why. What was she looking for, if anything?'

'I'm not sure she was looking for anything,' said Ian. 'She let herself in with a key. I'm pretty sure that despite what everyone thought, they were still in touch.'

'The robe!' said Libby, sitting up straight. 'The person who attacked Ben was wearing it.'

'Which means that whoever it was is involved in this case, doesn't it?'

'And Dominic could have given her the robe.' Libby frowned. 'So she must have been involved in the theft of the reliquary.'

'But it wasn't stolen.'

'Oh, bugger, so it wasn't.' Libby got to her feet and went to peer through the door through which Ben had been wheeled away. 'Why is he being such a long time?'

Ian laughed. 'You haven't spent much time in hospitals recently, then. And don't worry about him. I think this MRI is only a precaution.'

'But you hear such awful things about bangs on the head ...' said Libby.

'Not when everything's been so thoroughly investigated,' said Ian. 'And look, here he is now.'

Ben appeared in a wheelchair looking distinctly grumpy, with a young, tired-looking doctor beside him.

'They want to keep me in overnight,' he said. 'Ian, can't you talk to them?'

'I think it's advisable,' said the doctor, giving Ben a dirty look. 'It was quite a heavy blow. We can't see anything suspicious on the scan, but Mr Wilde ought to be monitored.'

'I think you ought to stay, Ben,' said Ian. 'I'll take Libby home and she can come and get you tomorrow.'

'Oh, can't I stay?' asked Libby.

The young doctor looked uncomfortable, but Ben forestalled him.

'No, you go home, Lib. You need to tell everyone what's happened, and you'll have to call Mum when you get home.'

Hetty had come out of the Manor when the ambulance had arrived, and, although appearing outwardly her usual calm and phlegmatic self, Ben and Libby both knew how worried she would be.

'All right,' said Libby with a sigh. She turned to the doctor. 'Is he going to be all right?'

The doctor gave a tired smile. 'I think he's fine. We just need to keep an eye on him.'

Libby bent to kiss Ben and found, to her surprise, that there was a painful lump in her throat and her lips were quivering.

'Go on with you,' he whispered. 'See you in the morning. Love you.'

Ian led a silent Libby outside to his car.

'Thanks,' she said, as he helped her into the car. 'It's out of your way.'

'I must take care of my star witness,' said Ian. 'I have the utmost faith in your ability to get to the bottom of the whole business in next to no time.'

'Liar,' said Libby, obscurely comforted, and relapsed into silence.

Half an hour later, Ian drew up outside number 17.

'Are you OK? Do you want me to come in with you?' he asked.

'No, thanks, Ian. I'll pour myself a large whisky and

phone Hetty and Fran. I hope I don't wake them.'

'It's only one o'clock,' said Ian. 'I expect they're both still waiting for news. Oh – and I'm told Peter and Harry came tearing up the drive after you'd gone off in the ambulance, so you'd better call them, too.'

'I will,' Libby promised, and leant over to kiss Ian's cheek. 'Thanks for being there tonight. I know you were there because it's your job, but still.'

'I needn't have come,' said Ian. 'It would have been normal procedure to have a uniform in attendance. I was there as a friend.'

'And you got us through in record time,' said Libby.

'Head injuries are always seen quickly.' He, in turn, kissed Libby's cheek. 'Off you go. I'll be in touch.'

Libby let herself in, idly stroked Sidney's head as he looked up from the sofa, and poured herself the promised whisky, after which she phoned Hetty, who answered immediately.

'All right, gal,' she said after being reassured. 'I'll come with you in the morning.'

Fran was also waiting for the call.

'I wasn't worried,' she said. 'I don't know why.'

'That's actually reassuring,' said Libby. 'But listen to what Ian told me.'

Fran agreed to discuss it in detail the following day and to speak to everyone who might need to know, then Libby called Peter's mobile.

'I thought it was Hetty when I saw the blue lights,' he said. 'Why didn't you call me?'

'You couldn't have done anything,' said Libby. 'He's OK, a bit sore and grumpy, but all you would have done is go haring off into the darkness and probably got hit on the head, too.'

'Bloody woman,' Peter grumbled.

'Me?'

'No, that Estelle. I knew she was trouble the minute she turned up on the doorstep.'

'We don't know it was her,' said Libby.

'Hmm,' said Peter. 'Can I come with you tomorrow?'

'No, Pete, Hetty's coming, and we don't want to overcrowd him. I'll ring you when we're home.'

Libby switched off the phone, finished her whisky and climbed slowly up the stairs.

'I'll never sleep,' she told Sidney, whom she had allowed to join her. 'I know I won't.'

But she did.

The following morning the phone woke her with a call from Bob the Butcher, who wanted to know if he could do anything. He was followed by various other members of the theatre company, until, in order to shower in peace, she switched off both the landline and her mobile.

When she was ready, she called the hospital and was told yes, she could collect Mr Wilde as soon as she liked. She called Hetty, who said she would be ready at the end of the drive, then left a message for Ian and set off.

They found Ben, dressed, with a bandage on his head, sitting at the nurse's station in his ward, clutching a large envelope.

'That's for your GP,' said a nurse to Libby, as though Ben were a child. No wonder he still looked grumpy, she thought.

'So how is it?' she asked as soon as they were back in the car.

'A bit painful,' said the patient with a sigh. 'But not too bad. I've had stitches,' he added proudly.

'Wow!' said Libby, admiringly. 'Everyone's been asking after you.'

'How did they know?'

'The village,' said Hetty succinctly from the back seat.

'Any news from Ian?'

Libby flicked him a warning glance. 'Not yet.'

'Right.' Ben subsided into his seat. 'I'll just close my eyes for a bit. You've no idea how noisy it is in a hospital at night.'

After they'd delivered Hetty to the Manor, Libby drove carefully back to Allhallow's Lane.

'Now, do you want to go to bed?' she asked.

'No, I want to know what Ian said.' Ben sat down carefully on the sofa. 'I'd like a decent cup of tea, though.'

Libby told him what Ian had said the previous night while she made a pot of good strong tea.

'Pete says it's got to be Estelle,' said Libby, 'and although Ian won't say it definitely is, I bet he thinks so, too.'

'I think it's got to be her, too,' said Ben, 'although, for a woman, she packs a powerful punch.'

'Perhaps she used the crowbar or whatever it was she was trying to get the lock off with,' said Libby.

'And,' said Ben, frowning, 'where did she get that from? If she's been hanging around on the estate all day since she left the hut, I bet she stole it from the yard.'

'Well, yes, if it was her, or if it was all the same person but not Estelle, but we don't know that, either.'

'We don't know if it was Estelle, and we don't know if it was the same person who was in the hut this morning.'

'Yes,' said Libby. 'Complicated, isn't it?'

'And you say Ian says she had a key to Dominic's house?'

'Yes. He actually said she let herself in with a key. I don't know how he knows that.'

'Perhaps they found a key that hadn't been there before?'

'You know what?' said Libby, 'you're thinking too much. You need to get some rest.'

Ben smiled. 'Trying to get rid of me already?' He sat up and held out a hand. 'Help me up, then. Are you going to undress me?'

'That would be bad for you,' said Libby primly. 'I shall watch you go up from the bottom of the stairs.'

'Spoil sport,' said Ben, and slowly climbed the stairs.

After checking that he was indeed in bed, Libby went back to the front room and poured herself another cup of tea before ringing Fran.

'Yes, he's fine. A bit grumpy, and he didn't sleep much, so he's gone up for a rest now. But what I'm wondering is, what will Estelle do next?'

'If it was Estelle who hit Ben and who was also in the hut yesterday morning, I don't think she'd try anything else, she'd be too exposed. She'd know the police would be all over the place.'

'Will they?'

'Of course. They'll be up there now, searching the estate.'

'Really? I must find out.'

'But what does she want?'

'Ian says she doesn't want anything, she's just hiding. If it is her.'

'But hiding from whom?'

'Well, the police, I suppose,' said Libby.

'That doesn't make sense. Until she broke into Dominic's house – which is debatable, anyway – she hadn't done anything wrong. So who is she hiding from?'

'If it is Estelle,' said Libby firmly, 'she's certainly done something wrong now, by walloping my Ben.'

'Yes, but she was hiding before that. Have you told Susannah?'

'No, not yet. I suppose I should. Will she tell David, do you think? You don't think he could have anything to do with last night?'

'We don't know what David has to do with any of it,' said Fran. 'And to be honest, I don't think we can keep this quiet. All the cast know what happened by now. It's possible, even, that David knows already.'

'Oh, dear,' said Libby. 'I'll call Susannah, then.'

But before she could do so, the phone rang again.

'Libby, it's Andrew. I tried you and Fran just now, but you were engaged.'

'Yes, we were talking,' began Libby.

'Listen a moment. I've left a message for Ian, but I thought both of you would want to know.'

'Know what?'

'Cornelia Fletcher is also a descendant of May and Albert Glover.'

Chapter Thirty-three

'She's *what*?' Libby sat down with a bump. 'Good God!'

'You remember I told you Albert and May had three children?'

'Yes, and Estelle is their great-granddaughter, from their son – er –'

'Robert. That's right. And last time I told you about Jessica and Edgar?'

'Yes?'

'Albert and May's third child was Caroline, who had a daughter Jean who was Cornelia's mother.'

'So Uncle Edgar is hers, too,' said Libby. 'Do you think she knows?'

'That would be first cousin once removed Edgar,' said Andrew. 'I wonder if either Mrs Fletcher or Mrs Butcher know? It's not the sort of thing you brag about, is it?'

'Ian and I were talking about it – lord, only yesterday morning – and speculating that Estelle knew. It's just as likely that Cornelia did, too.'

'Well, Cornelia's family were a different kettle of fish from Jessica's and Robert's. Her grandmother Caroline was the eldest of the Glover children, and she had friends among the solid middle classes of children who grew up between the wars. She was taken under the wing of another girl's family, and met and married a young man who, while not exactly aristocracy, was certainly upper middle class. Sadly he died in the war, and never saw Jean, Cornelia's mother, but Caroline and Jean were taken to live with his parents and were very comfortable.'

'So it's unlikely she ever knew Uncle Edgar?'

'She might not even have heard of him, but it's hard to believe that when you look at the circumstances.'

'I suppose it could just be coincidence,' said Libby, doubtfully.

'That she was attacked in front of the reliquary that it's almost certain her relative murdered for and stole?' said Andrew.

'So what about her husband?' asked Libby after a moment.

'Nothing. Middle class parents, grammar school, music degree and postgraduate diploma. All I can see is the bare facts, I know nothing about how he met his wife, nor when they separated, but apparently they aren't divorced.'

'I knew that,' said Libby.

'You did?' Andrew sounded startled.

'Yes, when I was talking to Martha – Cornelia – before all this began. She said before she joined the Abbey she'd been married and still was.'

'Well, it strikes me that there must be a connection,' said Andrew. 'I wonder if the cousins knew each other?'

'I wonder,' said Libby. 'Was Robert Glover's family well off? Middle-class?'

'Fairly ordinary, I think, but there's no way I can find out if they kept in touch with Caroline's family. As far as I can tell, they didn't live near each other.'

'Oh, dear, isn't this frustrating?' said Libby. 'Do you think Ian will challenge Martha with this?'

'You know him better than I do,' said Andrew, 'but he'd be foolish not to, wouldn't he?'

'He would,' said Libby, 'but he keeps saying she mustn't be worried.' She frowned. 'I wonder why.'

'Because she had a bad knock on the head?'

275

'Well, so has Ben, but he doesn't seem too worried about that,' said Libby.

'What? You didn't tell me that!'

'I didn't get a chance,' said Libby. 'That's what Fran and I were talking about on the phone when you tried to get through.' She explained about last night's events, including the possibility that Estelle was the perpetrator and the illegal occupier of the Hoppers' Hut.

'It does seem as though she might be dangerous,' said Andrew. 'And what's she after, do you think?'

'We did wonder if she thought the reliquary had been stolen, because it was never reported that it wasn't,' said Libby. 'She might be looking for it.'

'In your Hoppers' Huts?' said Andrew incredulously.

'Well, no, but in Dominic's house.'

'She knows he's dead and he died in the monastery,' said Andrew. 'He couldn't have got the reliquary out, could he?'

'No.' Libby sighed. 'Oh, I give up.'

'I doubt that,' said Andrew. 'I'll let you know if I find out anything else, or if DCI Connell gets in touch.'

Libby immediately called Fran and reported the conversation.

'What do you think?' she finished. 'Do you think Martha's involved?'

'With what? She was one of the victims,' said Fran.

'Well, of course she's involved to that extent,' said Libby. 'But she's actually a Beaumont/Tollybar descendant and cousin-in-law to the main victim. There's got to be a connection.'

'She never showed any sign of knowing Dominic, or he her,' said Fran, 'although I suppose they didn't come into contact much.'

'If the families had lost touch she probably wouldn't

know who he was,' said Libby, 'and from what Andrew says, it's quite likely they didn't even know of each other's existence – Martha and Estelle, I mean.'

'Meanwhile, what do you suppose Ian will do about this?' said Fran. 'Will he talk to Martha?'

'I don't think he can avoid it,' said Libby. 'I wonder if the Abbey would let me in to talk to her?'

'Libby! Of course you can't! What were you thinking of doing? Questioning her before Ian could get to her?'

'Well …'

'Don't be silly. If there's anything Ian wants us to know he'll tell us.'

Libby went into the kitchen and took her frustration out on leeks and potatoes for soup, and swore when the phone rang again.

'I'm bringin' a stew down for yer dinner, later,' said the laconic voice of Hetty. 'Save cookin'.'

Feeling ashamed, Libby put the vegetables in a stock pot and trailed up the stairs to see how Ben was. She found him staring out of the window, a frown on his face.

'You're supposed to be sleeping,' she said sitting on the edge of the bed.

'I can't,' said Ben. 'I keep thinking about the bloody case.'

'Well, before I bring you some soup – do you want soup? – I shall fill you in on the latest,' said Libby.

'Bloody hell,' said Ben, when she'd finished. 'So what happens next?'

'No idea,' said Libby. 'Fran and Andrew and I all think Ian will go and question Martha. She might know nothing about Estelle and Dominic.'

'Isn't that unlikely? A bit too much of a coincidence.'

'I suppose so. I want to talk to David.'

'Ian said you mustn't.'

'I know,' sighed Libby. 'It's so frustrating. I'm desperate to know who attacked you.'

'Funnily enough, so am I,' said Ben. 'What about that soup?'

Ben did fall asleep after lunch, and when Hetty turned up with her stew, she offered to sit and watch Libby's television instead of her own, allowing Libby to go out.

She wasn't sure where she wanted go, but back up the track on to the estate land seemed a good idea. The sky was grey again, so the old anorak and trainers were once more pressed into use, but this time Sidney declined to accompany her, as there was a new lap to sit on.

Despite the grey sky, the birds were still singing. Libby's favourite blackbird called to her as she left the house and from deep in the woods a variety of birdsong assured her that it *was* summer, even if it didn't look like it. She retraced her steps from the previous day, which now seemed like weeks ago and eventually came up to the Hoppers' Huts.

The blue–and-white police tape fluttered across the door, and all was still. Libby walked round behind the huts and peered at the ground. No sign of a vehicle, but then she would have seen that yesterday, if there had been one. There were plenty of tyre tracks in front of the huts from the police vehicles and Ben's car.

Libby carried on across the field until she came in sight of the yard where Ben kept his tractor and tools. It wasn't secured in any way, even though Ian had told him in the past about the many farm thefts the force had to deal with each year.

This afternoon it looked much as it always did. Libby wandered in to have a look at the tools but couldn't have guessed if any had been moved or if there were any missing. She looked up at the gallery, once a hayloft, and wondered if Estelle had hidden up there during the rest of yesterday until she came out for her attempt on the theatre. The rusty ladder didn't look as if it had been used, but Libby doubted she knew what to look for.

Anyway, she told herself as she left the yard, perhaps it wasn't Estelle. But if it wasn't, who else would be hiding in the hut? A random thief? A prisoner on the run? She wandered along the track towards the bridge, and finally on to the track that eventually led to the Manor and the theatre, remembering the first time Peter had brought her to look at the huts before they'd been renovated. It was always Peter or Harry forcing her into long and uncomfortable walks, she thought, grinning to herself, although her fitness levels had increased since living in the village.

Finally gaining the drive, and with no more idea of what had gone on yesterday than she had before her walk, she carried on into the high street and went into Nella's farm shop to buy Ben grapes.

'Are they for Ben?' asked Nella, putting them into a paper bag. 'How is he?'

'Everyone seems to know,' said Libby. 'He's fine, just a bit sore. His mum's sitting with him at the moment, but he'll be up and about tomorrow, I bet.'

'Give him our best,' said Nella. 'Awful thing to have happened.'

This was repeated all along the high street; Ali and Ahmed came out of the eight-til-late and Bob came out of his butcher's shop. By the time Libby reached number 17 she was glad to sit down and stop talking. Hetty made tea, took a cup up to Ben, and announced his intention of coming down for dinner.

'I hope he's all right to do that,' said Libby, 'although he seemed fine earlier.'

'He's good as gold,' said Hetty. 'Hard old head.'

Libby smiled affectionately at her mother-in-law-elect. 'Good genes,' she said.

Ben appeared half an hour later, showered and dressed, and looking, except for the dressing on his head, perfectly normal.

'It occurred to me,' he said, sitting on the sofa next to Libby, 'that no one checked inside the theatre last night, did they?'

'Yes,' said Hetty. 'Peter and Harry did, after you'd gone. With those policemen.'

'Ah. No one inside, then.'

'Well, of course not,' said Libby. 'You scared whoever it was off.'

'You don't think she was hiding inside and was just breaking out, realising she'd been locked in?'

Libby and Hetty looked incredulous.

'Are you sure you're all right?' Libby asked.

'I was just thinking what a stupid place it was to try and hide out, that's all,' said Ben. 'If that's what it was. After all, there's nothing to steal in the theatre, is there?'

'Our tech equipment and lights,' said Libby, 'but that would need a van to take it away. No, I don't think the theatre was being burgled.'

'No.' Ben sighed.

'I went and had a look at the yard this afternoon,' said Libby. 'I couldn't tell if anything was missing.'

'Did the police look at it?'

'Fran reckoned the police would have been all over the grounds this morning.'

'They were,' said Hetty. 'Come and ask permission. Don't know where they went. Left 'em to it.'

'Just have to wait until we hear from Ian, then,' said Libby. 'If we ever do.'

The three of them ate Hetty's stew sitting round the kitchen table, with Sidney perched hopefully next to the Rayburn. Ben heroically refused wine and consumed most of his bunch of grapes instead. Libby refused Hetty's offer of help to wash up and Ben declared his aim of escorting his mother home.

'Don't be daft,' she said. 'Supposed to rest. It's still light, ain't it?'

As soon as she'd left, Ben called Peter and asked him to watch out for her.

'He told me not to be an old woman, that my mother was walking home in broad daylight in her home village in full sight of people she'd known most of her life,' said Ben with a grin. 'I think that bump on the head must have affected me after all!'

Libby left him on the sofa while she went to tackle the washing-up and heard the phone ring again. Ben appeared in the doorway frowning, the phone still to his ear.

'Yes,' he was saying, 'but honestly, I think you'd better talk to Libby. She's right here.'

'David Fletcher,' he mouthed, holding out the receiver. 'He wants to talk about his wife.'

Chapter Thirty-four

'David?'

'Yes, Libby. Look, I'm sorry to bother you, but I know something's been going on with my wife, but I can't get anyone to talk about it. You're all blocking me every time I try and find out.'

Libby thought for a moment. 'If you'd been honest from the first it might have been different, but we were warned about you by the police.'

'The police?' David's voice rose several notches. 'What on earth for?'

'To find out that a person's estranged husband is making enquiries about her immediately after a murder and a vicious attack, seemingly under cover, is enough to make anyone suspicious,' said Libby. 'Have you spoken to the police now?'

'No, of course not. They wouldn't tell me anything the first time I asked.'

'Well, I should, if I were you,' said Libby, 'because whatever you tell me I shall pass on, and it would be better coming from you.'

There was a short silence. Then:

'All right. I'll call them now. Do I use 999?'

'No, I'll give you the number to use, just hold on a moment.' Libby reached for her mobile to look up Ian's official number. 'He wants to talk,' she whispered to Ben. 'What shall I do?'

'Ask him here,' said Ben, 'and I'll make sure Pete

knows he's coming in case of trouble.'

'Here you are,' said Libby into the phone, and gave David the number. 'I expect you'll have to leave a message. Meanwhile, if you're not doing anything, do you want to come over here and talk about it? I can't guarantee that we've got any answers, but we might have.'

'Would you mind? I don't seem to have endeared myself to any of you over the last couple of weeks.'

Libby sighed. 'No. Blame our suspicious minds. But do come over. We might be able to sort a few things out. Do you know where we are?'

'Aren't you at the Manor?'

'No, Ben's mother lives there. We live at number 17, Allhallow's Lane. Come down the hill from Nethergate, pass the Manor and theatre drive and it's the next on the left.'

'Half an hour, he said,' said Libby, switching off the phone. 'How much do we tell him?'

'I think we'll have to let him talk and just confirm where we can,' said Ben. 'I've called Pete.'

'We won't even know if he really has called Ian, either,' said Libby, turning back to the sink.

'Oh, I think he will have done, because he knows you will,' said Ben. 'And this, if I mistake not, Watson, will be our client now.' He answered the phone. 'Hello, Ian. We were just talking about you. Yes, we know, he's coming here to talk to us about it. What do we say? Oh, right. Half an hour – yes, that'll be fine. He'll be spooked, though.' He switched off the phone. 'Yes, David left a message and Ian's coming here, too.'

'You're right, he will be spooked. What do we say in the meantime?'

'Play it by ear,' said Ben with a grin. 'As if that isn't what you do all the time.'

By the time David knocked at the door, the washing-up was done and the big kettle was whispering to itself on the Rayburn.

'Coffee?' Libby offered, as he sat down in the chair opposite the sofa. 'I thought you wouldn't want a drink as you've got to drive home.'

'That would be lovely, thank you.' David looked round. 'Lovely cottage.'

'Thank you,' said Libby. 'I won't be a minute.'

She made coffee in a jug and put it on the tray with milk and mugs.

'So, what is it you want to tell us?' asked Ben, when they were settled.

'It's more what you can tell me,' said David. 'I read – or heard, I can't now remember – that my wife, Cornelia, had been hurt in an attack at St Eldreda's Abbey, and there was also a murder. I called the Abbey, but they wouldn't comment, neither would the police, so I decided to come down here and find out myself. I called Susannah because we've worked together several times and it was pure coincidence that you'd just asked her into your show.'

'Why did you want to find out about Cornelia?' asked Libby.

David looked surprised. 'Wouldn't you? If it was your husband?'

'But you no longer live together. She's cut all ties, she told me so herself.'

'So you do know her!' said David in triumph.

'Yes, I do, but as I said, she told me you'd cut all ties.'

'She did. Nothing to do with me. I wasn't surprised to hear that the attack had been in an Abbey, though.'

'Oh? Why?' said Ben.

'One of the reasons for the split. She had become more and more – well, religious, I suppose. And St Eldreda's, of

284

all places. I knew there must be something up.'

Libby and Ben looked at each other.

'Because?' asked Libby.

'Oh, something to do with her ancestors. There was a casket, or something.'

Libby sighed. 'Yes, we know all about that. Didn't you see it mentioned in the paper?'

'No.' David looked from one to the other in apparent bewilderment.

'What did you see, then?' said Ben.

'That an actor who'd been performing in a play in the Monastery had been murdered and my wife had been the victim of a brutal attack.'

'You didn't go back to find out what the play had been about?' said Libby.

'No. It mentioned you, which was how I was able to track you down.'

'Me?' said Libby. 'Or the Oast House Theatre?'

'The Oast,' said David.

There was a sharp rap on the door. Libby got up.

'I'm sorry,' she heard David say, 'I didn't ask about your head. What happened?'

'Ian, come in.' Libby held the door open and allowed Ian to pass her.

'David, I don't think you've met Detective Chief Inspector Connell, have you?' said Ben.

David looked pole-axed.

'Mr Fletcher.' Ian pulled out one of the upright chairs and sat down.

'Coffee?' asked Libby. 'I'll fetch a mug.'

'Look,' David stood up. 'I'm sorry I interrupted. I'll –'

'Sit down, Mr Fletcher. You obviously wanted to talk to me, so I've come here for you to do just that.'

David looked round at the three expectant faces and sat

down again. Libby poured a mug of coffee for Ian and handed it over.

'David has just been telling us how he came to be looking for his wife, Ian. Would you like him to repeat it?'

David gave a précis of what he'd said and when he'd finished, looked anxiously at Ian.

'And I'm sure Mrs Sarjeant has told you she knows about your wife's ancestry? And the links to the reliquary?'

'The what?'

'Come, Mr Fletcher. I'm sure you know exactly what I mean. After all, it must have come up when you were talking to Mrs Butcher last Sunday.'

David's jaw dropped.

'And did she stay with you?' asked Libby. Ian frowned at her.

'Yes, she did.' David sighed heavily. 'If you know about Estelle, I'd better tell you everything that happened.'

'It would be best, sir,' said Ian.

'Cornelia and Estelle are cousins,' began David.

'We know,' chorused Ben and Libby.

'Is there anything you don't know?' snapped David.

'Yes. Why you met Estelle,' said Libby, equally waspish.

'When I saw the murdered man's name, I knew it was Estelle's husband. I couldn't believe it was a coincidence, I thought they must have patched up their differences and become friends again – Estelle and Cornelia, I mean.'

'Had there been a family argument?' asked Ian.

'I believe the cousins had been quite close when they were children, but there was some kind of – I don't really know – a difference of opinion. They'd kept in touch, though. Anyway, I thought I'd call Estelle.' He fell silent.

Ian put down his mug. 'And then?'

'Well, she was in a state. I couldn't quite make out what

she was going on about, but she said she was down here already and they wouldn't let her into Dom's house. She also said she knew nothing about Cornelia being attacked.'

'So you met her at Creekmarsh Place?' said Ben.

'Yes. How do you know?'

'Sheer coincidence,' said Libby. 'We know the owner. We were there raiding the vegetable beds.'

'Oh.' David shrugged. 'Well, we drove miles away and had a pub lunch, which Estelle spent complaining that the police and the theatre company were being obstructive, and why couldn't she go into Dom's house. I said all the right things about Dom, I think, although I'd never liked him. Never liked her, much, either. I said all I wanted to find out about was Cornelia, but she just wouldn't talk about that. Anyway, I said she could stay in the cottage that night.'

'And the next night?' asked Ian.

'No, but she did turn up on Tuesday. I let her use the washing machine.'

'Ah,' said Libby. Ian frowned at her again.

'And the next time you saw her?' said Ian.

'I haven't seen her since.' David looked round at them all. 'Look, what is this all about?'

'It's rather complicated,' said Libby. 'Much of it is about Cornelia's family history.'

'Really?' He looked puzzled.

'Do you really not know the history of the reliquary?' said Ben.

'I know it was a jewelled casket that had belonged to the family years ago and was something to do with St Eldreda.'

'Which family?' asked Libby.

David looked surprised. 'The Glovers, I suppose.'

'It's far more complicated than that,' said Ian. 'Did you get any hint from Mrs Butcher that the item featured in her husband's murder?'

'She said she thought it had been stolen, and it was family property anyway. It didn't seem to be her main worry, though.'

'Oh.' It was Libby's turn to look surprised.

'So you don't know where Mrs Butcher's been since Tuesday?' said Ian.

'No.'

'Not last night, for instance?'

'Last night? No!'

'You didn't go to the theatre?'

'No!' David looked from Ian to Libby. 'You told Susannah I wasn't needed last night.'

'We did.' Libby nodded. 'And Estelle didn't turn up on your doorstep last night?'

'I've already said, no. And why? Why do you need to know about her last night? What's happened.'

'This,' said Ben, pointing to his dressing.

'You said –'

'It happened at the theatre,' said Ben. 'It did. Someone was trying to break in and I interrupted.'

'But why should it have been Estelle?' asked David, now looking thoroughly confused.

Ian calmly explained how Estelle was suspected of breaking into Dominic's house and the Hoppers' Hut and the reasons.

'Why haven't you asked Cornelia about her?' said David when Ian had finished.

'We've been protecting Mrs Fletcher since the attack in case someone decided to finish the job,' said Ian.

'Oh, I see! That was why you wouldn't let me near her!' Ian inclined his head.

'So can I see her now? Where is she?'

'We've only got your word so far that all you want to do

is find out how she is, Mr Fletcher, so until we find her attacker and Mr Butcher's murderer, she's staying just where she is.'

Libby broke the awkward silence.

'So, did Cornelia tell you much about the family? She and Estelle weren't first cousins, were they?'

'No, their mothers were,' said David. 'They were close when the girls were born. And they both used to talk about their favourite uncle.'

'Oh?' said three voices.

'Yes, Edgar. Uncle Edgar.'

Chapter Thirty-five

'So does that leave us any further on?' asked Libby, when David had gone, with assurances that they would tell him anything they thought he ought to know in the future.

'It's become a possibility that both Cornelia and Estelle knew about the stolen reliquary from Uncle Edgar,' said Ian.

'But they were only little girls! He wouldn't have told them,' said Libby.

'Simply because of that,' said Ian. 'Can't you see a slightly disreputable uncle showing his little nieces a secret? They'd have loved that. And when he sold it he disappeared off to the Caribbean and became even more romantic in their eyes.'

'Hmm. And when they grew up they realised what had really happened?'

'Maybe not until the reliquary came on the market,' said Ian.

'So it begins to look as if Estelle is the murderer?' said Ben.

'Except that David said Estelle didn't seem interested in Cornelia. Wouldn't she be worried that Cornelia would point the finger if she recovered?' said Libby.

'She was wearing the missing robe, we think,' said Ian. 'Perhaps she was sure she wouldn't be recognised.' He frowned. 'It doesn't ring true to me, though.'

'Who else could it be, though?' said Libby. 'Are there any other suspects you haven't told us about?'

'Yes, there are,' said Ian with a laugh. 'But all boring ones as far as you're concerened.'

'What do you mean, boring?'

'Debtors, mainly. He was in with some very nasty people.'

'But could they have got down here and into the monastery?' said Ben. 'Unlikely, surely?'

'Very,' said Ian. 'But there is one other, of course.'

'Who?'

'David himself.'

Libby's mouth dropped open.

'Didn't you believe him?' asked Ben.

'I think a lot of what he said was true. But don't you wonder just a little about his rather urgent wish to see his estranged wife?'

'The recognition thing, again,' said Libby. 'So what did he lie about?'

'Only hearing about the case after it had happened,' said Ian. 'Everything else is substantially correct, I expect. It still doesn't explain Estelle's actions, though.'

'Oh, but it does!' said Libby. 'She's discovered what's going on and is in hiding from him. That's why she didn't go back to his cottage to collect her washing!'

'Possible,' said Ian. 'We just need to find her – not least because she may have put you in hospital, Ben.'

'Couldn't that have been David, too?' said Libby.

'Why would he need to get into the theatre? He's been perfectly safe in his cottage.'

'Oh – yes.' Libby's face fell. 'Still, it's a good theory about Estelle, isn't it?'

'It is.' Ian smiled and got to his feet. 'Thanks for arranging this evening. If we've started a hare, so much the better.'

'I've just realised,' said Libby, as she accompanied him

to the door, 'we all referred to her as Cornelia. No one mentioned Martha. Does he still not know?'

'If he does, he was being very careful not to admit it. Now don't worry about it any more, Libby. Go and look after Ben. Not that he looks as if he needs it.'

'He doesn't,' said Libby. 'I'd say he was a fraud if it wasn't for how much he worried me last night.'

'I heard that,' said Ben, as she went back into the living room. 'I shall now demand a whisky.'

'Should you?' said Libby doubtfully.

'Yes, I should, and so should you. And after that, we should have an early night.'

On Saturday morning, Libby decided to go to the Abbey during their open hours and see if it would be possible to see Martha.

'Don't tell her anything, though,' said Ben. 'You don't want to upset any apple carts.'

'I know,' said Libby, 'but last time I saw her I felt sure there was something she wasn't telling me. If I could get her to open up it could be the answer.'

Sister Catherine was delighted to see her, but confessed she was worried about Martha.

'I know the police are happy for her to be here,' she said, as she led Libby into a part of the Abbey she'd not seen before, 'but she seems to be scared all the time. I've told her no one can get at her here, but it hasn't made any difference.'

'Is it her husband? Does she know he's around?'

'I don't think so. Honestly Libby, I'm really quite worried about her.' Sister Catherine shook her head. 'I wish I didn't feel this was all my fault.'

'Oh, don't Cathy,' said Libby, involuntarily. 'Oh – sorry.'

'That's all right, Libby.' Catherine patted her arm.

'You're a friend. Here we are.'

She knocked on a door and stuck her head round. 'Libby Sarjeant's here to see you, Martha.'

Libby was pleased to see Martha's face light up as she entered the room.

'How are you feeling?' she asked after bending to kiss Martha's cheek. 'I see you're up and about now.'

Martha was sitting in a chair by the window, which looked out over what was obviously a private courtyard. Two of the sisters were sitting on stone benches.

'Yes, I'm fine, now. I ought to be back at work.' Martha's eyes slid to the sisters. 'I should be helping.'

'Better that you should be completely well first, though,' said Libby.

'Yes.' Martha looked thoughtful. 'So, is there any more news about the murder?'

'Not really,' said Libby. 'Not directly.'

'Directly? What do you mean?'

'I mean nothing that points to Dominic's murderer.'

'But something else?' Martha's eyes were wide – with fear?

'Background stuff, I think,' said Libby. 'Martha – what are you afraid of? No one can get at you in here. No one even knows where you are except me and the police.'

'I know.' Martha looked at the floor. 'But I keep thinking ...' she looked up and her eyes went out of focus.

'You're reliving that moment, aren't you?' said Libby gently. 'It isn't because you've remembered something about who hit you?'

'No,' Martha said quickly.

'Well, never mind. I'm sure it will get easier. I must tell you about the show – it's going so well. Susannah's a brilliant accompanist and –' she stopped and recovered herself, 'everyone's remembered their songs and sketches really well from the last time we did Music Hall.'

'I'm sure she has remembered something, though,' Libby told Fran later on the phone, having brought her up to date on the events of yesterday evening.

'And she's scared,' said Fran.

'Yes. You don't suppose she thinks she was attacked by a – a – a supernatural thing, do you? St Eldreda come to life or something?'

'It's possible, I suppose. That bright light I saw – if that's what she saw, maybe that's exactly what she thinks.'

'And she's scared because she feels she's being punished – but what for? She protected the reliquary.'

'I don't know,' said Fran. 'Not being religious I can't get inside the workings of her mind. But I won't scoff.'

'Good.' Libby yawned. 'I don't seem to have slept much over the past couple of days. I might have a nap this afternoon.'

'You're getting old,' laughed Fran. 'Let me know if anything else happens.'

Ben appeared from the kitchen.

'Let's be all normal,' he said, 'and go and have a lunchtime drink.'

'Then I really will have a nap this afternoon,' said Libby.

Several members of the theatre company were in the pub, and all wanted to know how Ben was and what had really happened. He basked in the attention for a while, then pleaded exhaustion and steered Libby to a quiet table.

'That was a bit too normal,' he said. 'I suppose, actually, I do still feel a bit shaky.'

Libby looked at him thoughtfully. 'I'm not surprised. Martha's not back to normal yet and she was hit weeks ago.'

'She was in a coma, though. Hers was more serious than

294

mine.'

'Hmm. But to all outward appearances she's better. So if she's still claiming illness it must mean she's scared of something. I asked her this morning.'

'Wasn't that risky?' said Ben.

'I don't think so.' Libby shrugged. 'I was trying to be reassuring, telling her no one can get at her in the Abbey. Which, if she's shamming, she knows perfectly well. So she's hiding.'

'You don't know that,' said Ben. 'And wouldn't she have told the police if she was afraid of someone?'

Libby repeated the supernatural theory. Ben laughed.

'I don't think so, do you? Really?'

'Not really, but she does seem a bit strange. Not like she was during the play. She was perfectly normal then.'

'We're back to "normal" are we? So do you think I'm going to be a bit peculiar when I've recovered from my bump?'

Libby grinned at him. 'I shall make no comment!'

They finished their drinks and Libby deemed it safer to leave after one, as Ben was looking tired and pale. Once home, she packed him off to bed and went back downstairs to have the nap she'd promised herself.

The phone woke her an hour later.

At first there was nothing.

'Hello?' repeated Libby irritably.

'Libby – I've remembered.' Martha's voice almost whispered. 'What shall I do?'

'You've remembered who attacked you?' Libby shot upright.

'S-sort of. What shall I do?'

'Call the police, straight away. Have you got the number?'

'No. Could you do it for me?'

'That wouldn't really –'

'Please.' Martha's voice broke. 'I'm so scared.'

'Yes, I know. Who was it then?' Libby held her breath.

'No, I can't tell you. I'll tell the police.'

'All right. Stay where you are. Someone will come back to you as soon as possible.'

Libby ended the call and rang Ian's personal mobile.

'Who is it?' he said, when Libby relayed Martha's message.

'She wouldn't tell me. I said someone would be back to her as soon as possible.'

'Where is she?'

Libby was surprised. 'At the Abbey, I suppose. She was there this morning, too scared to go out.'

'Right. We're on our way. Will you call the Abbey and warn them?'

'If they aren't praying,' said Libby.

She rang the number Sister Catherine had given her, and was relieved when the nun herself answered.

'The police are going to arrive to talk to Martha again,' she said. 'Will you be in the chapel?'

'Not until Vespers,' said Catherine. 'I'll fetch Martha to the front office, then they won't have to disturb anyone. What's it about?'

'She rang me and asked me to tell the police she'd remembered. She wouldn't tell me any more.'

'Oh, thank the dear Lord,' said Catherine. 'I'll go straight away.'

On impulse, Libby ran upstairs and woke Ben.

'I'm going over there,' she told him. 'It might be less scary for her.'

'Be careful,' said Ben. 'Don't forget your mobile.'

The sky was so overcast it felt like winter, Libby thought, as she drove towards the Abbey for the second time today. She slowed down as she reached the place where Patti had first shown it to her. It looked peaceful, the ruined arches blending completely into the backdrop of hills and trees.

Her mobile rang.

'Where are you?' It was Sister Catherine.

'On my way to you. Why?'

'Martha isn't here.'

Chapter Thirty-six

'Have you told the police?' said Libby, yanking on the handbrake.

'I can't find the number!' Sister Catherine sounded almost tearful.

'I'll do it. Sit tight and we'll all be there very soon.'

Libby called Ian and then Fran.

'Where could she be?' she asked. 'What do you think's happened?'

'Someone's got at her,' said Fran. 'That's why she rang you earlier.'

'But why wouldn't she tell me who it was?'

'He was there?'

'If he was there, why would she ring me at all?'

'I don't know. You'd better carry on to the Abbey and find out.'

When Libby arrived at the Abbey, Ian's car and a squad car were both on the drive. Ian appeared in the doorway and came straight towards her.

'Are you sure she said nothing else?'

'No – I told you. And she was whispering.'

'Why wouldn't she give you a name?'

'There couldn't have been someone there, she wouldn't have called at all.'

'If she'd seen someone outside her room she might have done,' said Ian.

'Or perhaps,' said Libby with sudden inspiration, 'she was forced to make the call?'

Ian looked at her with rare approval. 'Perhaps,' he said.

A uniformed officer approached from the monastery side of the building. 'No sign round there, sir.'

'If someone's got her,' said Libby, 'where would he take her?'

'Nowhere obvious,' said Ian. 'We've put out an alert, but we don't know what we're looking for.'

'No unusual cars?'

'No. Look, Libby, I know you want to help, but believe me, the best thing you could do is to go back home in case she calls again.'

'She'll call my mobile, and I've got that with me. Can I have a look in the monastery grounds?'

'They've got to be searched properly,' said Ian. 'I don't want you trampling over evidence.'

'Can I go in and see Sister Catherine, then?'

Ian sighed. 'Yes, go on. But don't get in the way.'

Sister Catherine was in the hall with two other, older sisters.

'Oh, Libby! she said, clasping Libby's hands. 'Whatever is going on?'

'I don't know, but I just had an idea.' Libby glanced over her shoulder to where Ian was talking into his mobile. 'Can we go through to the atrium?'

Surprised, Catherine nodded and led the way through the corridors until they came to the now empty atrium, looking out over the ruins of the monastery.

'Could she have got out this way?' said Libby. 'She had the keys at one point.'

Catherine moved across to the doors and pushed. They swung open. She looked round at Libby, fear in her eyes. 'Now what?'

'I suppose we tell Ian. Why didn't he find this?'

'He hasn't had time yet,' said Catherine. 'I'll go and

299

fetch him.'

Libby stepped outside and turned left. Just round the corner was the gardener's shed they had used as a dressing room. She found her heart thumping and her legs trembling. She didn't know what had drawn her here, but she was quite certain that this was where Martha was, alive or dead.

And then she heard Estelle's voice.

'What are you doing?' hissed Ian behind her.

'Estelle. She's got Martha in there.' Libby suddenly felt weak and leant against the wall.

'Stay there.' Ian moved backwards and signalled to someone out of sight.

'Don't you need back-up?' whispered Libby.

'No time. It's on its way.' Ian went forward, two uniformed constables approaching from either side. Then with a sudden movement, he lunged at the door and pulled it open. David Fletcher's face stared out at him and there was a scream from inside the hut. Libby started forward.

The three policemen were inside the hut. Libby was aware of Sister Catherine beside her wringing her hands, and the sound of sobbing. Over this she became aware of sirens and before anyone could emerge from the gardener's hut, the garden was full of police in protective clothing.

Catherine had her arm round Libby's shoulders. 'Come inside,' she said. 'Your nice policeman will let us know what's happening when he can.'

They sat in the visitor's room and a worried-looking little nun brought them tea. Eventually, there was a brief knock and Ian came into the room.

'Is it over?' said Libby.

'Yes, it's over. A lot of loose ends to tie up. I'll let you know when I can.'

Libby shook her head. 'I just didn't believe it was

David, even though I thought it might be Estelle.'

Ian's eyebrows rose. 'Oh, no,' he said. 'Dominic's murderer was Martha.'

It wasn't until the following day, when they were at the Manor for Hetty's Sunday lunch that Ian called.

'I'll come by and tell you as briefly as I can what happened,' he said.

'We're at the Manor having lunch,' said Libby, 'but Hetty won't mind if you come. You can have pudding and coffee.'

'How can I resist?' said Ian, sounding tired.

'I bet he hasn't been to bed,' said Libby, as she switched off her phone. 'At least we're all here so he only has to say it once.'

Fran and Guy had come, and Harry was due to arrive when his last lunchtime guests had gone.

Ian did indeed look tired when he arrived, and allowed himself to be seated in the biggest Windsor chair and supplied with apple crumble and cream.

'I shall go to sleep after this,' he said, smiling round at them all. 'How many times have we done this over the last few years?'

'Just like Poirot,' said Libby, 'only you're not accusing any of us.'

'You nearly dived straight into the middle of it yesterday,' said Ian.

'I didn't though, did I?' said Libby. 'I stopped as soon as I heard Estelle's voice. What was she –'

'I'll tell you what happened from the beginning,' said Ian, 'and you can ask questions afterwards. Where shall we start?'

'The last night of the show. The murder,' said Fran.

'Oh, I think we'd better go back further than that.' Ian

301

spooned up the last of his apple crumble. 'It all started when Uncle Edgar told two little girls all about this beautiful box which belonged to their family. We can't prove that he killed Bernard Evans, but it looks likely. From what I can gather from Estelle, they were given the impression that the box was theirs by right, to improve their fortunes, but of course he'd sold it on. Over the years, Estelle tried to find out about it.'

'Can I ask if we've confirmed that it was Bad Jack Jarvis who pinched it when he went abroad?' asked Libby.

'I don't think we'll ever know, but it seems likely, given where it ended up, and the fact that Albert and Ronald Barnes were both his descendants. Anyway, back to Martha – or Cornelia. She was different from Estelle. Always of a religious turn of mind, she didn't approve of the reliquary being sold for profit, but she also researched its history. She knew all about it, and that was, in fact, why she came to St Eldreda's Abbey. It was no coincidence. The catalyst for all the events was the appearance of it for sale. It seems Cornelia kept an eye on all sales of religious artifacts, and she spotted it. It was she who informed the nuns, although anonymously, and she was delighted when it came to the Abbey where she thought it ought to stay.'

'She actually said that to me,' said Libby.

'The next thing in the chain of events was Dominic finding out about it. He knew perfectly well that Estelle had always thought it was family property, and thought it could make some money. He told Estelle.'

'Were they separated?' asked Fran.

'Yes, but they got together to hatch the plan, which was, as you already know, for Dominic to stay behind and steal the reliquary. He obviously knew Martha came down to check on it in the middle of the night and thought it would be easy enough to overpower her. Estelle was there, as a

302

member of the audience who stayed behind, to take the reliquary away, so it wouldn't be found on Dominic.'

'Did Dominic mean to kill Martha? Even in his robe she would have recognised him,' said Fran.

'Estelle says she didn't know, but I would imagine that was the idea.'

'What went wrong?' asked Ben.

'Martha did come down in the middle of the night, more to worship it than anything else as far as I can tell, and when Dominic tried to overpower her, she recognised him and killed him. Estelle saw it all. Apparently, she said Martha was quite mad. After she'd got over the shock, realising she couldn't get out of the grounds, Estelle waited for Martha to reappear and then challenged her. She says, although I'm not sure it's true, she meant to tell the police. But then, of course, Martha attacked her.'

'You'd never have thought it, would you?' said Libby.

'The result of that was that Estelle fought back and Martha fell back on the stand and knocked herself out. Estelle thought she'd killed her, and went and hid until she could get out of the gates. She kept the robe Dominic had got for her.'

'Yes, why had she got the robe?' asked Ben. 'She didn't need it while she was in the audience.'

'Dominic wanted her to be robed so no one would recognise her if they were interrupted during the night. She kept it because she didn't know what else to do with it.'

'So what was she doing skulking round the huts and the theatre?' asked Peter.

'Literally, hiding. She'd been in touch with David Fletcher – or rather – he'd been in touch with her after he heard Dominic had been killed. But of course, she didn't know Martha was still alive, she thought, in fact, that she might have killed her, so she wasn't very forthcoming to him. She didn't want anyone to connect her with the crime scene and was worried about any evidence Dominic might have left at his house.'

'Did she hit me?' said Ben.

'Yes, and got even more terrified. She was wearing the robe in an attempt not to be recognised.'

'So what happened yesterday?' asked Fran.

'Estelle finally got in touch with David again to tell him that Cornelia was Martha and to confess to the whole thing.'

'How did she find out that Martha was still alive?'

'Believe it or not, Martha called her.'

'I didn't know she had a phone!' said Libby.

'Nobody did. But she called Estelle and said she was ready to tell the truth.'

'Why on earth did she call me?'

'When David and Estelle arrived, she met them in the ruins and led them to the gardener's shed. She had only expected Estelle and was planning to kill her and claim it was self-defence. She called you as a sort of proof that she was scared of Estelle.'

'Why wouldn't she say it was Estelle?' asked Fran.

'She thought you might call Estelle, or tell the police. She didn't want that. But David put a spoke in her wheel. She had Estelle at knife point in there.' Ian frowned down at the table. 'She was quite demented.'

'Why did she kill Dominic in the first place? She could have raised the alarm easily,' said Peter.

'She seems fixated on the reliquary, and keeps saying it should be kept at the Abbey. I think she was going to try and steal it herself and hide it somewhere.'

'She'd never have got away with that!' said Libby.

'No, but she's not in the least rational,' said Ian.

'Oh, I know – did you find out who called the Abbey

saying he was the beneficiary?' said Fran.

Ian smiled. 'Think about it. Who told you about the phone call?'

'Well, Martha did,' said Libby, 'but that was before Dominic's attack.'

'There was no phone call. Think about it a bit more.'

Fran, Libby, Ben and Peter looked at each other.

'No,' said Ben. 'Give up.'

'Dominic had done a dummy run, by all accounts –'

'Yes, he wasn't there a couple of times after rehearsal,' said Peter.

'So – he knew Martha was in the habit of coming down to check on the reliquary in the middle of the night.'

'To worship it, you said,' said Libby.

'Exactly. But, I told you, as far as we can make out from what she's saying, she intended it not to leave the Abbey. The phone call appears to have been a rather inept attempt at laying a false trail, hoping you would think someone was after it.'

Libby sighed. 'She certainly put on a good act. When I went to see her in hospital that time, I could have sworn she had no idea when Dominic was killed, or anything about it.'

'And Fran's bright light?' asked Guy, reaching out and taking his wife's hand. 'What was that?'

'Martha hitting her head on the reliquary stand,' said Libby and Fran together.

'That's part of the story I couldn't possibly answer,' said Ian, smiling. 'Yes, please, Hetty, I'd love coffee.'

'Poor David.' Fran shook her head. 'I don't suppose he'll want to do the show now.'

'Why won't he?' said Harry appearing in the doorway. 'What's been going on?'

'Oh, Harry!' came the chorus.

305

Epilogue

David did do The End of The Pier Show, confessing that he'd known Cornelia/Martha was a bit of a religious fanatic.

'The reason we never divorced was she didn't believe in it,' he told Libby, on their first night at the Alexandria. 'I would have done it eventually. Poor woman. He shook his head. 'Poor all of us.'

'And Estelle is going to be cautioned but not charged, which is good,' said Libby, 'even if she was planning to steal the reliquary.'

David shuddered. 'I never want to hear of that thing again.'

'No, neither do the Beaumonts,' said Libby. 'They said it has caused enough trouble.'

Peter wandered across the stage towards them. 'I don't either. And just remind me next time I get an idea for a play, Libby, not to write it.'

First Chapter of *Murder in the Dark*

The white-rimmed undergrowth crackled and the grass crunched underfoot. In the moonlight shapes loomed up on either side, threatening. The murderer paused, listening, but all was quiet. Then turned and crept from the scene, leaving the victim on the ground, staring silently and sightlessly through the branches at the stars.

Adam Sarjeant glanced over his shoulder at the creeping mist. Through it, the trees were vague outlines, giants moving noiselessly towards him.

'Mog,' he called. 'We can't go on much longer in this can we?'

His employer pushed back lank dark hair and looked up from the paving slab he was lining up. 'No. Just bring the tarp over and we'll cover it all. With any luck it'll be better tomorrow.'

Adam turned away from the new swimming pool he and Mog had been landscaping towards the covered pile of materials at the edge of the lawn. Beyond a wall, the house swam eerily like a great half-timbered ship. There was a rustle over to his right, and a figure burst through the hedge.

''Ere, Adam! Mog!'

'Johnny?' Mog stood up. 'What is it?'

'Bleedin' body, innit? Fuckin' 'ell.' Johnny suddenly bent double, stringy pony tail swinging forward over his shoulder.

'Johnny?' Adam ran towards him. 'Are you all right? What do you mean a body?'

Johnny lifted his head. 'Course I'm not bleedin' all right. Call the cops.'

Mog arrived at Adam's side. They looked at each other.

'Had we better check?' said Mog.

'It's a bleedin' woman, I tell yer. Dead as a dodo. Call the cops.' He sat down suddenly on the ground, his head in his hands.

Mog pulled out his phone and pushed buttons, while Adam ineffectually patted Johnny's shoulder.

'Yeah,' he heard Mog saying. 'No, I'm just working on the garden. The caretaker, he found it. Dark House, Dark Lane, between Steeple Cross and Keeper's Cob.'

'They say to stay here.' Mog looked nervously towards the gap in the hedge where Johnny had burst through. 'Where is it, Johnny?'

'Just outside the grotto. They won't make me go back, will they?'

'I don't know,' said Adam. 'They might.'

'I can't.'

'Did they say how long they'd be?' asked Adam.

'No, and let's face it, this house isn't exactly on a major road, is it?' Mog felt in his pocket for his tobacco. 'Want a rollie, Johnny?'

'Yeah. Ta.' Johnny looked up and watched as Mog rolled two slim cigarettes.

'It's going to be dark soon,' said Adam. 'Have we got a torch, Mog?'

'Don't know. Might have in the van.'

'Shall I go and see? If I walk about at the front the security light will come on and the police might see it.'

Mog nodded, leaning down to light Johnny's cigarette.

Adam walked towards the gate in the hedge that led to

the lawns at the back of the house and made for the drive at the side. The security lights came on and he walked to the gateway to see if he could see anything coming, but the lane, narrow as a cart track, twisted away in both directions shrouded in unbroken mist.

More Libby Sarjeant Murder Mysteries

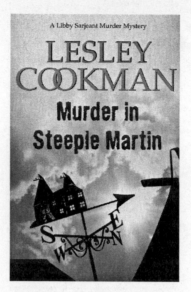

A Libby Sarjeant Murder Mystery

LESLEY COOKMAN

Murder in Steeple Martin

Murder in Steeple Martin

Artist and ex-actress Libby Sarjeant is busy directing a play for the opening of a new theatre in her village when one of her cast is found murdered. The play, written by her friend Peter, is based on real events in his family, disturbing and mysterious, which took place in the village during the last war.

As the investigation into the murder begins to uncover a tangled web of relationships in the village, it seems that the events dramatised in the play still cast a long shadow, dark enough to inspire murder.

Libby's natural nosiness soon leads her into the thick of the investigation, but is she too close to Peter's family, and in particular his cousin Ben, to be able to recognise the murderer?

ISBN 9781908262806

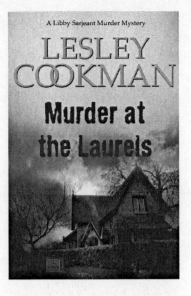

Murder at the Laurels

Steeple Martin amateur detective Libby's friend, and sleuthing partner, psychic investigator Fran Castle, suspects that there is something suspicious about the death of her aunt in a nursing home. When Fran's long-lost relatives turn up and seem either unconcerned or obstructive, Libby and Fran are sure something is wrong, particularly as the will is missing.

As usual Libby needs little persuasion to start investigating, even if she doesn't see herself as Miss Marple. They discover surprising links to Fran's own past but, as the murders multiply and the police take over, can the amateur sleuths keep on the trail?

ISBN 9781908262813

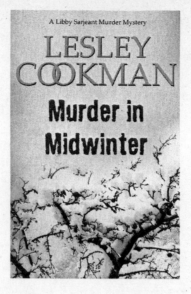

A Libby Sarjeant Murder Mystery

LESLEY COOKMAN

Murder in Midwinter

Murder in Midwinter

Kent village sleuth Libby and her psychic investigator friend Fran befriend Bella Morleigh, who has inherited a derelict theatre. When an unknown body is discovered inside the theatre, they feel duty bound to help with the investigation.

Although Libby is rather distracted by the preparations for her friends' Civil Partnership ceremony, she's getting the hang of using a computer to dig for information. However, when a second body is found it is one of Fran's psychic moments that makes the connection between the deaths; a connection with startling results.

ISBN 9781908262820